THE SHIP BREAKERS

THE SHIP BREAKERS

Peter Tonkin

This first world edition published in Great Britain 2007 by
SEVERN HOUSE PUBLISHERS LTD of
9–15 High Street, Sutton, Surrey SM1 1DF.
This first world edition published in the USA 2007 by
SEVERN HOUSE PUBLISHERS INC of
595 Madison Avenue, New York, N.Y. 10022.

British Library Cataloguing in Publication Data

Tonkin, Peter
   The ship breakers
   1.   Mariner, Richard (Fictitious character) - Fiction
   2.   Russia (Federation) - Fiction
   3.   Suspense fiction
   I.   Title
   823.9'14 [F]

   ISBN-13: 978-0-7278-6486-4

All Severn House titles are printed on acid-free paper.

Typeset by Palimpsest Book Production Ltd.,
Grangemouth, Stirlingshire, Scotland.
Printed and bound in Great Britain by
MPG Books Ltd., Bodmin, Cornwall.

One

O f the ten people hurrying seawards towards the deep-water end of Archangel's half-kilometre Komsomolskaya Pier on that rainy autumn afternoon, eight were ship breakers. The other two were Richard and Robin Mariner, nominal owners of the hulk *Prometheus*, towards which they were all rushing through the freezing drizzle. If anyone could be said to own a supertanker *in name only*, thought Robin, glancing up through the gloom at the monstrous vessel ahead and trying not to think too fondly of the air-conditioned, leather-seated elegance of the big Mercedes limousines left at the pier's distant security gate.

Much to the anger of their Russian hosts, the big main gates to the pier at the end of ulitsa Komsomolskaya had been locked and deserted. A glitch that had simply added to the already tense situation caused by a less than impressive lunch at a restaurant which spectacularly failed to live up to its reputation. Not only the favourite haunt of Felix Makarov, their host, but also the restaurant of the hotel where Richard and Robin were staying. A double own-goal, if such a thing could be said to exist, she thought. Certainly, Richard had tasted little of the bewildering array of starters, soups, hot courses and desserts that had swept before them, mostly comprised of fish and mushrooms, all accompanied with black bread and sour cream.

Robin hadn't been tempted by any of it, even though it was more than twenty-four hours since she had eaten anything other than airline food and snacks. It had all seemed too much, somehow, overwhelming her tired, queasy stomach with its abundance and its richness. Starving though she was, and all too well aware of her condition and what it would do to her mood if nothing else, she had nevertheless been unable to bring herself to touch a thing. And to make a bad situation worse, she had spent a good deal of the meal making sure the companion to her right was not touching her.

The disappointment would have consequences for the kitchen staff and management, she had no doubt, glancing across at the still-furious face of the leader of the Sevmash Consortium; Tsar of the ship breakers.

Robin shivered with apprehension as well as starvation, exhaustion and cold. She hunched her shoulders, bringing the thick warmth of the faux-fur of her coat collar up around her freezing cheeks, releasing as she did so a heartening wave of Chanel's most famous fragrance. She hoped that she and Richard would be able to present the interior of the super-tanker with more impressive efficiency, even though she had only arrived at Talagi Airport yesterday afternoon, hadn't eaten and had hardly slept and hadn't been aboard *Prometheus* in nearly ten years.

Looking at the state of the vessel now, she frankly doubted it.

The tanker towards which they were half running was long decommissioned. She had not sailed in the Heritage Mariner fleet in a decade – since she had been retired as flagship and been sold on, first to a Greek consortium, then to others more obscure. She was only briefly passing through the ownership of Richard and Robin, through Heritage Mariner's books and under the red duster of the British merchant fleet. And thank God for that, thought Robin, looking at the state of her. A couple of years rusting at anchor off the German coast had not been kind. She looked like a long-sunken wreck recently refloated, her upper works all blistered, pocked and running with blood-red rust; her windows filthy, cracked and broken; her brightwork dark or green; her long black hull seemingly dangerously thin and frail. She looked almost ghostly – as though Disney were setting another episode of *Pirates of the Caribbean* on oil tankers. Robin was surprised Richard had even been able to swing enough insurance cover to get her moved at all. But he had; energetic and indomitable as ever.

Heritage Mariner tugs had taken her under tow at Wilhelmshaven a fortnight ago and pulled the powerless water-ballasted rotting hulk round Denmark, Sweden and Norway, down the Kola Peninsula, through the White Sea this far. Russian tugs would pull her across the Dvina Bay and into

Severodvinsk within a very few more days, where she would be broken up at the massive yard once called Shipyard 402, now owned by the Sevmash Consortium. Controlled by Felix Makarov and his cohorts. If Richard and Robin could finalize the agreement with the Consortium that existed only on paper thus far. On paper and in Richard's wild and restless imagination, she thought grimly, glancing across at her husband.

As she did so, the wind gusted once again, a stiff north-westerly coming in across the Kola Peninsula, low over the nearby Arctic Circle and across the icy White Sea, driving the drizzle over *Prometheus* and into their twisted faces. Only Richard did not flinch at the icy – probably radioactive – bite of it, Robin observed sourly. The rain seemed to stream backwards off the shoulders of his British Warm overcoat as though he were an animated piece of the heroic statuary so popular here. But his animation was beginning to have some effect: Makarov and the nameless man beside him both cracked a smile.

The wind came again, snatching away Richard's amusing words and making *Prometheus* groan and howl as it pushed her hard against her fenders and roared through her deckwork, her bridge house and bridge wings, her open windows and vacant passageways. This close, it also brought the simple stench of her, a compound of rotting metal, rotting paint, rotting linoleum, rotting rubber and rotting wood. Against it, the reek of ancient oil seemed almost wholesome. Robin sank her face nose-deep into the fragrant cloud of her collar as the tails of her long black cashmere coat whipped about her booted ankles.

The pier had nothing in the way of protective walls or safety rails. It was little more than a man-made peninsula, a flat-topped breakwater thrusting out into the deepest channel of the bay so that big vessels like *Prometheus* could dock. So there was nothing to cut the wind or contain the stench. The wind gusted freely. The smell came and went. But, like the sound the ship was making, it intensified as they got closer.

When they stepped into *Prometheus*'s wind-shadow, the wet foulness closed around them while the groaning, keening howl became so loud that even Richard was forced into a tempo-rary silence. Fortunately, the need for speech was obviated by the obvious requirement that they climb the unsettlingly steep companionway that led through three turns to the main deck. The three turns made it seem like they were climbing three storeys of a tall house. And certainly, by the time they reached the main deck, they seemed to have climbed half the height of the grim grey buildings that backed whatever prospect led up and down from the Komsomolskaya crossroads. The wind had dropped in the interim and the drizzle had died away.

So that as Robin stepped on to the slippery foulness of the deck itself, watery sunlight broke through the overcast sky to bathe the Great Patriotic War monument looking vigilantly to all four quarters of the compass, the huge statue of Lenin and the public buildings along Trotsky Prospect to the south, dominated by the twenty-two-storey skyscraper of the Municipal Building on the corner that from this angle half obscured even Lenin. Which, under the circumstances, seemed apt enough. The men who were accompanying Richard and Robin aboard were what Richard called *novirusskaya* – men who were more interested in modern skyscrapers than in ancient statues of Lenin.

The White Sea in between it all seemed to turn to silver-gilt, the filth and the pollution of the water suddenly hidden by the golden brightness. But there was no warmth in the thin light. Robin folded her arms across her breast and snuggled her head down into her collar once again until the faux-fur sable met the faux-fur sable of her square Russian-style hat.

'Richard says you used to be the captain of this tub?' wheezed a breathless voice all too close behind her.

Robin turned, aware that her eyes were watering from the dazzle. Perhaps from more than the dazzle. 'That's right. When I was younger. When we all were.' Did I catch a whisper of self-pity in my own tones? she wondered.

'I've heard of child brides, but child *captains* . . .'

The gallantry was wasted on her. Her companion was the most repulsive of Richard's business partners. Fashionably hairless, like all of the others, he resembled a scrawny toad but obviously fancied himself as quite a ladykiller. He was certainly confident enough in his charm and his St Laurent wardrobe to feel that deodorant and mouthwash would be wasted. And indeed, it seemed to Robin that only a kind of miracle could keep the halitosis going in the face of the inordinate amounts of vodka he had been gargling since they met. Dutch courage, maybe, as he tried his hand with her. Or perhaps, like so many others, he just assumed that she was eye-candy that wouldn't object to the occasional *sucking* in a good cause. That's where many of the bright young businesswomen here seemed to fit into the pecking order. Or so she had heard.

Whatever the truth of the rumour, Fedor Gulin had been making passes at her all day, seemingly impervious to her iciest reserve. He had grabbed her thigh under the luncheon table and had been lucky to get away without a soundly slapped face. Only the thought of actually touching his warty skin had stopped her.

Richard was going to get a piece of her mind the first time they were alone together, she thought. She smiled her most brittle smile. 'You're very kind, Mr Gerkin . . .'

'Gulin . . .'

'But I'm afraid you flatter me. I have two children at university . . .'

'HA! *Also* a child bride! I knew this! I said—'

'You're too kind. But let's hurry up, shall we? The others . . .'

The others were just stepping into the bridge house over the lip of the 'A' deck outer door as they caught up. The atmosphere started Robin shivering at once in a way that her expensive coat could not begin to combat. Memories of experiences crowded round her as real as ghosts in a haunted mansion and as poignant as nightmares. She was close to being overwhelmed by the disorientating vividness of her feelings and would have walked carefully in any case. The state of the ancient lino beneath her feet made careful walking even more of a necessity.

As though in a dream, she looked around herself. Doors stood wide along both sides of the corridor where she trod so carefully in her sensible knee-high boots. Half-lit, day-grey and shadowy offices, work and recreation spaces jostled with each other to bring a poignant memory to life. On the one hand, the first mate's office and lading-control room, the officers' wardroom; on the other the galleys, the dining areas, the ship's Infirmary. Away ahead, beyond the companionways leading up into the accommodation, work and command areas or down into crews' quarters, cargo-handling and engineering, lay more recreational facilities. The ship's gym, the library, TV and video room.

Gulin seemed to remain oblivious to all this but he nevertheless stumbled several times before he ushered her on to the companionway then laboured up behind her, five more storeys, on to the navigation bridge. Again, she trod carefully, for she had no intention of touching anything that looked – or smelt – like the shrivelled plastic of the handrails.

The view from the bridge was breathtakingly wide, and could have been simply magnificent. It overlooked the Lomosov Theatre, the Naval Museum and the twin spans of the Dvina road and rail bridges beyond, down towards Severodvinsk itself. If only the buildings had any kind of style about them, she thought, it could have been a breathtakingly memorable view. And, in the gathering murk of early evening, it was lit up, as though someone somewhere thought this was St Petersburg.

But even the bay, the river mouth, the White Sea and the land crowding in upon them were simply overwhelmed by square, threateningly brutal low-Soviet architecture. Like Felix Makarov in concrete. All she could really see were disturbingly soulless, monstrously utilitarian blocks of grubby grainy grey, squared with pallid piss-yellow windows, stretching down to metal bridges as badly rusted as *Prometheus* and the distant slum-shipyards towards which she was headed.

But who am I to complain? Robin thought, bitterly, turning. For she was at least partly responsible for bringing this reeking, haunted hulk here. The once-good ship *Prometheus*, in such a disgusting state that it made even the most soulless concrete abortion seem insouciantly stylish. And, turning, she found herself face to face with Felix Makarov himself.

The Russian had come up behind her so silently during her bitter preoccupation that she had no idea he was so close to her. Now, as she turned, she found him towering immediately in front of her, close enough to catch her. In an embrace. Or in something worse. Only her pride stopped her stepping back. Only the steel in her stopped her face betraying shock or fear. She stood there, therefore, looking defiantly upwards. Her level grey gaze meeting his broodingly dark one, her golden curls, turned into a simple riot by the combination of wind and rain, not quite tickling his chin.

Except that he was also hairless, Makarov was the exact

opposite of Gerkin. In no way a mere *biznismen*, he was almost Richard's equal in height, power and enthusiasm. His face was all high cheekbones, deep, slanting eyes and square chin. The massive expanses of his cheeks were pitted so deeply it almost seemed that he had survived smallpox, or a youthful rash of acne in direct proportion to the levels of testosterone in his powerful body. For he seemed to burn with a kind of sexual power that Robin found particularly disconcerting. What was the name of that film producer in old Hollywood, she wondered inconsequentially, who had to have sex with a starlet every afternoon or he'd start chasing his secretaries around the desk? Independently of the fact that he was a powerful party animal outside office hours? And, she thought, a happily married family man to boot. Makarov seemed to be cast in the same almost infinitely insatiable mould, but she had to admit that he carried it off with some style.

Makarov's wardrobe and footwear, like Richard's, seemed to have been cut, personally fitted and hand-stitched in London. His British Warm was fawn where Richard's was navy, darkened almost to chocolate on the shoulders where the rain had begun to penetrate the merino wool. But his icy eyes were almost black where Richard's were dazzling blue. The brows above them were thick and level – showing how bear-like his face would have been had he not shaved fastidiously from the nape of his neck to the pit of his throat. At the pit of his throat there sat, perfectly Windsor-knotted in the elbow of his immaculately starched and snowy collar, the golden silk of a tie marked in black with Fabergé eagles. His ears were surprisingly small and neat. His lips were perfectly sculpted and as pink as a girl's but his nose was broad. His chin was uncompromisingly square. His teeth were brilliantly white. And when he spoke, the understated musk of his Eau Sauvage cologne was overlain by an unsettlingly familiar odour from her childhood: a hint of Parma violets.

'Your husband says that you are as enthusiastic about this venture as he is himself?' His voice was light baritone; unsettlingly so – she somehow always expected the deepest rumbling bass. His accent, like all their accents, was Harvard Business School. He and his Consortium were *novirusskaya* – modern Russian businessmen after all. But they *were* all men, of course.

They weren't *that* modern, thought Robin.

'Of course . . .' she answered, then hesitated and cleared her throat as she assessed her tone of voice. Was there just a hint of uncertainty there? A trace of bitterness from a mother who had dropped her babies off in their university digs for the first time and then headed eastwards to this God-forsaken place without even seeing them settled into their undergraduate courses?

If he heard it, he did not say so. Not yet, at any rate. 'And you were captain too?' he persisted, quietly, almost as though they were alone here.

'Yes. A decade or so ago . . .'

'Like my colleague Mr *Gulin*,' he emphasized the name just enough to tell her he had heard her calculatedly insulting alternative, 'I find that hard to credit.'

'You are as charming and gallant as your colleague. But I assure you that it is true.' Was it dangerous to be so icy with Makarov? On the one hand it might damage the deal; on the other, it might present him with a challenge.

'Then perhaps you would do us the honour of guiding us around your old command.'

This did surprise her enough to break her reserve a little. She glanced across at Richard. He gave a lopsided, sheepish grin and a shrug of his navy shoulders. *Typical Russians*, it seemed to say: *always go for the girl . . .*

'You husband will add his own thoughts to yours, I am sure . . .' purred Makarov.

'You'll have a hard job stopping him,' she observed drily, almost automatically.

And Makarov gave the ghost of a conspiratorial wink. Which was somehow even more intimate than Gulin's hand upon her upper inner thigh at lunch. Which unsettled her more than anything else so far.

'Yes, of course,' she said, stiffly, suddenly glad of a reason to turn and move away from him. She crossed to Richard's side. Her bright gaze settled on the middle distance at last and she realized she had been avoiding it. After the far vista of Severodvinsk and the all too intimate close-up of Makarov, his tie knot and his unsettlingly intimate winks, it was something of a shock to look around the equipment, windows, walls, deck and deck-head that had all, once, been hers to command.

'We're on the navigation bridge,' she said, her mind racing. 'So this would be a good place to start.'

But as she looked around the unloved messy wreck of the place, she wondered, just for an instant, where on earth she *could*, actually, *begin*.

Two

R ichard had explained about the Sevmash Consortium to her on the drive in from the airport the night before. They were what he called *novirusskaya*. New Russians. 'It's a slang term, but lots of people use it,' he said. 'It signifies that they want to get away from the old ways. Not just the old Soviet ways of pre-glasnost, pre-Yeltsin, but from some of the bad things since. They are trying to get their business enterprises working along legitimate Western lines. They see themselves as old-fashioned capitalists – Rockefellers, Howard Hugheses. In more modern terms, Bill Gateses if you will. They want to steer clear of the Al Capone, Don Corleone, Mafia sort of associations.

'And their forward-looking, cutting-edge business enterprise is the Severodvinsk Shipyard. They've acquired a controlling interest. They've put in capital and everything else needed to bring it up to world-class status. And while they're just what I need, Heritage Mariner is just what they need. It could be a marriage made in heaven. If we get this last bit right.'

A marriage made in heaven, thought Robin, looking up at Felix Makarov, Tsar of the *novirusskaya*. *If I get this right*. No pressure there, then. She drew in a deep breath.

'I don't want you to think of *Prometheus* as just some rotting old hulk,' Robin began decisively. 'I'm sure you can tell better than I can what potential profit there is for your Sevmash Consortium and your breakers' yards in the simple bulk of iron and steel that she comprises. Remember, like all the *Prometheus* series, she is double-hulled, so as well as the hull you see, there is another, slightly smaller but equally substantial, within that. Two solid hulls, even before you get to the skins of the tanks. Tanks which of course are themselves internally strutted, supported and subdivided with a massive amount of metal, like great steel cathedrals subdivided into naves and chapels.'

'We have seen the specifications and the design drawings,' inserted Makarov, smoothly. 'We've gone over them with our experts at the yards and they have calculated what percentage might be recoverable by us down at Severodvinsk. We have highly accurate computer models of how age, external weathering, internal stresses and shears, and, of course, chemical reactions with everything from salt water to the various types and compositions of crude oil will affect the range of iron, steel and other metal types involved.'

'But you will have only estimated what she represents in recoverable metals,' persisted Robin, equally smoothly, getting into her stride now. 'And like one of the Fabergé eggs that go with your pretty tie, Mr Makarov, she represents more than mere melt-down worth. And that may not have been so evident from whatever paperwork Richard sent you!

'It is obvious that a certain amount of cannibalization and simple pilferage has been going on. I was able to see that as Mr Gulin and I were coming up here, for I saw into many of the cabins and work areas I passed on the way, but it seems to me that much of the navigation equipment is still here and will be recoverable. A certain amount of work will make it fully functional and saleable again, I'm sure. And you may not have understood immediately what extra financial benefit this might also bring. Everything you see around you, from the GPS system to the collision-alarm radar and the ARPA over there was state of the art when fitted. Most of it was manufactured and fitted by Kelvin Hughes and still worth quite a bit. Certainly, I have seen ships quite recently sailing with far inferior equipment. The radio in the shack over there isn't computer-controlled – we didn't stretch to Hagenuk 4000s in those days like we do today in our big *Sissy* series tugs – but as practical marine kit goes, it would still do the job for me. And there's all the backup in there as well, so far as I can see.'

With Richard towering at one shoulder and Makarov at the other she proceeded; but it soon became clear that the men paying most attention to her words were Gulin and a couple of nerdy friends who supplemented their bald heads with thick black-rimmed spectacles. The equipment buffs, of course. One of them had a hand-held computer on to whose little screen he was scribbling notes with a stylus as she spoke.

Having surveyed the bridge and the radio shack, she led them down, glancing into the larger suites – the owner's suite and the captain's office and day room. A certain amount had been looted out of here, but the place was still surprisingly habitable. An oasis of cleanliness in the rust-bucket of the whole. Some things still existed in place. The cabling for a computer on the blistered veneer of the captain's desk, though the computer itself was gone. The porcelain also – both basins and toilet bowls – though where they led to now that the bilge pumps were offline was a moot point. And both taps and flushes looked in pretty good repair. 'There will be complete air-conditioning systems in these walls, of course,' she persisted, leading them right into the owner's suite. 'And of course, enough pipework and electrical cabling to bring light, power, water and sanitation to a sizeable block of flats. The bunks are wooden sided and seem quite solid, though the veneer surfaces don't seem to have lasted well in a damp salt atmosphere. Like the mirrors . . .'

'I've seen worse,' said Gulin.

'I'm sure you have,' she agreed sweetly, and led them on down from one reasonably preserved cabin to the next. From 'C' deck, to 'B' deck and on down to 'A' deck.

All the bottles, cans and glassware had gone from the officers' bar, but the tables and chairs had survived. And at least one pair of eyes lit up at the sight of a full-sized traditional English mirror-backed pub bar. The videos and DVD players had all been taken from the library but the bookshelves seemed promisingly full – until Robin tried to take a volume down only to discover that time and damp-ness had reduced it to papier mâché. Everything was gone from the gymnasium except the parallel bars on the walls and the equipment attached to them, but, again, the sprung wood of the flooring, still marked out for basketball and five-a-side football, seemed to have survived surprisingly well.

Miraculously, all of the massive IBM lading and cargo-control computers were still in the first officer's work area and lading room. 'If those can be brought back online they should be worth something,' Robin observed to the feverishly scribbling nerd. He nodded so vigorously that his glasses slipped down his nose.

'What *I* wonder,' insinuated Makarov quietly, 'is why the last owners of this vessel didn't get all of this stuff off her and sell it if it's worth so much.'

'We may have been lucky there,' said Richard a little brusquely. Robin, who knew his every tone and undertone, suspected at once he was dissembling. She had never known him actually lie, but this sounded dangerously close to it. Would Makarov pick up on that as readily? she wondered. 'Her final sub-leasing was to some section of the German government, apparently,' Richard persisted airily. 'I don't know which one. But it seems that civil servants can sometimes be just a little more lax in these matters than a commercial enterprise might be. Even German civil servants.'

'I see,' said Makarov smoothly. 'Certainly, I cannot imagine a properly run company letting such assets slip their fingers.'

'Might have gone bust,' said Robin, just for the sake of argument. They clearly weren't going anywhere for a while. Gulin and his nerds were all over the computer banks like flies on dog droppings.

'I take your point,' Makarov maintained his sinisterly silky charm. 'A lot of shipping companies have gone to the wall during the new millennium. They have lacked the . . . ah . . . *spirit of adventure* that keeps Heritage Mariner so buoyant.' He nodded in the direction of Richard and Robin; a slightly old-fashioned courtesy. Almost a bow. 'But even so, if a company folds, the receivers are usually as keen to capitalize upon its assets as anyone else might be.' He looked around the room. 'Yes. You have been lucky here. There is much for *us* to capitalize upon.'

'And more to come,' insisted Richard and Robin, speaking together.

'Down below,' Richard finished. Then he emphasized, 'There's a good deal more below.' She looked askance at him and he nodded vigorously, eyes sparkling with excitement. He clearly knew much more about the treasure trove

aboard the hulk than she did. And he, like she, could see
that Makarov was all but hooked. They were making a
historic deal here.

When Gulin's acolytes seemed satisfied for the time being,
Robin took them onwards to the section of the bridge house
she had been talking about when Richard interrupted her;
another area glimpsed through a half-open door on the way
along the 'A' deck corridor to the companionway.

The medical facilities were in an odd sort of disarray.
The sickberths were made up, sheets and blankets damp but
not yet mildewy, unlike some of the linen in some of the
cabins above. The treatment room, which was almost a basic
little operating theatre, had been rifled. But very little of
the ship's original medical supplies had been taken. True,
they were as basic as all the rest. The Heritage Mariner
supertankers carried a ship's doctor, and the supplies were
the practical minimum such an officer would require. She
passed over everything as though it was all much as she
might have expected and passed on down the corridor,
leaving one of Gulin's men still drooling and muttering
about supplying the local hospital.

The dining facilities had never distinguished between
officers and crew aboard Heritage Mariner ships. The dining
room was miraculously well fitted. Tables, chairs, all well
preserved. Cutlery – all stainless steel. Some glassware,
even. Crockery. Hotplates, urns. The ship's silver tea service
was beyond reclaim as far as she could see. The Victorian
teapot, coffee pot, milk jug, sugar bowl and tongs all looked
as black and crusted as one of Richard's barbecue meals.
But you could front a sizeable restaurant with the rest of
the stuff – and do it tonight by the look of things. Though
you'd have to supply new linen.

And, through a pair of squeaky doors, lay the galley that
would back the new-born restaurant to perfection. The ovens,
ranges and grills were all still there – all stainless steel and
as unsullied as the stainless-steel knives and forks. The
fridges and freezers, again commercial-standard brushed
steel. Only door seals, fastenings and, no doubt, some motors
needing work. Except for the fact that the cooker hood had
been raided. The extractor was gone. The opening into the
big square air-con system gaped wide. But, for a wonder,

the chef's equipment all still in place. Knives, choppers, boards, pots and pans. Everything. Robin paused, struck, as Gulin and two other acolytes checked and noted – this time with a pen on a little pad of paper. 'What?' asked Makarov, catching the change in her.

'Nothing. I was just struck by this. It's all so complete, isn't it? Spookily so, even allowing for the fact that there must have been some kind of a watch kept on board during the tow from Wilhelmshaven. I mean if you hooked up a generator, you could almost use this place now . . .'

'That is good for us, I think.' Makarov seemed to have missed her point entirely. Like Richard he had no intention of sharing her dark, disturbed mood.

'Funny you should say that, my love,' chimed in her ebullient husband. 'I happen to have a generator down below . . .'

It was a German oil-powered generator and it was aptly enough in the engine-control room. It was small but surprisingly powerful and because it was German it started the instant he pushed the green button. Its first cough brought to flickering life a series of lights that stretched away through engineering with sufficient power to allow them to switch off the torches they had carried down into the stygian gloom below decks. Robin flashed hers around before she did so, however, relieved and impressed to notice that the generator was venting into the air-con ducts. It wouldn't do to have it pumping carbon gases into the atmosphere in here. Monoxide or dioxide – they could both be deadly down here. But whoever had put this all in place and strung the lights it lighted through into the main engineering areas had done a good solid job. The watch-keepers who were aboard between Wilhelmshaven and here had found it in place all ready to go, she thought. That's what Richard had told her, far too pleased with the discovery to question where it had actually come from.

'Look,' persisted Richard, who had clearly taken over as guide now. 'If you thought the computer system up in lading was impressive, what do you think of this lot? Full engine-management system. Lading and cargo-control backups. Automatic fire-fighting system. The list goes on and on. You could use this lot in a medium-sized factory or refinery almost as it stands. And look at this pipework. I'll show you pump-rooms with sufficient pipework to plumb another block of flats. And the pumps to make it work. And enough electric wiring to get halfway to the moon. And there are spares of almost everything. But look at *this . . .*'

Richard hurried them out of the engineering-control room and into the engine room itself where the massive three-deck-deep space was all but filled with two mighty motors. They crouched like a pair of sphinxes side by side. Gleaming still, festooned with screens and dials, shrouded in ladders and walkways, surrounded with lesser monsters that Robin recognized as gear housings and shaft covers.

'Those are Rolls-Royce RB211 engines,' Richard breathed, almost awed; as though he had forgotten until now. 'Twin engines driving twin shafts to twin variable-pitch propellers. The same on every *Prometheus*. And look – the spare's still here. Fully serviced to Rolls-Royce spec. and ready to go. You could shove that thing straight into Concorde or a jumbo jet and it would fly. And all the spares you need to keep the three of them going for as long as you need.'

The last two Consortium men were off like whippets. Gulin followed more slowly. So that was the pattern, thought Robin. Makarov the chairman, the leader, the suit. Gulin the *biznesmen*. Two computer nerds, two general-specifications men, one of them a medico and another maybe a chef. Two engineers. Someone had prepared for this part of the survey well. Someone had read Richard's specifications thoroughly. And from what Makarov had said earlier on the bridge, their ships' architects had already discussed the hull itself, the double bottom and the tanks. Down in the yards at Severodvinsk.

Maybe Richard had chosen his partners wisely after all. And maybe these were the men to help Heritage Mariner get even further into the environment business. Making a tidy profit out of recovering and disposing of their super-annuated tankers in an ecologically friendly way. Reusing, recycling, disposing responsibly of anything too toxic. And the shipyards at Severodvinsk were just the place to do it – for they had just finished disposing – responsibly – of the Soviet Arctic Fleet's nuclear-powered vessels. If the

Sevmash Consortium were going to prove as good as their word.

But there was still the lingering ache of Gulin's fingers on the well-toned muscle of her inner thigh. And she still couldn't make her mind up about Makarov.

'You see?' called Richard. 'Even the safety equipment's all still here. Breathing apparatus, fire-fighting stuff, the lot . . .'

'But it's all so out of date,' persisted Makarov, speaking to Robin as he hulked in the shadows just beside her. 'Rolls-Royce motors, maybe. But for Concorde? Concorde hasn't flown in years and years . . .'

'Quality over modernity,' she answered clearly. 'There'll always be a market for Rolls-Royce kit. And there's so much Rolls-Royce equipment out there they'll be calling for spares for years. Even if those motors never turn over in their lives again, they'll still be supplying parts to vessels for another decade and more. When you've got it right, it stays right and people are always wanting to use it.'

Robin swung round to face Makarov full-on, as close to him now as he had come to her up on the bridge. 'It's like guns,' she persisted to cover the unsettling frisson of his nearness. 'There have been lots of newer and better guns brought out in the last twenty years. But every kid in Chechnya's still got his AK47! Know what I mean?'

She stopped, half-horrified. She had meant to say Africa. Chechnya just slipped out. Who knew what effect her words might have on him? A lot of Russians had lost a lot of relatives in that long-running situation. Might Makarov be one of them? Might he have served there himself? There was, she suddenly realized, something almost military about him that she had not noticed until now. She narrowed her eyes, trying to read his expression. But the shadows beneath the overhanging brows were impenetrable. The lines astride the broad nose, wide mouth and square chin seemed absolute, as though carved in stone.

But then the edges of his cavernous eyes crinkled slightly, the lines deepened by the dramatic light. The corner of his mouth stirred. 'You're in the wrong line of work,' he said. 'You should be . . .'

'A used-car salesman?' she finished for him, too stressed

suddenly to wait as he lingered almost sensuously with his thought.

'An arms dealer,' he concluded with a dry chuckle.

And that, like the intimate wink, unsettled her more than she cared to admit.

Three

The moment they reached their 'luxury' suite, Robin began to pull off her clothing. Richard too shrugged off his overcoat and reached for the house phone to call for room service. 'What are the chances of getting this lot dried off before we go out again?' he wondered.

'Heaven knows.' Robin laid her coat ready alongside his for surrender to whoever came in answer to his call then carried on stripping.

Richard turned from his brief chat with reception to find her in her underwear, reaching back for the hook on her bra. The breasts that had been such a focus for Gulin bulged palely over the top of the plain black silky cups. 'Hmm,' he said. 'Now, what were our plans for later? And can they hold back for an hour or so?'

'Hold your horses, sailor,' she answered with the ghost of a smile. 'The only hot and steamy experience this girl's up for at the moment is a shower.' The calming effect of her words was more than a little undermined by the way her breasts swung free as the bra came off.

'OK,' he temporized cheerfully, reaching for his tie knot. 'The least I can do is scrub your back for you.'

'Oh no you don't!' she said, stepping out of a wisp of silk that might have been a thong except for the edging of lace. 'I know where back-rubbing gets us. I'll shower alone, thank you very much. Your mission is to get the name of a really good restaurant from the bellboy when he comes to get our wet things.'

'This place has the best restaurant, even though lunch went a little off the rails,' he called after her as she padded through into one of the few en-suite facilities in the hotel. 'We can book a table for later and I can still scrub . . .'

She paused in the doorway and looked back over her shoulder. 'Out,' she insisted. 'I want to eat out. Afterwards, who knows?' She twitched her hips just enough to keep his hopes up. The movement gave a twinge of discomfort to the little bruise on her thigh left by Gulin's all-too personal attentions. And that reminded her that she still had a bone to pick with Richard. More than one, in fact. But so much had happened since her first dull anger with him that she wanted a little time to think things through.

The little by-play went some way to cheering them both up and lightening the atmosphere, for they had both found the meeting aboard *Prometheus* stressful. Robin in particular had been affected by the ghosts resurrected by the tour of her old command, and by something indefinable that had nagged at her subconscious all the way through the guided tour. But mostly, she was concerned about the whole deal and the personalities involved in it. After Makarov's innuendoes and Gulin's outright lechery it was pleasant to remain the one object of desire for the one man she wanted to be desired by.

As Robin waited for the shower to reach the required temperature, just a little short of scalding, she thought about Richard's partners in the project. Makarov had been the personification of sinister charm while Gulin had simply been charmless. Like a pair out of a James Bond film. Like Goldfinger and Oddjob, like Scaramanga and Nik Nak, like Carver and Stamper. Both of them in very marked contrast to Richard with his bluff, almost innocent British ebullience. And that was worrying, of course, because Richard was no 007. Or it would have been worrying, she told herself bracingly, if Gulin had been more like a henchman and less like a toad.

But the case they had all made was compelling enough. And especially Markov. There was a fantastic deal to be done here, even with ships that were far older, even more battered and much less well equipped than *Prometheus*. And perhaps Richard was right. Perhaps the deal had the potential to be truly ground-breaking.

Over the rumble of the shower and the roaring of the water system, Robin heard the bellboy at the door, and Richard's 'Come in and look at these please. Oh, and could you recommend . . . ?'

She stepped into the safety of the steam-filled stall without further thought. The water was perfect. She allowed it to come foaming over her breasts for a moment, then she turned and allowed it to pummel her shoulders, sending a river of blessed warmth down her spine into the valley of her buttocks.

She stretched sensuously, feeling the water bring its blessed warmth to her bones. Perhaps she might invite Richard in to scrub her back after all, she thought, and let her rumbling tummy go hang. But then, on the other hand, there were still things here that she simply did not like. As she soaped herself, she thought back to the sudden shock awaiting them as they ran back though the drizzle along the pier towards the pair of big black Mercedes limousines.

There had been uniformed officers waiting at the security gate as they arrived back from *Prometheus*. Sufficient numbers of them to be crowding round the Mercedes limousines. Big, hard, unsmiling men in uniforms Robin did not recognize. Well armed with guns that she all too clearly did recognize.

'Nothing to worry about,' said Makarov, a little steel behind his ready smile. 'Just GAI traffic police . . .'

He took aside the man who looked like the senior officer and chatted easily to him. Gulin made a more anxious third, their bodies grouped together, keeping their hands concealed. Their hands and anything that might be passing between them. Though, thought Robin as she clambered aboard the Mercedes simply glad to get out of the freezing rain, the officers seemed suspiciously interested in *Prometheus* for simple traffic cops.

'Just as I said,' schmoozed Makarov as he climbed in beside them. 'Traffic policemen checking up on our vehicles. Nothing to be concerned about.' But when Robin casually glanced back, the security gate was up and the officers' own less luxurious vehicles were rolling determinedly along the increasingly distant pier. The Mercedes containing Gulin and his men turned right and disappeared towards the distant Dvina Bridge.

'Look,' said Richard, a propos of nothing other than that they had turned right at a major road junction, one block further on than Gulin and Co., 'that cinema there is showing a season of Eisenstein films. Perhaps we should go, Robin. I've never seen Eisenstein's films on the big screen. That poster looks like *Alexander Nevsky* and that one is *Ivan the Terrible*, I'm certain.'

'That is the Snezhok cinema,' confirmed Makarov. 'It usually shows Western films. I saw *Casino Royale* there last, I believe. But there is a Classic Russian season running. You have missed *Battleship Potemkin*, I'm afraid . . .' His tone was odd once again, as though he was keeping back something vital to tease his ignorant guests. Like the winks, it made Robin uneasy.

The Mercedes swept down ten city blocks, across ten more junctions until it rolled effortlessly past the skyscraper of the Central Administration Building and Detsky Mir into ploschad Lenina where the man himself towered in black rock the better part of twenty metres high. Robin knew this area well enough to expect a left turn up to the telephone office and the hotel where they were staying. But no. They rolled onwards past the Premier Supermarket, general store and restaurant and the Dvina hotel next door before swinging into Trotsky Prospekt between more soulless grey building-boxes.

As they swung left, Makarov leaned sideways towards her. 'I have ordered this little diversion for your benefit,' he said. 'It seems to me that we are keener on Richard's enterprise than you are. And the only reason I can see for this is that you do not understand what a solid basis it is founded upon. I am a Muscovite, you must understand. My colleague Gulin is from Archangel and his associates are local too. They are from Severodvinsk, of course. They are Pomory. I am therefore not ashamed to show you some things they might be less . . . ah . . .' He searched for the right word as the Mercedes whispered through the rapidly darkening afternoon towards the early blackness of an icy, drizzle-filled autumn Wednesday evening. 'Less *eager* to have you see . . .'

The Mercedes came on to another thoroughfare and swung right. Almost immediately, the grey blocks were snatched away. Or they were in the foreground at least, thought Robin, for they stood solidly in the middle distance like a crowd of grey-suited adults looking down upon a line of children in fancy dress. And there, framed against the backs of the towering concrete apartments lining the next crossroad north, stood a row of crazy little wooden houses. Wooden walls, wooden-tiled roofs, wooden verandas and wooden doors. Wooden walkways stretched before them, heaving up and down where the land, like the timber, was warped. Some of them had glass windows but most of them had waxed paper or closed shutters. The window frames like all the rest were too far out of true to support anything like glazing – let alone double glazing. None of them stood straight or square. They sagged and leaned, bulging and boarded. There was some scant greenery around them – nothing that could be called a garden or anything like one. Robin saw goats tethered. Dogs prowling.

It was as though they had slipped back a century or two like time-travellers in a TV series. There was no obvious source of municipal power here; no street lighting. In the gathering shadows there seemed to be a pinpoint of light here and there such as might come from an oil lamp. Smoke issued from some of the chimneys as the residents took some action against the cold as well as the dark.

In Germany or Austria, Norway or Sweden, such a sight would have been a tourist treasure brightly painted and well maintained, staffed with locals in period dress, cheerfully dispensing entertaining history lessons while gathering in the tourist dollars. But Robin could see at a glance that this was real. These houses were more or less as they had been when Ivan the Terrible founded the place, except that they were unloved, dilapidated and slowly being torn apart by the way the ground heaved as it froze and thawed year on year. And people really lived in them. Though what sort of life they lived, Robin was hard put to imagine. Everything here was the architectural equivalent of a down-and-out dosser wrapped in a blanket in a doorway.

The Mercedes slid to a stop at the roadside. The three of them sat in the kind of comfort, enjoying the kind of amenities, that these sad little wooden hovels would never know.

'What I want you to understand,' said Makarov quietly, 'is that Archangel is a great city. Of course it is older than New York – which great city is not? It is a great centre for trade, a massive port for commercial as well as naval shipping, for sea traffic from all over the world as well as for river traffic from the interior. It has been so for centuries. And much of the trade that has made it great in the past has been with Great

Britain and what used to be her colonies. You have seen the
barges, I am sure. And the wood that floats down from the
Taiga. In the past also there were huge markets supplied with
trade goods from your British Empire and in more recent
times from the British and American war efforts. It has
remained a great city, even when the Soviet Union became
more inward-looking. Millions of people live and work here.
There are only half a dozen cities in the old Russia that equal
it. And this is a good place. A *happening* place. Even the
maliskaya are beginning to spread some wealth down into the
middle classes. As are business ventures like ours. Overcoming
the drugs, the prostitution, the Aids; opening markets almost
as massive as those in China. The maliskaya are doing this –
what you in the west call the Mafiya or the ROC, Russian
organized crime. What more can legitimate businessmen such
as ourselves achieve in a place such as this? It is beyond
dreams. Beyond visions!'

Makarov leaned even closer to Robin, the smell of Parma
violets on his breath giving his words an added authority, as
though her grandmother were telling her these things. 'But
look at the basis from which we begin. Look at these houses,
these . . . what would you call them? These *hovels*. Look at
them and think of the equipment you have towed into the
harbour aboard the rotting hulk you would discard like a piece
of trash with hardly a second thought.

'Even the glass in the bridge-house windows will find a
ready market here. One of the hotels will take all the cutlery
at premium prices as though it has come from Harrods or
Bloomingdales. The sheets are damp and mildewed? They will
clean up, dry and sell as readily as those from Premier. And
the drugs in your little surgery? We have doctors in rural hospitals who would kill to get hold of them. Don't you see? What
is junk to you can be treasure here. And, as Richard so clearly
knows, the computers by IBM, the engines by Rolls-Royce
are almost beyond price. The steel of the hull will make us a
profit. What is hidden away in the bridge house will make us
rich! And if there are many more in such a state then we will
all have dachas in the country before the end of the year.
Dachas in St Tropez and Bermuda.'

As if to emphasize his impassioned words, an ancient tram
wheezed out of the darkness and clanked past the shining

limousine. Something which, like the Parma violets, would have been familiar to Robin's grandmother. And she could see his point, even if the vision of dachas in the South of France and on the far side of the world left her cold. But he had more to add.

'*Even* here. And if you think this place would benefit from some simple Western input such as half a dozen apparently useless supertankers could supply, you should see some of the outlying areas. And some of the other independent states that are just beginning to open up. Latvia. Lithuania. Estonia . . .'

Behind the tram came a couple of battered-looking cars with official-looking markings largely obscured by dirt. They all had official-looking lights on the top which marked them as officers in yet another of the state security and control services. Where in England there would just be a part of the police force, here there seemed to be overlapping, independent armies of authority. Armies that were variously equipped and funded. Armies in constant competition with each other, worrying every incident and crime like wolves around a tasty carcass. One light on one car lit up as they swung in behind the stationary Merc. Makarov carried on regardless. 'But on the other hand, even if we forget the extras and simply consider the hulls, the strength of cities such as this lies in their simple, old-fashioned manufacturing ability. Like China, we can take steel and make anything out of it at really competitive prices. Nowadays, getting raw materials out of the interior is more problematic – unless they can be moved on barges.

'But you bring us basic supplies from outside. And how many supertankers are we talking about? The better part of a dozen in the Heritage Mariner fleet alone? Three million tons of steel in meltdown just for starters. And once we get working, we'll widen the net and go for any old shipping we can strip and recycle . . .'

There would have been more, but a sharp tapping at the driver's window interrupted the flow. Makarov looked out and frowned. Because the uniform at the window asking them to move along now was another GAI traffic cop. 'Time to return you to your hotel,' Makarov said, with absolute finality.

And, Robin realized now, as she thoughtlessly soaped her tummy with the Imperial Leather which she had been lucky to get in

Premier this morning, that the second GAI officer moving them on outside the little wooden huts had looked nothing like the men who had gone up the pier towards *Prometheus*. Not his uniform, not his car, not the old-fashioned-looking gun whose barrel he had been tapping on the driver's window . . .

Four

R obin strode back into their hotel suite as naked as the day she was born except in the matter of some bright blonde curls. And in the matter of a number of diamond-brilliant water drops from the boiling shower which glittered on her skin. She was, literally, steaming. Her face was folded in a frown of deep concern.

Richard didn't even glance at her. He was looking at a guide book. 'The bellboy's taken our coats,' he called over his shoulder. 'He'll put them in the hot room of the sauna downstairs and keep an eye on them. No one's using it so they'll be warm and dry when we need them on our way out. Now, he recommended that place, if we don't want to eat in here,' he said, gesturing to a card on the table. 'I'm just checking it.'

'Richard . . .'

He didn't pick up on the worry in her voice. 'Looks promising. Just the sort of place we'd want to try. Very ethnic. And right down by the sea.'

'*Richard!*'

He picked up on that and turned at once. His eyebrows rose. 'I thought you didn't want your back rubbed until after we had eaten,' he said, his tone still light, playful.

Now it was her turn to pick up on tone. She looked down at herself. 'Chuck me that robe off the bed,' she demanded. 'This is important. I want you concentrating.'

'What's worrying you?' he asked as he did what she requested.

'Those weren't traffic cops who stopped us at the security gate when we came off *Prometheus*,' she explained, shrugging herself almost angrily into white terry towelling.

'Weren't they?' He didn't seem all that concerned. 'It's hard to tell. There are so many state and local forces here. Not to mention private security firms. And that's even before you get to what we would call policemen.'

'But they went on up the pier towards *Prometheus*.'

'Maybe they were customs and immigration, then, or the Archangel equivalent. England isn't the only place in danger of being flooded with illegal immigrants, you know. They have an immigration crisis here as well. Mostly Vietnamese, I understand . . .'

'Then why . . .'

'Why look for illegal immigrants on a ship inbound from Wilhelmshaven? I don't know. Maybe there's some German illegal immigration as well. Or more likely they think Germany's a stop-off on whatever route the snakeheads and people-smugglers use. Maybe people are meeting with ships at sea and bringing them in. You know very well how good criminal organizations like the Mafia are at smuggling people all over the world. Especially women for the sex trade.'

Richard's remark referred to an adventure they had experienced a few years back setting up a super-cat service between Thunder Bay in Canada and Chicago. They had found the bodies of women floating in the water and traced them to Russian freighters, which had been involved in people-smuggling.

'No! That's not what I mean and don't change the subject. This isn't the Great Lakes. It's Russia, for God's sake. Why did your friend Makarov say they were GAI if they weren't?'

'No idea. Knowing him, he just thought it would put our minds at rest while he got on with negotiating the deal.'

'But he'd only do that if customs and immigration were going to be a worry. Are they?'

'No. There's no one aboard. Not even a harbour watch. You'd have seen anyone who was there, just the same as the rest of us when we looked around her this afternoon.'

'That's not quite true, and you know it. Supertankers are huge. We didn't go into every space by any means. The hull could have been packed with stowaways and we'd never have noticed a thing.'

'It's not very likely, though, is it? I know you don't trust Makarov as much as I do yet, but think about it. The towing watch who came all the way round from Wilhelmshaven must have noticed something and we know all of them well.

Personally. As individuals, especially after the work we did towing *Quebec*. You must admit that they would have noticed something if there had been anyone living secretly aboard. And they would have told us. No question. I mean they were quick enough to report the generator they found down in engineering, weren't they?

'Well, the guys who were aboard for the voyage left at the weekend aboard *Sissy* when she sailed back out. She was clear of passengers then and she's clear of passengers now. So immigration won't be a problem. And I've got customs clearance for the hulk and everything aboard her. Even for the generator the towing crew rigged so they could check out the motors for me on the way over. And anyway, customs don't want to be a problem. Think about what Makarov said. Think about what *Prometheus* and the others like her could mean for the local economy. Nobody in Moscow wants a problem. It's doubly certain that nobody in Archangel wants a problem either.'

'Yeah!' Her riposte was taken from her daughter's teenage vocabulary. It ranked with *whatever!* and was almost derisive. 'It all comes back to Makarov, doesn't it? And how much we can trust him. How much we can trust what he says. How much we can trust his honesty. How much we can trust his business connections or his political contacts or whatever. How much we can trust him to deliver on what he says. I mean, look at that tie he wears.'

Richard, frowning, fixed her with his steadiest stare. He could see that she was worried, out of her depth and almost frightened. He'd felt that way a little when he first started doing business in Russia himself, but he was more confident now. And he believed he had formed a good working relationship with Felix Makarov.

'Felix is *novirusskaya*, New Russia,' he answered slowly. As forcefully as he was able. 'As I told you on the drive in from the airport, that means he's fiercely capitalist, money- and market-driven. No time for the old slow Soviet kick-back ways. As sharp as any American. The whole Sevmash Consortium set-up is. They want inward investment, at almost any price. They've fixed up or broken up the whole of the old Soviet Navy's Arctic Fleet, surface vessels, submarines and support. That was a huge job and they've done it well. Made themselves cutting-edge in some aspects – especially in nuclear disposal and environmentally friendly oil cleanup. And they've done some excellent work for us, remember, turning old *Typhoon* nuclear submarines into our *Titan* series of submersible oil tankers. And look what a profit that has made for Heritage Mariner – enough to fund this next scheme at the very least!'

Robin nodded, using the motion of her head to assist the towel-drying of her riot of golden curls. Her expression had softened, but only from worried to sceptical.

Sensing victory somewhere up ahead, Richard ploughed on. 'Now, they've one of the world's biggest, most modern and environmentally sensitive shipyards over in Severodvinsk and they don't want it standing idle. They want this deal as much as we do – and they have full backing of the authorities. Look, darling. They are all legitimate and above board. I mean, look at the transport . . .'

'Two huge black Mercs. So? I thought they were obligatory, whether you were in business or in government or in the Mafia or whatever. Standard issue,' she added a little more gently.

'Perhaps. But the point of having *two* limousines is that one of them holds you and your guests or associates while the other holds your bodyguards if you're up to anything risky or shady. Felix's second Merc held Gulin and the number-crunchers. All legit and above board. I mean Gulin and Co. couldn't be further from the average Russian bodyguard, could they? They couldn't knock the sugar off the top of one of the pear tarts at this restaurant we're going to. The best pears in puff pastry in the world, according to the guide book . . .'

Robin said nothing. But her tummy spoke volumes for her in a long, low rumble. Richard had checkmated her concern by cheating in a way that only he, perhaps, could do. Well, if not quite checkmated it, he had at least reordered her priorities and put it on the back burner for the moment.

As Robin thoughtfully stepped out of the white robe like Venus rising from the surf and reached for the Chanel No. 5, Richard remained sensitive to her mood, like the master of gamesmanship that he was. Aware that he had not quite managed to convince her of his point, of his trust in Felix Makarov and

his colleagues in the Sevmash Consortium, or of his satisfaction with where they were and what they were achieving
here. He used a swift shower and shave to clarify his thoughts
and came out into their suite talking as though they had been
having a conversation in the interim.

'Besides, you know as well as I do what the British government is proposing to do in the next Environment Act.' He
slapped on a little Roger and Gallet aftershave. 'Treating tankers
like *Prometheus* and all equivalent vessels as though they were
as dangerous as guns. And I suppose, for the environment, they
could be.'

She was dry and fragrant now. She reached for clean underwear. As he stepped into cotton shorts she stepped into a black
all-in-one that required a good deal of wriggling, huffing and
puffing as she pulled it over the cleavage of her buttocks and up
past her waist. With his vest safely if unfashionably and
unromantically in place, he stood behind her and helped her
ease the top of her garment over her breasts. The effect of it
was to make her slim, strong figure almost girlish. And, like
his vest, it was also practical. And, above all, it was warm.

'If the government brings in a sort of end-user certificate
for shipping, then we'll already be well ahead of the market,'
he persisted quietly. 'Everybody else will be huffing and
puffing, trying to trace their old vessels and take some kind
of responsibility for decommissioning them. Or more likely
coming up with excuses as to why such a lengthy and expensive procedure is impossible for them and should be done
by the government or yet another quango if the environment
is so all-fired important. But we'll already know where all
ours are and be under way with the work.'

Confident of his abiding desire for her, Robin put sense
above sex appeal and shrugged on a cotton vest before reaching
for a thick silk blouse with a high neck and long sleeves.
Richard, still talking as he buttoned the snowy whiteness of
his shirt, eyed the thick tights on the bed somewhat askance,
however. If you put those on, my darling, there'll be no back-
rubbing for the rest of the month, he thought to himself.

'And, as with carbon emissions, the end-user certificates
for ships will be tradable,' he continued, with the authority of
a man who has counted government ministers amongst his
closest associates and confidants through more than one

decade, Parliament and administration. 'I mean, there's already a lucrative market that allows countries and companies to buy and sell each other's responsibilities for cleaning up the carbon-dioxide emissions they cause. You know they're even talking about pumping the stuff into the deep oceans so it can liquefy, sink and stay there. People who are on top of their carbon emissions are making absolute fortunes.'

Robin sat on the bed and inserted her right foot into the right leg of the tights. Moments later she was standing with the elastic waistband under the hem of the vest and the tail of the blouse. Richard stepped into his heavy woollen socks and pulled them up almost to his knees, hopping from one foot to the other as he did so, reaching for his heavy woollen suit trousers and stepping into them in turn. Actually, he thought, the tights set off her hips and bottom surprisingly well. She looked like a principal boy in a pantomime; androgynously sexy. *Hot* in the alternative, slangy way to the one she intended, now that they were dealing in the teenage slang so precious to the distant, absent twins. There might be some back-rubbing later after all.

'And it'll be the same for us with this new system,' he persisted as he buttoned his trousers. 'If we are on top of our own responsibilities, we'll be in a position to pick up others' at a tidy profit. Imagine what Sevmash could get *not just* out of decommissioned supertankers but out of superannuated bulk carriers, container vessels, cruise liners. Imagine what people might well pay us to take away their messes and their responsibilities under the law . . .'

'OK,' she acquiesced, stepping into a heavy pair of trousers that had been lovingly and expensively tailored to her figure. Precisely as his had been hand-tailored to his own. She tucked in vest and blouse and zipped up, closing a button and tightening a stylish but redundant belt. 'There's a potential demand that might be enormous. A ready market. Contacts in place and ready to go. You've made a perfect case.'

Richard, braces in place, was standing in front of the mirror putting his quietly expensive silk tie into a full Windsor knot, cufflinks gleaming as he worked. 'But . . . ?' he asked gently.

'But I'm still not convinced. There's something I can't quite put my finger on.' She reached for the jacket that matched the trousers, then changed her mind and sat on the bed, reaching instead for a pair of practical but near-priceless knee-high leather boots.

'That's the main reason you're here, of course.' Richard settled the tie, tucked one end into the loop behind the other, checked the points were exactly the same length and took a pair of silver-backed hairbrushes from the night stand. 'You know I get carried away by enthusiasm for a project. I miss detail sometimes. If I'm missing anything now, you'll see it. By the same token, doing deals in Russia has a pretty dicey reputation. If we close a big one here I don't want you worrying. So if there are problems I haven't seen, you'll find them and we'll pull out. If there aren't any problems after all, then when we go ahead, you'll know what and who is involved and you won't need to worry about it.'

He finished brushing the wings of hair above his ears back into place below the blue-black waves that sat so thickly on his broad scalp. Robin was tugging a round brush through her own golden curls and as it passed, they were falling almost magically into place. By the time she had finished she looked as though she had spent an hour or two in a beauty salon. She reached for her eyeliner, lip-gloss and a box of slightly glittering face powder. 'Not long now,' she said, glancing across at him in the mirror.

'Gilding the lily,' he grinned.

And, oddly, that was the vision of her that remained in his memory most vividly during the next few hellish hours after they had informed him she was missing presumed dead. Staring fixedly into the mirror with that slight frown of concentration she always used when applying the minimum of makeup to the flawless perfection of her face.

'Felix knows we need some time alone to put our heads together,' he persisted, blissfully unaware of the relentless approach of the impending tragedy. 'That's why he agreed we'd go out to dinner alone tonight. Otherwise, you know, he'd be wining and dining us himself.'

'It's not so much that I want to be with you,' she teased, putting down her eyeliner and placing one of her hankies over her breast like a bib. 'It's just that I have to get away from the foul Gulin no matter what it costs.'

She plunged a big soft-bristled brush into the powder and accentuated her cheekbones and jawline with a few deft flicks.

He shrugged himself into his suit jacket and reached for hers as she pulled the spotless handkerchief free. He held it out so that she could slip it on and button it tightly across her tummy. She settled it in place and glanced at herself in the mirror for one last time.

'Ready?' he asked, pocketing wallet, keys and mobile phone. His worked properly here whereas hers still refused to do so.

'Ready for anything,' she answered, reaching for her handbag.

And she actually believed that she *was* ready for anything. But of course she had no more knowledge than he did of what was actually going to happen next.

Five

The concierge looked up as Richard and Robin arrived in reception. He glanced across at the bellboy, who vanished towards the sauna. 'Are your associates picking you up this evening, Captain Mariner?' he asked.

'Not tonight, Sergei,' answered Richard easily. 'Can you call us a taxi, please?'

As he dialled 20-40-60, the concierge continued his urbane conversation. 'And may I enquire where you are off to? It may be better if I tell the taxi driver . . .'

'Just down to the harbour. There's a restaurant there that we've been recommended to try. Izba.'

'Of course. A popular choice – if you haven't booked a table at *our own* excellent restaurant . . .'

'Not tonight. We had lunch here, after all.' Richard was far too tactful to mention that he had hardly had a mouthful and that Robin, preoccupied with Gulin and his attentions, had not eaten anything at all.

'Of course.' Sergei launched into a few sharp phrases of Russian down the phone line. Robin recognized only the word *Izba*. Then the bellboy returned with their overcoats. She put her handbag on the counter and became preoccupied with shrugging herself into the warm soft luxuriance of the silk-lined, fur-collared, black cashmere he held respectfully open to her. In one pocket were her warm-lined leather gloves, in the other the faux-fur hat that matched the apparent sable of her collar. She felt she looked very Russian indeed as she crossed the lobby and paused in the doorway, hugging her bag against her ribs as though that would ease the growling of her hungry stomach. Like a bit-player in *Dr Zhivago*.

Behind her, Sergei said something to Richard about the fare

to their destination. A brightly coloured vehicle that resembled a big American Ford eased to a stop. The doorman ran down the steps, opened the rear door and looked expectantly back towards her.

Without further thought, Robin braved the freezing drizzle, crossed the pavement and stepped into the back of the waiting cab, automatically wrinkling her nose against the smell of cigarette smoke that clung to almost every public space here. And a good few private ones. Richard squeezed in beside her at once. The doorman closed the door. Richard leaned forwards towards the cabby and said the word 'Izba,' in confirmation of what Sergei had said, and another word she did not recognize, which she assumed meant 'drive', because the taxi eased forward into the drizzly darkness of the evening.

The taxi swept swiftly and efficiently through the traffic, avoiding impatient pedestrians, scooters, motorbikes, other traffic and trams. It swung left and followed a big, busy thoroughfare down to the inevitable ploschad Lenina, then past the statue and the skyscraper on down towards the Krasnaya Pristan Pier. Most of the daylight had gone now, even the early sunset smothered by thickening overcast. Some of the *novirusskaya* businessmen of the local chamber of commerce had invested in some public works of late, however, thought Robin. Lenin's statue, the more distant war memorial and all the most attractive buildings along the prospekt overlooking the sea were bathed in searchlights as though this were the Naval Museum and seafront at St Petersburg.

Izba was in one of these fortunately illuminated erections. The taxi eased to a stop outside a big wooden door surrounded by what looked like the complete frontage torn from one of the crazy little cottages Felix Makarov had taken them to see. Robin eased herself out of the taxi then stood, trying to get her head round the unsettling sight as the cab eased forward another couple of metres to join the bright queue of a waiting cab rank. A cottage front had simply been nailed to the wall of a tower block, its door over the doorway in the dull grey concrete. It was bizarre, like some kind of architectural crucifixion. The doorman opened the cottage door for her. He too looked like something out of *Dr Zhivago*. Something out of the starving peasant sections.

'"Izba" means cottage, apparently,' said Richard stepping
up behind her. 'The whole place is themed on a traditional
Archangel cottage – food, decor, the lot. This should be fun.
And the food is to die for. Which will be of primary concern
to you, my love, I'm sure . . .'

Izba was packed but Richard had asked the bellboy to
reserve a table. The decor was as rustic as the cottage front
outside had led them to expect – except that the place reminded
Robin irresistibly of Dr Who's Tardis. The tiny cottage frontage
gave no indication at all of how large the rooms behind it
actually were. Floor space was considerable and well packed
with tables. Wooden ceilings were high and heavily beamed.
The floors of course were wooden; so were the tables and
chairs. The lamps were small and oil-filled. Large ones hung
in golden galaxies from the ceiling in rustic chandeliers; small
ones sat on the tables, gleaming away into the shadow distance
like fading constellations. Robin didn't want even to start
thinking about the fire risk. But the heat from the lamps gave
a friendly fug and, crucially, stopped the cigarette smoke from
gathering too thickly.

As someone took their coats and put them in the cloakroom area by the door, Robin looked around. The clientele
presented a range wide enough to raise one of her perfectly
sculpted eyebrows. Sailors in from the vessels in the nearby
harbour. Officers in variously smart uniforms variously accompanied by wives and girlfriends. Crew in groups who had
obviously saved their pay for the experience. Some of them
had shaved and some had not. Some of them had changed out
of their work clothes. Some had not. All of them had loud
girls in tow whose makeup was too thick and whose bright
blonde hair lacked the indefinable authenticity of Robin's own.

Beside the sailors were solid middle-aged businessmen in
old-fashioned, pre-glasnost suits. Dark jackets of thick mate-
rial which seemed more like cardboard than cloth. White shirts.
Dark ties. Here and there a badge a-gleam on a lapel. Honours
from the military or the Party. Their companions were too
young to be their wives. In some cases they looked too young
to be their daughters. But they hung upon every word with
worshipful attention, like Party hacks listening to Leonid
Brezhnev in the old days.

And there were Richard's *novirusskaya*: young men in

Armani, with cellphones glued to their ears and cigarettes waving extravagantly as they talked, creating intricate smoky patterns in the bored faces of their Gucci-clad trophy-dates. What glittered here were the golden cufflinks, the platinum rings and wrist chains. Watches by Breitling, Patek and Rolex. And the women dripped with jewellery too.

The bellboy either had influence or had made a powerful case for his guests. Richard and Robin were shown to a secluded, smoke-free table beside the window. As they settled themselves Richard enquired whether they were too late for *obed*. Robin looked down across the illuminated Dvina Bay and the White Sea surging gloomily out of the shadowy waters beyond. In the distance, she could hear the relentless rumbling of the surf between the hulls that packed the docks or heaved through the rolling waves where the river currents and the tides were eternally at war.

'Is that what you'd like, darling?'

It took a moment for her to pull herself back out of the restless, threatening gloom. To realize that Richard was talking to her.

'Is that what you'd like, darling? *Obed*?'

One of the frustrations of the meal that Robin had missed courtesy of Gulin was that it had been *obed*. This was the substantial main meal of the early afternoon; a full dinner, taken at late lunchtime. It was more likely that the lighter *uzhyn* supper would be on offer now. And Robin was a trencherwoman.

The waiter smiled and put Richard's mind at rest as she nodded in hungry response to his anxious enquiry.

Yes. If *obed* was still available, they should go for that.

Obed was indeed still available on request, the eager young waiter assured them. There would be *zakuski* appetizers, *pervyye blyuda* second-course soups, *goryachiye blyuda* hot main courses and *deserty* on offer. He passed the menu. Robin stopped trying to separate *Prometheus* from the shadows away behind the illuminated curve of the bay and focused on the food.

The waiter spoke English well and was happy to guide them, no doubt knowing good tippers when he saw them, like any waiter worth his salt. Soon they had settled on *ikra krasnaya*, the cheaper, saltier red salmon caviar, for it was produced locally, unlike the black caviar. The *ikra krasnaya* would be served with *olivie* salad, blini and sour cream. For the lady, this would be followed by *lapsha*, chicken-noodle soup; and for the gentleman, *borscht*. There would be black bread, butter and sour cream. For the hot course, the lady would enjoy a *zarkoye* of beef, mushrooms, vegetables and potatoes stewed in a clay pot and served with black bread and sour cream. The gentleman would prefer *galupsty* of cabbage leaves rolled and stuffed with savoury, seasoned beef, served with *kartoshka* potatoes, boiled in their skins and served with butter, and, as was essential at this season, *griby* – wild mushrooms gathered by the locals and quality-assured by the chef. There would be black bread, butter and, of course, sour cream. Robin knew what *deserty* was going to be – pear tart and ice cream. She just doubted whether they were going to make it that far. Perhaps *uzhyn* would have been a better idea after all, she thought wryly.

Richard didn't drink and Robin wanted to keep a clear head so they didn't need to explore the drinks menu. They both settled for *chai*, the almost Chinese-sounding word for tea reminding Robin of earlier adventures in Hong Kong when the twins were very much younger – and packed off to boarding school rather than university. She had her tea *s sakharam*, with sugar. Richard had his *s faren'im*, with jam; just for the experience. There were also a good many bottles of *mineral-naya voda* available, though none of Richard's favourite naturally sparkling Malvern water.

Richard chatted amiably enough as they waited for the red salmon caviar and blinis. And there was enough domestic information to be passed to keep them going for a while. In spite of his best intentions, Richard never seemed to be there at the important steps in their children's lives. Robin understood the reasons for this but at the same time she remained unhappy about the way the situation kept recurring. He had to work hard to get out of her any kind of detail about how Mary and William had taken to their first experience of university life. How pleased, even, they had been with the new state-of-the-art phones he had bought them as their going-away presents when he himself had been going away. But with the arrival of the tea and a basket of black bread and butter, she began to chat a little more amiably.

Fortunately the twins were at the same university. Had they been going to different ones, Robin pointed out tartly, then his precious Russian deal would definitely have had to go on hold, even if it meant Heritage Mariner losing out. But then, as her mood lightened briefly, she explained the positive sides of the experience. The twins were able to get accommodation in adjoining single-sex halls – and would be on the lookout for a flat to share at the earliest opportunity. And, perhaps best of all, they were there to support each other through the rigorous social minefield that was Freshers' Week.

Robin had overseen the start of the settling-in process. She had even joined in some of it, amused by the simple youthful energy being expended all around her. But to be fair, had soon found herself out of place and eventually alone as the youngsters conquered the social scene and left her to her own devices.

'Like father, like son,' he said, wryly.

'Like father, like daughter,' she added, almost bitterly, her mood darkening again.

He gave a lopsided grin that wasn't quite an apology.

This was old ground. They had been over it before, time and time again. It was one of the few strains on their marriage. The way he went off on escapades in the cheerful assumption that she would be there to run the house, look after the kids and still come running if he needed her really got under her skin sometimes. And this was one of those occasions. One of the very few things that made her feel taken for granted, almost isolated.

A small red mountain of salmon eggs arrived together with enough blinis to feed an army and sufficient sour cream to sink a fleet.

'Enjoy,' said the waiter.

And Richard's cellphone went off. He pulled it out of his pocket automatically and looked at the screen. 'I don't know who this is,' he said, 'but it might be important. Only a very select circle of locals have this number. Mind if I take it?'

Half of the other customers there seemed to have their phones glued to their ears. 'Go ahead,' Robin said wearily, reaching for a blini. 'Knock yourself out.'

Unlike the *novirusskaya*, old-fashioned Richard excused himself and went off towards the door to talk in private. As he did so, something resembling Table Mountain covered in thick, creamy white snow arrived. This was the *olivie* side salad. 'Don't worry,' said the waiter, 'your black bread will be here momentarily.' He hovered anxiously until he saw Robin taking a bite of blini buttered with sour cream and piled with salty salmon eggs. When he moved away, Richard had stepped out of sight.

That was another thing, thought Robin as she munched moodily. Richard's cellphone seemed to work perfectly here. Hers did not. She must have a different provider, deal or tariff. That was something else for them to discuss when he returned to his meal. But the caviar was excellent and the blinis like savoury clouds. She tried some of the side salad and found, concealed under the snow-cap of cream, some delicious pink sea-trout a little overcooked but perfectly complemented by pickled cucumber.

The waiter returned with yet more black bread and butter. 'Your husband says not to wait for him,' said the waiter. 'The phone call is important but he won't be long . . .'

But when the *lapsha* soup arrived, Richard had still not returned. More enraged than worried, Robin ploughed on. She had not been here that long. The combination of nearness to the Arctic Circle and jetlag was playing havoc with her internal clock. The ups and downs of a very testing day simply added to her sense of loss and isolation. Looking out of the window at the bright foreground where the docks, piers and shipping stood amid the rhythmic heaving of the sea, she became almost hypnotized. The way the waves swirled in and out of the velvet blackness and lost themselves amid a welter of cross-currents under the counters of the barges, boats, ships, ferries and tankers thronging the vista ahead of her made her dream of past times and distant places.

Such was her preoccupation that she missed entirely the stirring by the cloakroom. The flash of an official-looking shoulder. The gleam of a badge that did not say GAI but which had been at the security gate this afternoon.

It was only when a waiter almost apologetically brought the fragrantly steaming clay pot of *zarkoye* beef and mushroom stew she had ordered to a table still piled opposite her with untasted caviar and unspooned *borscht* that she realized just how much time had passed.

She rose, disorientated, as though she had been asleep. Richard's beetroot soup looked like a bowl of blood with clouds of cottonwool floating in it where the sour cream was beginning to dissolve. The food in her stomach seemed to sour at once. She felt almost faint and increasingly nauseous.

'Where is my husband?' she asked. The waiter shrugged and she realized that this was a new man, not the cheerful, English-speaking youth who had guided them through the menu. This one was of the Brezhnev vintage, not the *novirusskaya*. 'Where's our waiter?' she demanded, obscurely more worried by the change of waiter than by Richard's continued absence. The man with the clay pot shrugged. Robin turned. 'Excuse me,' she said – though she doubted whether this new man understood. New man maybe but by no means new Russian.

She pushed past him a little unsteadily and went over towards the door. A man approached. She vaguely recognized the man who had taken their coats when they entered. 'Is there some problem?' he asked.

'No,' answered Robin uncertainly. 'I'm just looking for my husband.'

Over the stranger's shoulder she could see the lines of coats in the cloakroom. Her black *Dr Zhivago* coat was there with the black faux-fur hat above it. The peg beside it was empty. Richard's distinctive navy blue British Warm was gone.

Richard was gone.

Six

Robin crossed to the coat rack and froze, frowning. She reached out and touched the place where Richard's overcoat had been, as though she trusted her fingers more than her eyes, the intimacy of touch more than the distance of sight. Her fingertips told her of absence as clearly as her troubled gaze did. There was no doubt about it. For whatever reason, he had left her here alone. Automatically, she took her own coat down, as though it would find some way of telling her what had happened to his coat. What had happened to him. Instead it enveloped her in a warm, fragrant cloud of Chanel. She shook it out gently, deep in thought. Almost as though she would swing it over her shoulders and run away to look for him in the strange and shadowy vastness of the icy city.

But even had Robin actually considered running away at that stage, flight was out of the question. Her handbag was beside her seat under the table. Without that she would be truly helpless; utterly alone and totally forlorn. And she did not really consider it. She was not some silly girl. She was a ship's captain, she told herself bracingly. A captain who still held papers that would allow her to command a super-tanker had she felt the slightest desire to do so.

In her adventurous career, Robin Mariner had faced crises that had threatened her life at the very least. Occasionally her virtue and once or twice disfigurement and crippling. And she had faced them alone as regularly as she faced her domestic responsibilities alone. She was angry that Richard's inveterately workaholic lifestyle had forced her to put the twins into university without their father there to share the experience. He had left her to get them into boarding school. He had left her alone at prize days, school plays and sports days without number. But she was not about to be panicked by the fact that he had managed to leave her alone in a restaurant. Even one in the remoter parts of Russia. Enraged, certainly. Panicked – not yet.

Her first coherent thought was, *What is that bloody man up to now?*

Her second was, Shall I settle up and go back to the hotel at once or shall I at least try for the pear tart and ice cream? Her tummy, helpfully, added to the discussion with a quiet grumble. It at least was by no means satisfied yet. While she was deciding, she allowed herself to be guided back to the table by the man who had taken their coats, still clutching her overcoat thoughtlessly against her breast.

It did not strike her as odd at the time that he neither answered her question nor offered any kind of comment on her situation at all. It was only later that she began to suspect that he had seen what had happened to Richard and was acting under some kind of orders or duress himself.

As things were, however, Robin allowed herself to be guided back to her seat at the laden table. Still preoccupied with immediate practicalities, she placed her coat across the seat of the empty chair beside her own. She picked up her handbag from the floor beside her right foot and checked the contents. She glanced around as she did so, all too well aware of the danger of getting out wads of cash and piles of plastic in isolated, foreign places. Then she gave herself a mental shake. She would have been just as careful of doing so in a popular London restaurant.

There were roubles, euros and dollar traveller's cheques in her purse. But there was also a range of credit and debit cards, all of them accepted internationally, almost universally. All of them in healthy credit. The bill was not going to be a problem. She felt for the phone beneath the purse. As she did so, she noted several things. First, that there was a neat little tourist map of the city on the bottom of the bag beneath it, just above the jumble of keys and general stuff that always seemed to live there, whether of immediate use or not. Next, moving the keys to the Land Rover Discovery that was currently in a long-term car park at Heathrow, she touched the button of the little light on the key ring and illuminated yet more junk in the abyssal depths of the bag. Finally, she took out the phone. She flipped it open and switched it on. The screen brightened. An hour-glass whirled. The signal icon lit up. That was a novelty. She pressed the memory button and auto-dialled Richard's number.

Captain Richard Mariner's cellphone was unobtainable, she was informed by an eerily computerized female voice speaking in unapologetic and inhumanly accentless English. Would she like to leave a message?

Yes she bloody would, she thought. But she'd better not leave the first one that sprang to mind. You never knew who might be listening nowadays. She drew breath to leave a slightly less furious alternative. Connection faded. The phone went dead in her hands.

'Bloody thing!' she snarled, shaking its slender shape as though she was thinking of strangling it there and then.

The coat man – the maître d', she assumed – reappeared. 'Is everything all right?' he demanded, his eyes on her hands. His English was heavily accented as well as stilted and formal. If he got into sentences more than half a dozen syllables long she would have a hard time following him, she thought.

'Of course,' she answered, equally formally. She folded the phone closed as demurely as a child pressing a flower, put it back in her bag and zipped the whole thing securely shut. Then she launched into a social white lie that, later, would only add to her embarrassment. That would have added to it even more than it did, perhaps, if she had enjoyed the leisure or the inclination to think about it when irritation had turned to panic, panic had turned to fear and fear had turned to terror. All in all, that first white lie was one of the lesser evils of the fatal night.

'My husband has stepped out to take a call. You see my phone is not working properly in here. Perhaps the signal . . .'

His expressive eyes swept around the *novirusskaya* gabbling on their cells. None of them had any problem with a signal. But then his expression cleared a little. 'Of course,' he acquiesced. 'You will wait here for his return. In the meantime, is the food to your satisfaction?'

'Entirely.' She lifted the lid on her stew pot. The smell made her head whirl, even after the caviar, the salad and the soup. Her stomach burbled in unladylike anticipation.

'Perhaps you could keep my husband's food warm until he returns,' she suggested.

The maître d' bowed in continued acquiescence. Calculatedly so, to mask the surprise in his eyes that she should think her husband was likely to return. It was fortunate, he thought, that she was so well supplied with cash and cards or he would have been on to the concierge at her hotel to check her credit rating. Or on to the militsia to have a car and a police cell waiting for her when she failed to settle her account. Always assuming the authorities weren't on their way to talk to her in any case. But when he straightened, none of these thoughts was obvious at all. His expression was innocently bland once again.

'Are you sure you would not like some wine to accompany your meal?' he asked solicitously, if almost impenetrably.

Robin recognized the word wine, if little else. *What the hell?* she thought. It was bloody Richard who was teetotal. She was not. Never had been. Never would be. And certainly not tonight. 'Is there a red wine you could recommend?' she asked in a dulcet tone that Richard, had he been there, would have recognized as a most potent danger signal.

She did not recognize the label, though it was not in Cyrillic Russian as she had half expected it to be. The wine itself was rich and fruity, full of a peppery warmth that she accurately guessed to have been born under the fertile suns of the Southern Hemisphere. It complemented the beef and mushroom stew perfectly.

As Robin ate and drank, the untasted early courses were cleared away from Richard's place and they were not succeeded by the stuffed cabbage leaves, the wild mushrooms or the buttered potatoes he had ordered. She thought nothing of this, because it was exactly what she had requested. And in any case, her attention was distracted by a sudden explosion of sound at a nearby table. One of the suspiciously over-blonde girls reared unsteadily to her feet, spitting some kind of insult and a good deal of half-chewed food down at a group of sheepish sailors. There had clearly been a failure of negotiations about numbers, services or tariffs. The girl smoothed her micro-miniskirt over her fishnet-stockinged thighs so that the self-supporting tops at least were covered. She readjusted her cleavage in an almost savage manner. No silicone there, thought Robin wisely. She tossed her head, but with a care which told Robin at least that she was not absolutely confident that her too-golden locks were as utterly secure as her bosom. Then, clothed in hauteur every bit as absolute as Robin's black overcoat, she turned on her stiletto heel and strode away from the table.

For a moment Robin thought she was going to plonk herself down in Richard's empty place and begin to share her woes, sister to sister. But instead, the affronted woman pushed past Richard's empty place and twisted a handle Robin had not observed before. The window through which Robin had been looking up towards *Prometheus* swung open in a section that reached from the floor to two metres up the wall. A French window, clearly. The girl stepped out. An icy breeze swirled in, setting constellations and galaxies of lamp-flames flickering. The maître d' abandoned the cloak room and the reception desk to make sure that someone amongst the disappointed matelots was going to pay for their companion's food and drink.

Robin shivered in the icy blast, then returned to her dinner, dismissing the little byplay with a mental shrug. Even though women seemed to serve an almost medieval function in some places here, somewhere between slaves and trophies, she mused, they were nevertheless able to stand up for themselves. She glanced around the room hoping to share some sisterly solidarity in a speaking glance or two. But none of the women met her glance. Only the men did, their glances for the most part calculating, speculative and downright hungry. She returned to her food, still hungry herself, but on another level entirely.

But when her stew was finished and Richard had still not reappeared, she called the maître d' over again. It really was time to take the bull by the horns and get organized here, she thought, before the increasingly speculative group of recently forlorn sailors made a move to replace their departed companion with Robin herself. She could feel the weight of their lustful gazes on the back of her head like sunbeams on a summer beach. 'Is there a phone I can use to speak to my hotel?' she asked. 'My husband may have returned there

and forgotten to contact me. My personal phone isn't
working, as you know . . .'

'Of course. I will dial through for you immediately. It is
the hotel Zelyony, is it not? At the telephone office? Please
remain where you are. I will bring the phone to your table.'

She only understood part of this, really only the words
that described her hotel and its location. She watched the
man as he crossed to his desk with particularly close attention, therefore, trusting her eyes to tell her what her ears
had failed to understand. And so she saw the strangers the
very instant they pushed through the cloakroom. There were
three of them. They were all men. They were not wearing
uniforms but they behaved like a military unit, eyes every-
where. The leader crossed to the desk at once and stopped
the maître d' from making the promised phone call with the
flash of some kind of a badge.

She knew they had come for her even before the maître
d' furtively glanced towards her as he gabbled answers to
a rapid-fire series of questions. She was on her feet without
conscious thought. She discovered she had her coat over
her right forearm and her bag in her left hand. Only when
her feet began to move did she realize where she was
going. Her eyes were fixed on the handle of the French
window and her right hand was reaching for it before her
brain caught up.

If her almost catatonically disassociated mind was
thinking of anything then, it was gripped by a kind of
dawning revelation founded on almost everything conscious
and subconscious that had happened so far today. The men
at the reception desk were some kind of authorities or,
worse, some kind of organized crime. In a place such as
this, she feared, there would be a fatally thin dividing line
between the two. They had arrived because of something to
do with Makarov, Gulin and their Sevmash Consortium.
Their actions had been triggered by something to do with
Prometheus. *Prometheus*, which, conversely and confus-
ingly, was herself the only familiar element in the whole
fatal mess.

Their first action had been to take Richard. To arrest
Richard. Or to kidnap him. To hold him helpless and forbid
him to warn her that they were also coming after her. And

their second action was to come for her. To arrest her. Or to kidnap her.

And here they were.

It was only when the cold hit Robin like an avalanche that she realized she was outside the French windows. Still, her feet seemed to know what they were doing. They were running her up the side street away from the seafront towards the main road. Her brain was catching up now. She remembered that on the main road there was a rank of cabs, all with their motors running. No sooner had it realized this, than it began to search for the word Richard had used to make the taxi go. But it would not come to mind.

Gasping with fear and frustration, she swung round the corner and there was the cab rank. Its tail was a few metres along from the restaurant. Its head was another hundred metres further up the street. And her clever feet had taken her to the foremost vehicle. She opened the rear passenger door and slung her coat in, following it at once. She nearly brained herself on the sloping back of the doorway getting in, for at the very moment she did so, men came boiling out of the restaurant door and she turned to look at them, simply horrified. The three-man unit and the maître d' burst on to the pavement with enough force to set the whole false cottage front shaking dangerously. And all of them were clearly looking for her. With even more fervour and focus now. She finally realized that the maître d' must have seen what had really happened to Richard. Had been part of the plot all along. Had been cleverly manipulating her, ensuring that she remained at her table until the men who had taken Richard returned for her. Had been secretly laughing at her childish lies. Her cheeks burned as she blushed crimson for the first time since her teens.

Her golden curls brushed the door-jamb as her backside hit the seat and she slammed the door. '*Gastinitsa*,' she gasped. It was not the word Richard had used but it was the only one that came to mind. It meant *hotel*.

'*Gde?*' he asked, speaking slowly because she was a foreigner. *Where?*

'*Zelyony*,' she answered, naming her hotel with all the linguistic confidence that she could muster. Then, breathless and increasingly nervous in the face of his stolid inactivity she repeated, '*Zelyony. Telefonyy punkt*,' the three words she had understood from the maître d's last conversation with her. The hotel was also the telephone office.

The cabby nodded accommodatingly at last, signalled carefully and eased gently forward. Now they were in motion, she looked back again. Everyone except the maître d' was piling into a solid-looking square black car. The maître d' was pointing at her cab and shouting something. Telling the hunters he had seen their quarry getting into the taxi, no doubt. Her heart sank. Only her well-filled stomach kept despair at bay. And the disassociation arising from three-quarters of a bottle of Cabernet Shiraz at 14.5% volume. Doors slammed distantly. The pursuit vehicle swung out into the traffic without indication, hesitation or any consideration for other road-users. Tyres screamed as cars swung out of the way. Brakes and horns howled. Only the trams rattled on undisturbed.

The trams and Robin's taxi driver. Apparently unaware of the pursuit, or so used to such driving that it didn't really register, he eased forward to the end of the square and swung right. Traffic was not particularly heavy, but the driver seemed to see no need to hurry, and Robin couldn't remember the Russian for *faster* if she had ever known it.

The black car paused at the junction as though the driver was looking for them. And Robin suddenly realized that many of the vehicles around her were also cabs. Relief flooded her. She began to try and think ahead. There was a fair chance they might lose her amongst the crowd if they only knew they were following a cab. But they knew where she was going, for the maître d' would have told them about the hotel and the telephone office. If she went there, therefore, they would be waiting for her. She needed to go somewhere else, therefore. Somewhere she could think things through, then call the hotel and find out what was really going on here. But she couldn't rely on her cell. She needed a public phone, therefore. But of course the only place she was certain to find one was at the telephone office. Which was the one place she wished to avoid.

The taxi slowed for the next junction. Robin recognized

it. Down on her left there was a bookshop and then the square with the huge statue of Lenin. Her hotel was one block further on, also on the left.

'*Naleva!*' she called. *Left!*

Seven

'*Naleva?*' asked the cabbie stolidly.

She grabbed some roubles from her purse and waved them. '*Naleva*,' she confirmed.

He shrugged, checked his mirror, signalled, changed lanes. Approached the junction in the left-hand lane. The black car behind them remained in the middle lane, ready to go left, right or straight ahead. It was closing with them rapidly but it had clearly lost contact. Robin had the presence of mind to slip out her black hat and cover the bright telltale of her blonde curls. Though, she thought, more cheerfully, the girl who had left the sailors and her companions who had remained with their meal-tickets in the restaurant proved that blondes were as commonplace in Archangel as taxis on Troitsky Street.

Even so, Robin pulled the hat into place and settled back. The driver's eyes gleamed in the rear-view, then his gaze returned to the road. It was hot in here, after all. That's why they kept their motors running all the time, even when waiting for fares. So that they could keep the heating on at full blast. There was no real need for a fare to don coat or hat at all.

Robin leaned back further into the plastic of the seat covering and cudgelled her brains. Then she remembered the little map in the bottom of her bag. She pulled it out and consulted it. It was difficult to see and as near impossible to understand as the maître d's impenetrable accent. She felt for her car keys and tried the little torch but it wasn't much help either. Streets were named in Cyrillic and then in more familiar characters but apart from obvious, already familiar names like Lenin, Trotsky, spelled *Troitsky* for some reason, and Gagarin, there was little for her to see. Places of interest were numbered but she couldn't access the key, no matter how she folded and refolded the sheet.

As Robin struggled with the map, the cab swung left into the street with the bookshop. *Ploschad Lenina* loomed.

'*Pryama!*' she ordered, glancing up and recognizing where they were. *Straight ahead.*

'*Pryama,*' the cabby shrugged. And got in lane to cross the square and go on northward into Troitsky Prospekt. Then, as soon as he was settled, he reached into the glove compartment.

For a moment filled with the purest terror, Robin thought he was going to pull out a handset and radio in the whereabouts of the strange foreign fare he had just picked up. But no. He pulled out a pack of cigarettes and, driving one-handed, lit up. Her relief was so great that she didn't say a thing.

Robin put the map and keys away and looked back instead. She couldn't see the black car any longer. She breathed a sigh of relief and settled back into the seat. The heady fumes of the driver's tobacco added themselves to the alcohol and the adrenaline and other potent internally produced drugs that were washing through her system. Reality receded even further. The dazzling brightness of ploschad Lenina swept past. Lenin loomed massively then his shadow was swallowed by the shadow of the skyscraper on the corner. They crossed a junction heading north. The State Medical Academy loomed and vanished. The Internet cafe near its main entrance glittered and died. That was where the drugs in *Prometheus*'s sick room would be bound for, if Robin had her way. Better the Medical Academy than the open market available on eBay in the cafe at its street-level frontage at any rate.

The war memorial succeeded the Medical Academy. Four intrepid soldiers almost as tall as Lenin himself looked east and west and south and north. The great bronze hero facing eternally northwards watched Robin as she looked southwards once again through the taxi's rear window. But she could no more distinguish her pursuers amongst the bustling evening traffic than they had been able to discern her taxi amongst all the others.

They drove due north for six blocks as Robin strained her eyes looking south along their wake. But if the pursuers were there, she couldn't make them out. And given the manner in which they had entered the traffic flow outside the restaurant, she reckoned they would have been easy enough to spot, simply by the amount of disruption they caused to the traffic all around them. She breathed easier. She thought further ahead. But even as she did so, her sense of isolation grew. One cross-roads after another counted off how far away she was getting from anywhere she recognized. She checked the map one last time then folded it away and returned it to her bag. Her utter isolation was driven home relentlessly by every Soviet-clone grey concrete box of flats. Even with a map in her posses-sion, she had no idea where she was, where she was going or how to get back again.

Contacting the hotel must be her first priority. If she got no further help or information from Sergei the concierge, always assuming he was still on duty at the reception desk, she must contact the authorities. She had no idea where the local militsia station was. If it was marked on the map, which she doubted, she couldn't see it any more than she could see anything else. So, even if there was no good news about Richard when she contacted the hotel, she should ask Sergei, or whoever, to contact the militsia for her and have them waiting there when she arrived. She would go to the uniforms rather than the plainclothes of the three pursuers who would no doubt also be waiting in the lobby.

Easy choice, she reckoned. Job done.

The taxi eased round to the right, following a curve in the road, which in turn followed the shoreline one block west-wards. The movement was enough to disturb Robin's thoughts and she snapped back to near-reality. She recognized this place. They were coming up to the Komsomolskaya crossroads. And there on the corner a little way in front of her was the Snezhok cinema. The posters for Sergei Eisenstein's *Battleship Potemkin*, *Alexander Nevsky* and *Ivan the Terrible* blazed brightly in the drizzling gloom amongst others, equally lurid, which she did not recognize. Certainly, none of them were for *Casino Royale*.

Relief washed over her. She couldn't think of a cinema in all her wide experience which didn't have a public phone box somewhere in the foyer. '*Shtoi!*' she called. *Stop!*

The driver glanced questioningly over his shoulder and she gestured towards the cinema with the bundle of roubles snatched from her purse.

'Hokay,' he said, endlessly amenable. He swung easily right, eased up to the pavement on the corner, and stopped outside the brightly lit building.

Robin leaped out and almost threw her roubles at him. Only at the last moment did she think to keep some back in case the phone was cash-only. He gave a cheery wave and accelerated away with a little less care than usual. Clearly she had overpaid and he wanted to be well clear before she had any second thoughts. She turned on her heel and hurried in. Nothing could have been further from her mind than second thoughts.

There were three steps up to the main entrance of the cinema, with a steady surge of clients coming and going up and down them. Shrugging on her coat and securing her handbag over her shoulder and under her arm, Robin wormed her way through easily enough and slipped in through the entrance doors.

Snezhok's foyer was busy. Robin found herself fighting through a loose mixed scrum of men. There were no phones immediately obvious, so she began to work her way towards the ticket kiosk. Smoke billowed. Sweat stank. The noise was overpowering. She seemed to be surrounded by the four levels of masculine client from the restaurant. Working men. Men in uniform. Men in old suits. Men in new suits. It did not strike her immediately that the four levels of their female companionship were absent.

She made it to the kiosk. '*Telefon?*' she demanded, performing a quick pantomime with her right hand. Fist closed except for two digits. Thumb in her ear, little finger stretched towards her mouth. The universal shorthand for making a phone call. The pasty-faced and spotty young man in the kiosk nodded and rubbed his finger and thumb together. The universal sign for *pay up*. She gave over some of the roubles she kept back from the taxi driver. He gave her some change and a ticket. '*Telefon?*' she repeated, miming a little more desperately this time.

He gestured towards a door at the side of the foyer that looked exactly like the entrance to the main auditorium. Perhaps there was a telephone by the ticket collection point before the auditorium itself, she thought. She smiled her thanks and all but ran in the direction indicated. Someone tried to take her ticket as she hurried through the doors but she was too close to her goal to be distracted now.

Robin burst into semi-darkness. The noise and smell were disorientatingly overpowering. A combination of brassy, blaring music and exclusively masculine howling. The stench of cigarette smoke was deepened by the heady smell of alcohol. There were sweat and cheap perfume heavy on the air. Damp clothing and foul breath. There was no phone. She could see that immediately. She had come directly into the auditorium itself. On her right hand, a flight of seats rose tier above tier as though this were some kind of lecture theatre. All of the seats were packed with smoking, swigging, braying men. Immediately on her left rose a low stage, just where she might have expected there to be a screen, this being a cinema.

But instead of the heroic if celluloid Alexander Nevsky engaging invading hordes in his legendary battle on the ice, there was something utterly different on display. Something shockingly, disorientatingly different. It was a strip show. Robin stood, simply gaping, staring up at what was going on upon the stage. Three young women were assembled, apparently for afternoon tea, with tables and chairs and all the props. They had evidently returned from a ride in the country for two of them wore jodhpurs, boots and spurs. And they seemed to be carrying riding crops as well as some of the tack brought from the stables. Robin's disorientated gaze took in straps, buckles and reins on the chairs and chaise longue. What looked like Swiss rolls iced in bright pink, cream-coloured ice-lollies, cucumbers for sandwiches and bananas in a fruit bowl were piled up on the table.

Two of the girls on stage had evidently decided they would overpower the third, who was already wearing next to nothing and looking very sorry for herself as she suffered the increasingly suggestive demands of her dominant companions. Under Robin's unbelieving gaze, the unfortunate victim was relieved of the last of her clothing, and her companions began to get themselves ready for a little girl-on-girl action.

With a shock as physical as a punch to the solar plexus, Robin realized that what she had assumed to be tea-things on the table were nothing of the sort at all. Her cheeks flooded with blood as she blushed to the roots of her hair and the tips of her ears for the second time that evening. The noise reached new heights and Robin whirled once more, blasting the door open with such force that she nearly relieved the incoming customer of his teeth. He staggered back and half fell, yelling something at her as she pushed angrily past him.

Then she was in the bustle of the main foyer once again, so shaken that all thoughts of finding a phone and calling Sergei at the hotel were simply driven from her mind. She shouldered her way for the exit instead, heart pounding, stomach heaving, head whirling, cheeks burning, grey eyes flooding with tears of rage and outrage.

She pushed the outer doors open with exactly the same force as she had used on the inner ones. And the man whose face she came near to rearranging this time was the leader of the trio hunting her. The man who had flashed the Militsia badge or Mafia ID at the maître d'. Knocked off balance by Robin's dramatic exit, he stumbled back into the arms of the companion behind him. Then the pair of them, like circus clowns, fell back off the edge of the top step and went sprawling down the next two on to the pavement.

Robin was past them in a flash, and she suddenly found herself to be running for her life as her feet took charge once more. Snezhok was on the corner of Troitsky, which ran roughly north–south, and Komsomolskaya running east–west. She ran across the junction, heading west. She went that way largely because the lights were with her and she was able to get straight across Troitsky at the pedestrian crossing and run straight on down the next section of Komsomolskaya directly ahead. The next block was maybe two hundred and fifty metres of square, dull-windowed corporate clone-flats. Then another, lesser, junction. Then simple blackness. She ran towards this with the single-minded power of a woman who had given up jogging long since because she didn't find it exercised her sufficiently rigorously. It did not occur to her that her black coat, sable hat and dark clothing made her almost invisible in the drizzly thickness of the shadows. But so it proved.

Over the beat of her footsteps and the steady surge of her breathing, Robin listened for the sounds that would warn her of pursuit. Too wise to risk looking over her shoulder in the shadowy strangeness of the sparsely populated street, she concentrated with all her might on the things that she could hear. On the angry bellows far behind the steady snarling of the traffic released from the stasis of the pedestrian-crossing lights. The clanging of trams.

The hooting of horns. The slamming of car doors as the two men jumped back aboard.

The screaming of the tyres as the driver took off across Troitsky in the same way as he had pulled out from the restaurant. The blaring of horns. The screech of tyres. The squealing of a skid.

The shattering impact of one car slamming into another. More screeching, squealing, slamming, shattering. A *lot* more screeching, squealing, slamming and shattering.

Shouting.

Screaming.

Robin slowed. She risked a look over her shoulder. The whole of the junction that she had just run across was at a standstill. Sirens sounded distantly all around as the traffic police sought to become involved. From Troitsky away to the south, she thought, remembering the bits of the map that had made most sense to her. From Gagarina to the north. From Komsomolskaya away behind her down towards the centre of town. Abruptly, from straight ahead – and rushing nearer.

For the first time Robin looked further ahead than this end of the street itself. One hundred metres or so ahead of her there was a cross-street that looked almost deserted of traffic. Beyond that, only the darkness. Beyond that only the sea. The wind gusted towards her, full of drizzle, sea smells and something more. A car came up to the junction straight ahead, siren screaming and lights blazing. Before it turned right into Komsomolskaya itself, it swung a little to the left, avoiding a pothole or some such obstacle in the road. Then it came barrelling hell-for-leather down to the vehicle graveyard of the crash site.

Robin stepped back into the shadows of a doorway as it howled on past her, intent upon its own GAI traffic-police business. Then she stepped forward once again, her face folded into a speculative frown. She looked up the length of the street ahead of her, as though she could still see what the GAI car had fleetingly revealed to her. As though she could see all that and much more. She breathed in once again. In and in and in until her ribs ached. The smell in her nostrils would have reminded her, even if the vision in her memory had not.

In her mind's eye she saw the security gates at the near end of the Komsomolskaya Pier and the dark, silent, familiar and safe-seeming hulk of *Prometheus* sitting solidly at the far end, sending its graveyard stench of rotting, rust and rancid oil down along the wind towards her.

Eight

This end of ulitsa Komsomolskaya had been quiet if not quite deserted before the excitement started. The sounds of the crash and the shrieking sirens, however, pulled people out of their flats in ever-increasing numbers. A slow night on post-Soviet TV, clearly, thought Robin grimly. The promise of some good old-fashioned police-procedural live action here outweighing even the glossy fictions of New York, Miami, London or wherever.

Everyone seemed to looking east or heading east down to the junction with Troitsky, where the noise was all coming from and the dazzling action was converging. Doorways slammed open and closed. Windows squealed wide. People shouted questions that no one seemed to answer. Another GAI car screamed past down Komsomolskaya. More people came out.

Robin slowed, then lingered half in a doorway looking back, fearful of being the only one there heading west against the overwhelming flow of rubber-neckers. She felt she already stood out far too much in the gathering crowd. Everyone around her was dressed in clothes that ranged from overalls to dressing gowns depending on what they had been doing when the noises started. A good few of them had bothered with over-coats but none of them with hats. The cloth of their clothing was largely practical, workaday, heavy. And predominantly grey. Apart from the absence of flat hats, the men and women around Robin looked like extras from one of those sixties films set in a northern English factory town. Or a Welsh mining village in the thirties. *Saturday Night and Sunday Morning*, perhaps. *How Green Was My Valley*.

Robin queasily reckoned that someone looking like an extra from *Dr Zhivago* was going to linger in everyone's memory unless she was very careful indeed. And if anyone spoke to her expecting an answer then she would be utterly unmasked. She never doubted that when the immediate crisis was past, the three men in the black car would come down here after her. And they would be asking questions; looking for witnesses, trying to work out where she had gone to. And she hoped and prayed that *that* wasn't going to be jaw-droppingly obvious.

Robin stayed well back in the shadows, therefore, allowing the inquisitive locals to eddy past her. Doing her best to seem to be heading eastwards while, at the very least, staying roughly where she was. She noticed the odd glance flung at her, mostly from the passing men, but no one approached her. Summoning up her courage, she began to work her way along the road towards the still-distant gates at the near end of the pier and the hopefully unsuspected refuge of the good ship at its far end. In her head she was rehearsing the phrases she might need if anyone did come near her.

'*Ya zalbludilas!*' I'm lost.

'*Gde gostinitsa Zelyony?*' Where is the Zelyony Hotel?

'*Gde taksi?*' would be a good one to fall back on, especially as she had seen a taxi rank outside Snezhok. Not that she wanted to go back there. But still, if push came to shove . . .

'*Gde tualet?*' But only if things got really desperate. Especially as she couldn't remember having seen a public toilet anywhere at all, and she most certainly didn't want to get invited to use the private ablutions in any of the flats.

She wanted to avoid '*Ya ni gavaryu pa ruski*' and '*Ya gavarite pa angliyski?*' (I don't speak Russian, do you speak English?) as being just that bit too memorable, too. But, again, the words remained in her defensive armoury, just in case.

Blessedly, the noise soon began to quieten, the entertainment value to pall and the crowd to thin in proportion. After some minutes, more than five but less than ten she thought, Robin felt free to move forward more purposefully. No one seemed to be paying her any attention, for she was now moving with the flow of sightseers returning to the warmth of their homes. Her clothes might be out of place still, but her movement no longer was.

Robin paused at the corner of Komsomolskaya and looked across the last wide road that ran north–south between her and her goal. The road had seemed narrower and less busy than Troitsky from way back outside Snezhok but she saw now that this was something of an illusion. It was, of course, the closest thing Archangel had to a Marine Drive or Promenade. The trams and commuter traffic were supplemented by sightseers clearly just driving lackadaisically along, looking out at what views still remained in the almost pitch-darkness. The distant prospect of the Naval Museum, which did look a little like St Petersburg from away up here, under the steady beams of the searchlights shining up on it. The other illuminated edifices near ploschad Lenina added to the vista, all of them given some added beauty by distance and drizzle like the face of an ageing actress pictured through a soft-focus lens.

The span of the bridges. The snakes of traffic crossing the river. The sudden serpentine splendour of a locomotive, its siren sounding like a lost soul in a sudden seeming silence. The industrial brightness of the shipyards and factories beyond just beginning the night shift. The shipping out on the bay, still with yellow deck lights on as well as more colourful navigation lights. Ferries coming and going, throwing enough white light out and down to illuminate lively little patches of the sea.

Robin crossed at the pedestrian lights but was doubly careful as she did so. The drivers were hesitant to give way to pedestrians at the best of times, even in the face of red lights – when the lights were actually working. All too often seeming to see this small municipal revolt as a potent gesture against the long-dead system that put the lights there in the first place. And there would be an extra contingent here fixated with the view and not watching the road at all. On top of which, a black outfit that hid her from pursuers might well do the same from even careful drivers in the dull glow of the street lighting. On the one hand invisibility could save her. On the other hand it could also get her killed.

But not on this occasion. Robin made it safely across to the far pavement and swung briefly south until the security gates at the foot of the pier were at her right shoulder, standing back behind the broad entrance road running along the half-kilometre of the pier-top itself. It was the wide slip road blocked by gates which had served both Mercedes limousines and Militsia or GAI vehicles as a pull-in. Here Robin stopped once more and looked up, narrow-eyed. The gates were high, sectioned with diamonds of woven wire backed in turn with sheets of corrugated iron and topped with rolls of razor wire. On one gate hung a bright yellow sign which said in Cyrillic and in Western script *Komsomolskaya Prichal* – Komsomol Pier. And more writing in both scripts that meant, she assumed, the equivalent of Private Property and KEEP OUT.

There was more, both in writing and icons, but nothing, Robin very potently hoped, which meant, 'This area is guarded by vicious dogs after dark: Trespassers will be Eaten'. She couldn't be sure, however, for although the words and pictures were running like wet ink under the rain, there was something that looked suspiciously like the head of an Alsatian or a wolf.

She listened as carefully as circumstances would allow, therefore. But at least there was no sound of anything barking or snuffling around within. And Robin recognized the occasional dismal howling as the wind in the superstructure of the still-distant ship. Still desperate enough to be taking uncharacteristic risks, therefore, she proceeded. At the very least, the increasing, unbearably icy, downpour made her reluctant to linger any more than she had to.

There was a little metal doorway just beside the bigger gates. Robin knew this from her adventures of the afternoon. If that was still open, as it had been when Felix Makarov led them through, then she was in. She crossed to it, moving forward into the deepest shadows afforded by the dull street lighting behind her and some dim sodium security lighting that she now noticed above.

Even in the half-light, Robin saw at once that things were different now. There was no padlock – thank God! she thought – but there was some bright yellow-and-black plastic tape secured across the whole door. It was the type of tape familiar from the countless American cop shows her son William and his father occasionally enjoyed on the TV. *CSI Archangel*. It had a bit of a ring to it, she thought. The GAI or Militsia or whoever it had been this afternoon clearly didn't want anyone else coming back in here for the time being. She hesitated, trying to calculate the implications of action and non-action alike while water ran like a tiny glacier under her collar and down her neck. She would have hesitated further, with her hand upon the little handle, some serious, sensible second thoughts coming now that her panic was subsiding. But the sirens started up again and she glanced over her shoulder to see the brightly lit police cars speeding back along ulitsa Komsomolskaya. If she stayed here, she would find herself in the full beam of their headlights at any moment now. It was this thought more than any other that made her pull the tape aside, slide the bolt across and step through into the welcome shadows of the pier beyond.

As Robin closed the door behind her, so its edges were suddenly defined by brightness. The screaming of the sirens mounted, lingered and died. She took a deep breath and turned. She hadn't noticed the tall lamp-standards this afternoon, but she saw them now, each one giving off a faint leprous lemony brightness defined more by the drizzle seven metres up than by any actual light that made it to the ground below. But as she moved forwards into what resembled a yellow-roofed tunnel of shadows with nothing but howling blackness at its end, so her eyes became accustomed to the gloom. The flat stone pier top with its ruler-straight edges made itself apparent like some kind of ghost. The grumbling of the surf against the jumbled foundation of boulders and concrete blocks below began to gather. City sounds receded until they became one with the restlessness of nature. Even the occasional siren became indistinguishable from the keening of the wind in *Prometheus*'s invisible bridge house.

Halfway down the pier there was a little guard hut which, like the security lights, Robin hadn't noticed this afternoon. She crossed to it with a stirring of hope. There might be food and warmth in there. There might also be officialdom, detention and arrest. But it didn't seem all that likely. There were no cars beside it and only a madman like herself would walk up and down this pier at night. It was locked and dark. She had neither the skills nor the intention to add breaking and entering to her list of crimes that night, so it remained inviolate and she remained cold and wet. But at least the overhang of its roof gave her a moment's respite to pause and look around before she pushed on grimly once again. The wind brought squalls eastward into her face so lazily that she could see them coming, defining lamp after lamp in glittering succession, but not until she was almost alongside it did the light or the rain-squalls reveal her goal to her.

In the darkness, defined only by the faintest outwash of the sickly security light and the glitter of spray leaping up and out along her edges, *Prometheus* looked infinitely more derelict than she had even this afternoon. The graveyard stench of her had been intensified by the relentless rain, and the wind brought it whimpering down to her nostrils. Because the companionway was painted white, she was just able to make it out in the gloom. But when she reached the foot of it, she had to grope forward on to the high-sided upward slope that mounted *Prometheus*'s precipitous side. So it was that she discovered the companionway had been police-taped like the side door leading on to the pier itself. She had time and, blessedly, the self-preserving inclination, to step carefully over this and rearrange it behind her so that it seemed apparently undisturbed.

But no sooner had Robin done this than she paused yet again. This all seemed so mad to her, suddenly. So childishly silly. And yet, she remembered the face of her pursuers' leader. How he had looked as he ran out of Izba with sufficient angry force to make the wooden frontage tremble against the wall. How he had looked up at her from his position sprawling on the pavement outside Snezhok. She most certainly did not want to find herself alone with him or with any of his men. And, having come this far, she would have felt herself to be really stupid if she just went back on to ulitsa Komsomolskaya, flagged down the first GAI car she found and handed herself in. What could she possibly say? Where would they take her? Who would they tell? What if she got the wrong kind of car and handed herself over to the men who put up the tape on the pier?

Then the main gate half a kilometre east opened briefly and her mind was made up for her in a twinkling. Headlights beamed down the length of the pier as some kind of a truck pulled in, its square form outlined by the streetlights on the prom behind. Its engine coughed as it laboured to a halt. The driver's door squealed open and slammed shut. The driver went back and closed the main gate over before labouring back to his vehicle again. The ancient vehicle pulled forward almost half the length of the pier and stopped. The driver got out again.

Robin couldn't see what he was doing, but suddenly she

didn't need to. A door groaned wide, all but the first grating sound of its hinges lost in the cacophony of half a dozen barking, snarling, howling dogs. The man shouted raucously at them, sounding scarcely less wild and threatening than they. The change in the timbre of the sounds denoted to the stricken woman the near-certain probability that the dogs had been unleashed rather than that they were responding to their master. The growling, snarling spread across the street-end of the pier as though a pack of wolves had come hunting there. Which, of course, in a manner of speaking, they had.

Robin was running for the safety of the bridge house before the door on the back of the truck slammed shut again. She was at the first turn of the companionway when the truck got back to the main gate and the driver exited as deliberately as he had entered and dropped off the dogs. In the time it took for the truck to vanish into distance and silence, she had reached the second turning. She was labouring for breath now because the slope was steep, and she was running at little less than panic speed. The thought of what half a dozen nearly wild guard dogs might do to her put the big man in the square black car firmly into perspective, no matter how angry she had made him with her narrow escapes at Izba and Snezhok. No matter how much angrier he had become at the centre of the multiple pile-up he and she had caused at the crossroads outside the cinema. No matter whether he was militsia or mafiya or something she hadn't even heard of yet.

Robin hit the deck running, just as the first of the guard dogs came up against the tape at the bottom of the companionway. She lost her footing on the slippery deck and went flying. Her bag span away and slithered to a stop somewhere in the shadows, vomiting out its contents as it went. Fortunately, the dog paused, confused by the strange bars across its path. It turned its head and barked, summoning its companions. Then it stood alert and waited.

Sobbing for breath, Robin pulled herself up to her knees and knelt there, looking desperately around. The deck was almost pitch-black but her eyes had seen nothing but the sodium of the security lighting recently and were fully night-adjusted. She was just able to make out her handbag, and keeping her eyes fixed on the square of almost inter-stellar blackness she came up to a crouch and crept across towards it. Her boot-tips brushed against something unexpected. A whisper of distant bells. She reached down and retrieved her keys. Shading the brightness with a careful hand, she switched on the tiny torch on the key ring designed to illuminate nothing much larger than a car-lock. It showed her that she had been just about to tread on her phone. She retrieved it instead and slipped it into her pocket.

The barking at the foot of the companionway grew louder as other dogs began to arrive. Robin reacted by working more quickly. But she remained as careful and as painstaking as she dared. Anything left lying on the deck would make her weaker. Would make her pursuers stronger if they found it. Would at the very least give the impatient dogs a clearer idea of her scent. The torch-beam would have seemed insignificantly tiny in almost any other circumstances but Robin's eyes were as wide as they went, irises and eyelids stretched to their fullest extent. Only drugs or death were likely to widen them further. The map came next, then the purse, still blessedly shut. A cardlike silver oblong gave her pause, however. Frowning, she picked it up. And it too blazed with light, nearly blinding her. And she remembered. A gift from Mary, something that would slide out of the way it was so light, slim and small. But something designed to turn into a proper torch if you pressed the right bits. That went into her pocket with her phone. And the rest went back into the bag as she finally retrieved it. Then she had straightened and was in motion once again, for the barking had stopped. Under the restless sobbing of the wind and the sighing of the rainfall sweeping over a deck the size of two full football fields, she heard the determined, almost steely rattling of claws upon the slope of the companionway. She took to her heels then, running full-tilt up the deck towards the bridge house. She shut down all but the essential senses. Sight to guide her towards the pallid bridge house as tall as the flats on the road nearby. Hearing to warn her of the approach of the sinisterly silent hunters. Feeling as her fingers tore the tape off the door-handle. Simple naked desperate power as she wrenched the great steel portal wide and leaped into the lightless pit behind. Power to slam it shut across the very snarling muzzles of the pursuers at her heels. Feeling as she turned the handle and heard the bolts

slide home. Hearing again as she noted the baffled and frustrated rage of the wild pack mere centimetres behind her.
Centimetres, blessedly filled with solid steel.

Robin sank down then with her back against the door until
she was seated on the sticky foulness of the rotting linoleum.
It was disgusting. But she felt at home here. Strangely safe;
even more secure than she had supposed she would feel. She
took a long, deep breath in the absolute blackness. Blindly
she felt in her pocket for the familiar slimness of her cellphone. She opened it and stared at it with almost insane intensity as its screen lit up and the icons began to glow. The
sign for SIGNAL lit up once more. She pressed autoredial. The
dogs had gone and the wind had fallen. The silence was so
complete that she could hear the ringtone from here.

'Pick up, Richard,' she whispered. 'Pick up, you bloody
man.'

And so he did. For a mercy he checked the call ID as he
answered. 'Robin?' he said, his voice so distant he might
almost have been on the moon. 'Where are you?'

She almost knocked her teeth loose as she slammed the
handset to her head. 'I'm safe aboard *Prometheus*,' she shouted.
'Will you for God's sake come and get me!'

But the phone died almost immediately and in the sudden
silent darkness she heard a quiet snuffling growl that seemed
to come from inside the bridge house, sufficiently close at
hand to warn her that she might not be so safe after all.

Nine

Richard really only heard the first two words of Robin's call before contact was lost. It was lost because her faulty phone broke down again. It was lost because Richard himself was in the cellars of the Archangel Medical Academy and there was a lot of interference from the Internet cafe immediately above his head.

But most of all it was lost because Investigator Elena Onega of the Archangel District Prosecutor's Office gestured to Militsia Sergeant Voroshilov and, good Cossack that he was, the sergeant translated the subtle movement of her pale, artistic hand into decisively violent action.

Investigator Onega gestured, *Stop him talking*.

Voroshilov translated this as, *Take his cellphone*, and performed a borderline assault that would have had him up before a Police Complaints Tribunal had this been almost anywhere further west and a good few places further east into the bargain. Richard's phone flew out of his hand as Voroshilov tried to confiscate it.

'Hey,' shouted Richard. 'What the hell . . .' and he swung into retaliatory action in a way that surprised the sergeant and the investigator, neither of whom was used to being stood up to in quite this manner.

The phone skittered across the floor, vanishing under the stark steel table and sliding away until it came up against the solid sensible shoe that belonged to the pathologist, Alicia Kashin. Her shoe characterized her. She was a solid, sensible woman. Her thick black hair seemed to have been polished. It gleamed almost patent-leather against the snowy collar of her starched white lab coat. She also wore a grey rubber apron, white latex gloves and a blue face mask that concealed everything below her black-rimmed glasses but did not muffle her crisp, clear words.

Had Richard himself not reacted to the sergeant's assault so swiftly, he might very well have joined his phone at the pathologist's feet. But ever since the militsia squad had picked him up at the restaurant he had been as jumpy as a cat on hot bricks. Voroshilov didn't know it, but he too was lucky he was still standing up. But he was willing to take things further and escalate the violence, even here.

'*Voroshilov!*' spat Elena Onega, seeing that the massive Englishman was also quite ready to respond further, and in an even more forthrightly Cossack manner. '*Enough!*' She spoke in flawless English and was pleased to see that her words made the Englishman, as well as the sergeant, pause. The militsia patrol men who had brought their huge guest here were still outside but she really didn't want to call them in. Not yet, at any rate. She wanted to hear from at least one other set of their colleagues first. She narrowed the heavy lids over the deep gold of her almond eyes and watched him from under an abundance of sable-brown lashes. Only the slightest flaring of her fine patrician nostrils betrayed how tense and how deeply excited the investigator was. The tip of her tongue traced her lips, moistening them in a flickering instant, vivid pink against the deep and generous red.

Richard took a deep breath and steadied himself mentally as well as physically. Robin's words had been strange but reassuring. They echoed in his memory, 'I'm safe . . .'

Of course she was safe. Why should she not be safe? Investigator Onega had been waiting for him in the car outside Izba to which the militsia patrol had conducted him. She had assured him that Robin was fine and the English-speaking waiter serving them had confirmed things when he coincidentally stepped outside for a breath of air. If Captain Mariner would accompany the investigator, they had said, his wife would soon be on her way back to the hotel, the meal complete, the bill settled and everyone fine and dandy. Richard didn't know Investigator Onega well enough to doubt her words then or now. She appeared to be every inch the reliable professional, in her perfectly tailored business suit so severely cut it might almost have been a military uniform, the single button of the narrow waist emphasizing the athletic breadth of her shoulders, the generous depth of her breast and the sensuous flare of her hips. He had not quite registered yet that the investigator, like the prosecutor, like the Militsia and all the rest could and did wear military uniform for a range of occasions and purposes. And, serious though the situation seemed, he had no idea just what the investigator was dealing with – or the lengths she was willing to go to in her quest to clear the matter up.

Voroshilov stood back and shrugged, though he continued to glare at the *Angliski*, his brown eyes like gun barrels poking between the planks of a forester's wooden hide. Planks made of two thick and solid brown crossbars. The uppermost, his single eyebrow that reached straight across his forehead, un-interrupted above his broad pugilist's nose, almost immediately beneath his crew-cut. And the lower was the matching square-cut moustache above his rule-straight, scar-thin mouth and thick stubble chin. Voroshilov flared his nostrils: four gun barrels.

Voroshilov was a wildly displaced Cossack. Two hundred years ago he would have been an *ataman*, happily leading his Kazak clan from one *stanitsa* to the next along the River Don, raping, pillaging, stealing and destroying to his heart's content. Now he was an Archangel district militsia sergeant and he had little time for investigators or prosecutors. Or foreigners or women, come to that. Women in general and his boss on this case in particular. Especially as Investigator Onega's call had come, via the prosecutor himself, just in time to spoil a promising-looking evening watching the outrageous new strippers up at Snezhok. The only element of forgiveness he allowed Elena Onega was the fact that she was better built than any stripper he had ever seen, and he had seen a good few, one way and another. When things got slow he would simply begin to see the investigator in his mind's eye wearing less and less clothing. First the jacket would come off. Then the skirt. Then the blouse. Then he really had to start using his imagination. But it was always a pleasure to do so . . .

Voroshilov understood the investigator's near-perfect English well enough, and her whipcrack tone better still. He had only been roughly schooled by army intelligence during his time loosely attached to a tank regiment on the western borders in the days of his youth when such things had existed. His German, of course, was better. Like many others who spoke such fluent English, however, in all sorts of walks of modern Russian life, Investigator Onega had learned hers

working for the KGB before she had arranged an inspired
career change just before her old employers got a name change,
amongst other things. Still hardly out of her teens, she moved,
so they said, from the Foreign Intelligence Service to the
Seventh Directorate and then to Security. But she had moved
again to the Security section of the Prosecutor's Office before
the Seventh Directorate became the Federal Security Service,
the FSB. Voroshilov suspected that she still sometimes rode
two horses, however, like her little friend who moonlighted
as a waiter down in Izba, schmoozing the tourists, sleeping
with the occasional canary, feeding back titbits to the Militsia,
the Prosecutor's Office, Security and even Constitutional
Protection. While making a fortune in hard-currency tips, of
course.

Voroshilov wondered whether the big *Angliski* knew these
facts about the lovely investigator and her circle of associates. And what his reaction would be if and when he found
out. They would find out more about the *Angliski*'s reactions
soon enough. When he discovered just exactly what the lovely
but duplicitous ex-KGB Investigator Onega was up to here,
for instance. Or when he discovered that the wife who had
just called through was not, in fact, destined for her plush
hotel suite at all. If she wasn't in it already, she was destined
for the back of an unmarked militsia patrol car, with Vladimir
Paznak and his boys. And Paznak's team were very much
worse than the team that had brought Mariner himself here.
Sometimes Paznak and Co. were even worse than Voroshilov
himself, though they were from Belarus originally, and almost
Slavs. So they weren't always what Westerners would call *on
the ball*. What they were doing here instead of policing Minsk
was just another of life's little conundrums. Like what *exactly*
the investigator would have chosen tonight in the matter of
underwear.

Richard's eyes broke contact with the sergeant's unflinching
stare and he crossed the icy little pathology laboratory until
he could stoop and retrieve his cellphone from the floor beside
the pathologist's foot. He checked that it was working and
used the dialback function without any further thought at all,
his face grim and his shoulders squared just in case. Robin's
cell was unobtainable. He switched it off and pocketed it,
blessedly unaware that only Investigator Onega's firmest stare

had kept her sergeant under restraint – like a guard dog tugging at its leash.

'I'm safe . . .' Robin had said. Good enough, thought Richard, in blissful ignorance of the truth. And he put her right out of his mind for the time being.

Pathologist Kashin called them all back to reality with her first quiet words. She spoke in Russian and then, flawlessly and fluidly, in English. It was impossible to be certain whether she was addressing her assembled audience or whether she was speaking for the benefit of some kind of recording device. Richard thought she was probably doing both. It did not occur to him that the English translation was for his sole benefit. Not to begin with, at any rate. Until the full significance of his presence there really began to dawn on him.

'The cadaver is that of a male of middle years,' *Vracha* – Dr – Alicia Kashin began. 'It arrived without clothing or identification papers of any kind. It may be difficult to establish identity, therefore, especially given the swelling on the face and the fact that the top knuckles of the thumb and first two fingers of each hand are missing. It has been reported by Officer Repin of the Customs and Immigration Division that it was originally discovered that way. This pathologist has not examined the crime scene and may have more to add to the report after she has done so. In due course we shall be able to estimate the time and means of death. Time of death is currently being estimated by the taking of the cadaver's core temperature. Once this is established we may proceed to other means. It must be stated at this time, however, that the flesh is stone cold to the touch and it is unlikely that core temperature will be much warmer. The limbs are free-moving so we can surmise that rigour is long past. This supposition is supported by the fact that the flesh is without elasticity. Pressure is not returned. Fingermarks remain as though in putty. There is no obvious swelling or discoloration other than those caused by brutal misuse, so that decomposition does not appear to have begun to any great extent. That is all we can say about *time* of death at the moment. In the meantime, we can make some introductory observations as we search for *cause* of death.

'The cadaver's ethnicity is clearly Caucasoid, though of

southern and eastern subtype. Not Mongoloid. Caucasoid of
the Arabic or Middle Eastern sub-type. He could be a Chechen.
But not a Vietnamese or Thai. His skull is classically rounded
with much weight behind the axis of the neck. What we might
call long-headed. His nose seems to have been broken but I
estimate that it was originally large, well-formed and hooked
in the Arabic or Semitic manner. The lips appear to be corre-
spondingly full, though again there is damage and resultant
swelling. There is nothing remarkable about the lower
mandible, which is again free-moving, except for damage to
the teeth. He is well built though not fat. Again, his body
mass is greater than that associated with Mongoloids such as
the Vietnamese. His hair type and colour are lighter than the
Mongoloid races and the hairiness of his body is more
pronounced, in a manner to be expected in the Arabic
Caucasoid male.

   'His head has been shaved but he is bearded. The shaving
of the head was done long enough ago for some stubble to
have reasserted itself though it is not thick enough to obscure
the bruises beneath. And of course hair continues to grow for
some little time after death, like fingernails. He appears to
have been circumcized, but the state of his genitals makes it
difficult to be certain. Likewise, the colour of his skin would
seem to match the Arabic Caucasoid ethnicity surmised for
him, but the state of the body, which appears to have suffered
severe and prolonged abuse, makes it hard to be absolutely
certain. The flesh on the front of the body seems particularly
discoloured and marked with a pattern of parallel indentations
running from shoulders to toes . . .'

Richard's mind really began to catch up with the situation
then. Investigator Onega had brought him here to help iden-
tify a body. This body. How in Heaven's name did she expect
him to know anything about a random Chechen found naked
and dead in Archangel?

   But the body had been brought here by customs and immigration officers, he reasoned. By this Officer Repin and his
men. Therefore it must have been discovered in or near the
sea. And the pathologist was insisting it was *not* Vietnamese
in a manner that would lead you to believe that she had almost
expected that it *would be* Vietnamese. It had come off a boat

or a ship, therefore. Hadn't he just been telling Robin about the immigration problems the Russians had with Vietnamese?

This was exactly as far as Richard had got in his logic when the door opened and another officer appeared. Richard recognized the neat uniform and the angular face of the man who had talked with Felix Makarov and Fedor Gulin at the security gate this afternoon, although he seemed taller than Richard remembered him. And that shock of black hair, almost as dark as the doctor's, had been concealed beneath a uniform cap. Still, there could be no doubt. He was the officer Felix had said was GAI, but whom Robin had suspected not to be. And her suspicions were clearly well founded. Richard understood at once that this also must be the officer who had brought the body in. That this must be the Officer Repin named by the pathologist a moment ago, therefore.

And that forged the last link in Richard's mind, although he could not bring himself at first to face the inescapable logic of his own cool clear logical reasoning. Repin had gone from the gate to the ship. He had reported what he had found there to the authorities who had appointed an investigator. And the investigator had brought them all, Richard, Repin, and the investigating team to this airless place. He turned back to the brutally disfigured corpse of the young man on the table. His heart sank and his stomach clenched with simple horror.

Customs Officer Repin and his team had found this poor man somewhere aboard *Prometheus*, Richard told himself, though he could hardly believe it to be true. But nothing else made sense. And that one supposition made sense of everything else that was happening. He glanced furtively around the room. Only Sergeant Voroshilov appeared to be watching him. Everyone else seemed to be watching Pathologist Kashin as she continued to describe the state of the dead man on the stainless-steel pathology table in front of her.

Oh my God, Richard said to himself again underneath his breath, as though he needed the repetition to truly drive the point well home. *They found this body aboard* Prometheus.

Ten

'I will begin at the crown of the cadaver's skull and work my way down his front, listing exterior damage to begin with,' Pathologist *vrach* Alicia Kashin announced, reaching up above her head and pulling down the brightest light Richard had seen in Archangel so far. 'The shaving of the skull makes it easy to see five different clusters of bruises on the cranium though as I have observed there is stubble growing there. There is some swelling and a good deal of discoloration. So I surmise these bruises were inflicted some time ago and well before death occurred. Perhaps around the same time that the head itself was shaved. The foremost cluster goes over on to the forehead itself. The brows are swollen and the eyes themselves bruised, puffy and shut. I can just open the left eye, however, and observe that the eyeball is badly bloodshot. The pupil is dilated as far as I can see and, of course, fixed . . .'

As the pathologist continued to list the young man's external injuries, Richard's mind was racing. Where in God's name could Customs Officer Repin and his team have found a corpse aboard *Prometheus*? How could a corpse have been brought aboard? Who by? When? Why? As he had explained so airily and confidently to Robin, the towing watch from the tug *Sissy* had been aboard since taking her under tow in Wilhelmshaven. He had told her then they would have found and reported any stowaway. Surely they would have noticed a dead body lying around the place. Of course they would. And they would have been even quicker to report a corpse than a stowaway.

So either it wasn't aboard during the trip round from Germany or it had been pretty effectively hidden away.

Say it wasn't aboard. What then? It must have been smuggled aboard from somewhere in Archangel itself. How long had *Prometheus* been tied up at the Komsomolskaya Pier? Almost exactly forty hours from the time *Sissy* had sailed back north and Felix and Richard had brought Robin and the rest aboard. Had there been any kind of watch during the long night of her arrival, the next day, the night and morning before they went aboard? No there had not. But, as Felix found out the hard way, the customs men had secured the main gates to the pier, clearly in anticipation of the inspection. Though they had not, as Felix again had discovered, locked the small door at the side. It would theoretically have been possible to smuggle a corpse aboard, therefore, before the full inspection late this afternoon.

But practicalities started intruding into his calculations at once. How many Chechens were there in Archangel? How easy would it be to beat a young man like this to death in the first place? How easy would it be to hide and transport the body? And it must have been hidden. From the sound of things it had been dead for a good while. Perhaps for days. So where would it have been hidden? And then how on earth would one get it through the city? Through the security gates? Along the pier? Up the gangplanks and aboard? All without anyone seeing or suspecting anything? If the ship was open and unguarded at night it was certainly conceivable. But Felix had been quite specific about security; as well aware as Richard of the commercial value of the most apparently insignificant things aboard. There were guards at night. Dogs.

Getting the naked corpse of a murdered man past a team of attack-trained guard dogs suddenly seemed a much less likely proposition to Richard. Always assuming one had any kind of a sane reason for doing so. Though looking at the young man's terrible condition, *sane* was not a word that anyone was likely to apply to whoever was involved in this. So. It might be possible to move the corpse with some kind of freedom through the city at night, the pier itself would be effectively closed. And when the pier was unattended – by dogs at least – during the day, then moving the body around the city was most problematic. Especially a body without any clothing. And in such a state . . .

Richard shook his head. Back to first principles, then. And the alternative scenario. How could the body have been aboard when they took up the tow in Wilhelmshaven? Or even, given what the doctor was saying, *before* they took up the tow? Only if it had been in some part of the ship that the towing

watch did not visit. But that again was hard to imagine. They
were ordered to check every part of the bridge house and were
the sort of men who were punctilious about obeying orders.
It hadn't been lying around in the bridge house, then. Or, to
be fair, Robin, himself, Felix, Fedor Gulin and the rest would
have stumbled across it themselves this afternoon. What about
the engineering decks? Lots of dark and secret places down
there. Almost as many as in the main hull forward of the
cofferdam beneath the huge green deck, where the cargo tanks
were. And the service tunnels, galleries and walkways all
around them, above deck and below. But again, there was a
problem. Beaten, battered and bruised, the cold flesh on the
steel table might be. But it was also clean.

A fact emphasized upon Richard's very thought by the way
Pathologist Kashin rolled the corpse on to its face. The back
was much hairier than the front, thought Richard, surprised.
But then he realized. No. The flesh was simply paler than the
flesh of his front. He noted the fact, as he was noting every
word the doctor was saying in spite of his feverish speculation. He would go over it all again later, when and if he had
leisure to think calmly and coolly.

If the unfortunate Chechen had been lolling about undiscovered in the nether reaches of the engineering areas or the
unexplored warrens around the cargo tanks – even had he
been bundled into the work spaces at the forecastle head – he
would have been soiled with oil. But he was not.

Richard had reached this point in his deliberations when
something else occurred to him. And it was this. Even had
the murderer been someone local who had found some way
of smuggling the body aboard from Archangel itself, he must
have hidden it up in the bridge house away from the filth of
the engineering sections and the main work areas. No matter
where the corpse came aboard, at Wilhelmshaven or Archangel
or somewhere in between, it must have been hidden in the
bridge house.

Robin must have led them all past the dead Chechen, lying
hidden somewhere on *Prometheus* this afternoon. For it was
only as they were coming off that Officer Repin and his men
had gone aboard. The thought was so disturbing that it made
Richard, the most pragmatic and down-to-earth of men,
shiver.

At this point in his almost circular deliberations, Richard was sidetracked for a moment once again. He wondered, if the body had been so well hidden that ten people had walked past it all unaware, how Repin and his men had found it. And then, with that first stirring of the paranoia that had gripped his wife long since, it occurred to him to start wondering why Repin and his men had been looking for it in the first place. And here the paranoia took a slightly firmer grip, for it suddenly occurred to him that he had been thinking of the corpse simply as a corpse. Its ethnicity only seemed important in that it was not Mongoloid Vietnamese. But it was Arabic Caucasoid. Possibly Chechen. And although Richard had seen no one of Arabic appearance since his arrival here, there might indeed be people in Archangel capable of beating a Chechen to death if they found one and then hiding his body for as long as they liked before putting it wherever the hell they wanted. What did they call themselves nowadays? The Service for the Protection of the Constitutional System and the Fight against Terrorism. Constitutional Protection for short. One of the seven services that were, with two directorates, the subsections of the Federal Security Service, now known as the FSB, that had replaced so much of the old KGB.

'So,' concluded Alicia Kashin, 'we can surmise with some certainty that the exterior contusions and other marks of restraint, beating and torture, including what appears to have been done to the genitals or even the fingertips, are not likely to constitute probable cause of death. Either individually or taken in combination. Unless the victim suffered some internal weakness that magnified or intensified their effect. A weak heart, perhaps, or some other kind of weakness or infection. With the body in such a state it is hard to judge whether the lividity characteristic in stroke or heart attack exists. And of course we have yet to establish a time of death, without which all comment on the state of the corpse is largely academic. We must do this as far as possible, therefore, before we proceed to internal examination. I will begin the internal examination only when I have established, as clearly as I can at this point, the time of death. Or, which is more likely, when I have established that it is, for the moment, impossible to do this with any kind of accuracy at all.'

During the whole of the examination so far, the corpse had been pierced in several vital places by thermometers. The pathologist now removed these and read them carefully before proceeding. 'The core temperature of the corpse is very little elevated above the current ambient temperature outside. To wit, one degree Celsius.' At this point she snapped off a switch that clearly controlled whatever recording device she was speaking into. She stopped being the pathologist for a moment and spoke to them as a woman, her voice soft and shaking. 'The body is certainly colder than this room, in fact close observation might suggest that he is beginning to perspire a little under the light. He is not. It is actually condensation. And by the same token, those are not tears. He is not weeping. The dead do not cry. Not even in Russia.'

The doctor cleared her throat, switched on her dictaphone and proceeded formally once again. 'As the state of the body in general has led me to speculate, therefore, death occurred so long ago as to make the use of core temperature as any kind of a guide unreliable if not absolutely inaccurate. Only when this pathologist examines the crime scene itself will any further comment along these lines be made. Though I am assured that the cadaver was not discovered in any functioning refrigeration or cold-storage area.

'At this point I can only add that the cleanliness of the cadaver, taken in conjunction with the lack of any obvious growth of mould or infestation by insect life, is likely to make accurate estimates of time of death through the influence of outside organisms very difficult indeed. We may have to rely on the much more lengthy pathology of blood, tissue and internal fluids. Whose interpretation once again relies crucially upon detailed examination of the crime scene itself.'

'That will have to wait, I'm afraid, Pathologist *vracha* Kashin,' inserted Investigator Onega at this point. 'The crime scene remains isolated until tomorrow morning at the earliest. There are considerations that reach even beyond even your competence, I'm afraid. But rest assured, you will see all there is to see at the first possible moment.'

'Then I can go no further with time of death,' acquiesced *vracha* Kashin equably. 'All we know for certain is that he died sufficiently long ago for the core-temperature test to yield no results at all. Now. How did he die? I will proceed with the internal examination. I will make the standard incisions here. And here. And here . . .'

Richard had seen full internal post-mortems carried out before. And had, indeed, added his own vital observations to those of the pathologist. But he was not destined to see this one. As *vracha* Kashin made the first incision of the classic Y-shaped thoracic internal examination, Investigator Onega gestured with her head just forcefully enough to set her sable hair stirring on the shoulder of her severely tailored jacket. Voroshilov and Repin fell in on either side of Richard and led him out of the room. Kashin's monotonous report fell exclusively into Russian and began to fade behind them. The closing of the path. lab door cut it off altogether.

Richard automatically turned left, heading back towards the lift up to the entrance and the street, but Onega went right and her two henchmen guided Richard into her wake. The three militsia men fell in behind again. The seven of them went along a short corridor that led deeper into the building, six men following one woman like something out of a fairy tale.

'You brought him over here from headquarters?' threw Onega over one square shoulder. She spoke in Russian to Repin, clearly not wanting to give too much away to the Englishman at this point.

'Yes, Investigator,' answered Repin, also in Russian. 'Though I don't see . . .'

'It will save time. If we can get the first part at least sorted out quickly then poor Voroshilov might still stand a chance of getting up to Snezhok before the end of tonight's show. I hear the last few acts are so disgusting that the Public Prosecutor's Office is considering raiding the place, in protection of public decency, despite the hard currency the performances and the videos and DVDs generate. And the potential for other sources of information, income and influence they give rise to, of course. You wouldn't want to miss something sick enough to generate a raid, eh, Voroshilov? And I expect you could persuade Officer Repin to accompany you. It'll show him what to look for on his next sweep for obscene imports, at least.'

Repin shrugged and gave a weary grin. Voroshilov said

nothing, though the twin planks of his eyebrow and moustache came closer together and his eyes looked more like gun barrels than ever. He exacted his own revenge by drawing a very precise bead upon the perfectly sculpted bottom immediately in front of him. Then imagining the rear view of Onega without the benefit of skirt or panties undergoing some of the experiences the girls at Snezhok were supposed to suffer live onstage. Now it was his turn to lick his lips. And, as Elena Onega didn't actually have eyes in the back of her head, to smirk a little.

Richard only understood the words *Voroshilov*, *Repin* and *Snezhok*. And as he had no idea of the character-change the cinema underwent on a Wednesday night, he viewed the sergeant and the customs officer in an utterly new light. They were Eisenstein fans. Classic-film buffs. In spite of appearances to the contrary, Voroshilov was an intellectual! And so was Repin! Who would ever have dreamed it?

Onega opened a door and strode in with her two sensitive intellectual film buffs and Richard in tow. 'Wait outside,' she ordered, not even bothering to turn her head. The last thing she said in Russian for a while. The Militsia team obeyed in stolid silence. None of them wanted to get on the wrong side of the investigator's acid tongue.

The room was another pathology lab but instead of a corpse spread on the table there was a schematic. Richard recognized the diagram at once. And the man crouching nervously behind it. 'Hello, Fedor,' he said easily. 'What's all this, then?'

Fedor Gulin looked up nervously, his frog face almost as sweaty as the face of the corpse next door, his baggy eyes brimming with unshed tears. He did not respond to Richard's cheery greeting. 'Investigator . . .' he said instead, bobbing into something between a bow and a curtsey. 'I have brought everything you asked for.' He gestured to the schematics of the derelict supertanker. They were copies of the originals held in the vaults of Heritage House and were old enough to make the great ship look new and impressive.

'Show me,' Onega ordered Repin as though Gulin had not spoken. As though he didn't actually exist.

Repin crossed to the table and looked down. Frowning, Richard also crossed to the officer's side. Repin had to talk to Gulin, for the schematics were large and extremely complex. And there were sheet upon sheet of them, almost a book. One sheet for each deck, in fact, starting with the keel and bilges and building to the weather deck atop the bridge house. After 'A' deck, where there were only the bridge-house decks to map, there were two decks per sheet. Which only served to make things more complex for eyes unused to such things. 'Show us the area I described to you,' ordered Repin.

Gulin nodded and bobbed obediently. He folded back the top two sheets with their double boxes of diagrams. The third sheet down was the main deck. The green-painted deck that lay at the top of the embarkation companionway. Richard could see it in his mind's eye, stretching away in front of the bridge house past the Sampson posts away to the forecastle head. The lines and circles translated themselves into sheaves of pipes, into tank-tops, manifolds, pumps . . .

But Gulin was gesturing to the rearmost section of the diagram. To something inside the bridge house itself, something there on 'A' deck. Once again, the schematic's lines, boxes and boxes within boxes, translated themselves into corridors, work areas, recreation and accommodation areas in Richard's imagination. He followed Gulin's finger through the vessel just exactly as he had followed Robin herself that afternoon. Except that Gulin's finger, skating over one black line after another, didn't really bother with doors.

'Here,' said Gulin at last. 'It was here.'

The pudgy finger hovered over the galley. The short-chewed nail pointed with the little roll of flesh at the fingertip which showed that Gulin had not just bitten off his nail tonight under the stress of the investigator's summons as delivered by Repin and his men. The room reared in Richard's memory as vividly as if they were standing in it now. He remembered the well-stocked work areas with their full complement of stainless-steel utensils. He remembered how they had all commented upon them. How one might almost use the equipment, the ranges and the ovens to start a restaurant. A restaurant fronted by the tables and chairs, knives and forks in the dining area next door. A restaurant supplied from the massive brushed-steel freezers at the rear of the galley itself. Freezers large enough to feed forty hungry officers and crew through a full six-week voyage without calling into port. Had they discussed all this or had he just imagined it? Whatever. There had been no corpse visible. None there, in point of fact, or they must have seen it as they all trouped through. The only possible hiding place was the big freezer and hadn't the pathologist said Repin hadn't found it in a freezer or cold store?

And yet, the pudgy finger with its short-chewed nail was stabbing down there with unshakeable relentlessness. All Richard could remember about the freezer was that the seals looked perished and the motors probably needed some work. No one had opened them to look inside. Not even Gulin's men with their pads and pencils. What would have been the point? And in any case, he remembered with a twinge of regret, almost of guilt, he had hurried them on through, babbling about his generator down in engineering, keen to relieve Robin of the burden of answering Felix Makarov's questions.

Concerned and a little jealous, perhaps, that the big Russian found her quite so interesting.

But in the face of Gulin's determined finger, Richard could no longer remain silent. 'Did you find the corpse in the freezer, Officer Repin?' he asked. 'Is that where it was? In the freezer in the galley?'

Repin nodded, narrow-eyed.

'But we were in there. We looked at that freezer this afternoon. We noticed nothing.' He gave a half laugh. 'Nothing except some perished seals and rusty motors. How did you find him?'

'They didn't find him themselves,' supplied Onega, unwilling to let her dominance over the conversation slip. 'Their dogs did.'

'But we couldn't smell anything . . .'

'What?' probed Onega.

'Except the stink of rottenness all around us anyway.'

'Dogs have more discriminating noses,' Onega observed drily.

Richard swung back to Repin. 'That's all there was to it? It was as simple as that? You took some dogs on board and they led you straight to the freezer? Straight to the corpse? Just like that?'

Investigator Onega answered for the customs officer. 'Yes. They found this one in the freezer. On the lowest shelf. Face down.'

Just as Onega spoke, the door opened and the pathologist came in. Her gloves and apron were liberally smeared with blood, which looked as dark and thick as tar. 'It was his heart,' she said. 'If you return with me I will show you. He had a weakness in the left ventricle. The stress of the beating was too much for him. Elevated blood pressure. Pouf! It burst like a balloon.'

'Thank you, *vracha* Kashin, we will examine it later, perhaps,' said Onega gently, her almond eyes fixed on Richard, as gold as those of a hunting wolf. Waiting for the full import of her words to sink in. Watching for his reaction.

They found this one in the freezer, thought Richard. *This one*.

Oh my God.

That explained a great deal more about what was going on. Why they could afford to move the man next door away from the crime scene. Why they had secured the pier. Why so many police officials seemed to be involved in a solitary case. Why it so clearly had such a high priority. Why she had said that strange thing to the pathologist: *There are considerations that reach even beyond even your competence, I'm afraid*. Too bloody true there were! Why they were waiting for someone else, someone more senior, someone from the General Prosecutor's Office in Moscow, even. Someone who could assess the political and diplomatic impact. Someone to come up here and take a closer look. And he remembered with a deathly chill his earlier thought about the FSB's Service for the Protection of the Constitutional System and the Fight against Terrorism.

There were more corpses. Heaven knew how many more.

And they were still on board *Prometheus*.

Eleven

When the whistle sounded, Robin was overwhelmed by an almost unbearable feeling of relief. One moment she had seemed to be in the most terrible danger as the dog snuffled unerringly towards her through the absolute darkness of the 'A' deck corridor. The next she was safe once again.

To be fair, though, she thought, *sounded* was not the right word at all. There had been no real noise, simply a piercing summons that worked on an almost subliminal level. A super-auditory shriek that proved she wasn't ready for a hearing aid just yet, and which only someone such as herself who had once been a dog owner would have recognized as a whistle in the first place.

At the first bat-like shriek, the snuffling in the darkness stopped. Robin could almost sense the pricking of the ears, the raising of the wolf-like head. The swinging of the questing face. She could certainly hear the rumbling half-pant, half-growl. Warmth and dog breath moved through the dank stillness towards her supersensitive face. The whistling came again and with a frustrated snarl, the dog turned.

A gruff voice shouted something that would have been impenetrable even had it not been Russian and bellowed from such a distance as to assure Robin that its owner at least was staying obediently on the far side of the police tape. The gruff bellow was the dog's name, no doubt. And some kind of threat or promise. Couched in obscenely insulting terms, judging by the tenor and tone of it. The snarl was repeated and the dogs were cantering away, claws tapping eerily on the lino like Blind Pew's stick in *Treasure Island*.

Robin pulled herself to her feet and stood, her mouth wide, her breasts heaving, gulping down air as though oxygen alone could stop her pounding heart from bursting like a child's balloon. Her first thought was to run to the lading office and watch the dogs cross the deck once more and satisfy herself that they had gone down the companionway to their master on the pier. But a more immediate need for security drove her in the opposite direction. She walked determinedly straight ahead down the length of the 'A' deck corridor until her super-senses warned her she was near the starboard door out on to the weather deck. The blackness in front of her took on a lighter tone. A sense of infinite space existing beyond the realms of sight. Sounds gathered. The rumbling of the surf against the old ship's hollow side. The batter of the wind whose intrusive fingers slapped her icily on the cheek. Sea smells filled her wide-flared nostrils, washing away the ship's dead stench. She risked the light on her key ring and there, less than a metre ahead, the bulkhead door stood wide. She switched off the tiny light and then reached out unerringly to swing it closed, balancing sufficient speed to stop the hinges squealing with enough control to stop it slamming shut.

Robin turned the handle until the door was secure, let fall her hands and stood in the utter blackness, going through memories of this afternoon as though she was watching a film-show in her head. With a ghostly Felix Makarov at her shoulder, she revisited every office, room and cabin on this deck trying to assure herself that there was nowhere left open in case the dogs came back. It was only when she finished this process that she remembered with utter certainty that the door she had just closed had in fact been securely closed when she and Richard had gone ashore. Someone less careful had been aboard since. The men who taped the gangway, obviously. The men at the gate that Makarov had so airily dismissed as GAI traffic police.

GAI in a pig's eye!
In a pig's eye GAI!

She giggled at the ridiculous little rhyme. Then realized that she was actually laughing out loud. And finding it danger-ously hard to stop. She went straight back to her deep-breathing exercises. She cleared her mind and looked for something calming to think about. Russian. What was the Russian word for . . . *darkness*? Darkness was about all she could see. Yes. That would do nicely. She rummaged through her memory, actually seeming to consult the little phrasebook she had bought in preparation for the visit in her mind's eye until she found the word she was looking for. *Svet*. Yes, that was it. Darkness was *svet*.

And she was certainly awash with *svet* at the moment, she observed, beginning to giggle again at yet another dreadful pun.

This is all getting too much for you, old girl, she thought, blissfully unaware that she was wrong in any case.

Still breathing deeply and silently through a gaping mouth and flaring nose, straining the top of her black-lace all-in-one and putting her blouse buttons at risk, Robin proceeded along the corridor like a drowning zombie. Waiting for her heart to slow down and hoping she would soon lose the hysterical desire to start giggling helplessly once again, Robin picked her way back through the reeking bridge house. And this time she was planning to go into the lading office.

In the *Prometheus* series of supertankers, the lading office, where the first officer did much of the cargo-control work, was on the forward port corner of the 'A' deck in the bridge house. It was accessed through the first officer's office, which opened directly off the 'A' deck corridor almost opposite the door into the galley. Its forward-facing windows offered unrivalled views along the deck, but Robin was not interested in the view for the moment. She moved with the care of a blind woman through the clutter of desk, chairs, tables and computer equipment, relying on her visual memory of this afternoon's visit. And, as it turned out, on the protection afforded to toes and shins by a stout pair of knee-boots. For her memory was not quite perfect.

In spite of the painful temptation, however, Robin did not fall back on either the key-ring flashlight or the bigger credit-card torch from her handbag. She had plans for both of these. And good reason to take care. For, just as she was hoping to look out, she was all too well aware that people might be looking in. Her goal was to get to the little port-side window that looked down over the gangplank to the pier itself and look through this to spy out the land without letting anyone anywhere ashore suspect her presence aboard.

A careful, painstaking peek through this vital little spy hole established that the hut halfway along the pier's length was now occupied. It gave off light in sharp-edged beams, which seemed so bright to her night-adjusted gaze that even under the sodium glimmer of the security lighting it looked like some kind of alien spaceship recently settled there. A few more moments of concentrated watching established to Robin's satisfaction that there was one watchman who came and went through the alien inner brightness and occasionally loomed monstrously in the doorway.

The watchman was platoon leader to half a dozen dogs, a mixture of Alsatians and Dobermanns, who trotted about their patrols like soldiers, moving restlessly from shadow to shadow with silent and sinister purpose, noses to the ground, undeterred by the chill and the drizzle. Every now and then one of the patrolling canines would pause, look up and test the wind. Even under the dim security lighting, its eyes and teeth would glint. Its breath would smoke on the icy air as though they all were demons.

Robin shivered, but not with the cold. She was not about to go back out there. And only the solidity of the heavy metal bulkhead doors at either end of the corridor behind her made her almost perfectly certain that they wouldn't be back in here either. A situation that seemed to her very nearly perfect. For the time being. She noticed that at some point during her concentrated observation of the pier, her breathing and heartbeat had returned to normal. Her mouth had closed, much to the relief of her dry throat. She was breathing through her nose, much to the regret of her too-acute sense of smell. She turned and crept carefully back across the room, through the inner office and out into the corridor. As she went through the first door she closed it after her and risked the little key-ring light to save her suffering shins. Out in the corridor, she closed the second door and felt in her bag for the bigger credit-card torch.

By that light, Robin began to prowl through the bridge house ensuring that every door was closed tight. Along this corridor and on 'A' deck at least. For no sooner had she rid herself of her fear of the dogs than she discovered an unwelcome reversion to childhood night terrors had taken place within her. For she was suddenly afraid of the dark. Even thinking of it as *svet* didn't help. There were no more giggles left in her.

To be fair, Robin told herself, accepting the situation as she found it, she wasn't just terrified of the dark. Even in the dull light of the afternoon, this had seemed a sinister and ghostly place to her. The stench of death on such a titanic scale made the huge ship reek like a battleground full of corpses. The chilly dampness and mouldy, rusty, rotting stench of it put her in mind of what the trenches on the Somme must have been like. And the barbed-wired, corpse-packed swamps of the battlefields between them. With no Captain Blackadder or Private Baldrick to lighten the horror. Her simple plan had been just to wait for Richard to come aboard and get her out of here. But now she had a sub-plan to keep her busy and make the wait for rescue seem shorter. Like a proverbial kettle that was not in fact being watched while it boiled. For if she just sat around alone in this terrible place with nothing to occupy her mind, heaven alone knew what horrors might claim her.

Satisfied that every door nearby was safely shut and far too nervous to go further afield on to the upper decks where she would have to forgo the torch until all the doors up there were closed as well, Robin returned to the central companionway. Here she followed the bright beam downwards to the first turning where, upon a little shelf convenient to hand, stood the half-dozen torches Richard had given out this afternoon. She counted them and wavered, torn between the conflicting notions. Should she take them all, packing her pockets and hoping they didn't fall out and break? Should she just take one and leave the others where she would be certain to find them again? Or should she take the one with the brightest beam and fill her pockets with the batteries from the others so that she was sure she would always have the power to make more light?

In the end she gave herself a shake that was supposed to be mental but which became disturbingly physical. She took the first one to hand, telling herself severely not to get side-tracked into complicated plans. She was not here for the long haul. Richard would be here soon. When she switched her chosen torch on it nearly blinded her.

Even though Robin was absolutely delighted to have so much light at her disposal to fight back against the dark, even though she was utterly certain that a torch shining down a metal-sided stairwell could never be seen from the outside, especially as it was shining at the heart of a bridge house in which every door was safely shut, she shaded the beam with her hand as she went down into the lightless but windowless bowels below.

When Robin reached the first engineering deck, she followed the shaded beam aft along the route that Richard had taken them this afternoon with mounting confidence. And here, again, she was careful to close every door behind her. For she was planning on fighting the blackness with all the light that she could switch on. And there were a hell of a lot of lights down here.

The only part of this new sub-plan that gave her pause was the worry that all her careful planning might backfire, that she might cover her traces aboard so well, then make herself so invisible down here that Richard would not find her when he came. And, although she was certain that, after her message, he would tear his old command to pieces with his bare hands in search of her, she nevertheless decided on a regular series of patrols. Like the dogs, she would test the air every now and then to keep a close eye on what was going on outside. At the very least it would get some proper discipline into the situation, and give her something to do if the night watch got too long and the fear of the dark in this horrific place started to get too much for her to handle.

Twelve

The trusty German generator started on the first touch of the green button, as reliable as the Mercedes limousines or *machinas* so beloved of the Russian underworld and the Sevmash Consortium. Darkness was instantly banished from every place beneath the massive overhead octopus of wiring that had light bulbs instead of suckers strung along its tentacles. Robin looked around the functional engineering space. It was a depressingly masculine environment. All practicality and no comfort. Had there been chairs there originally, they were all gone now. Even through in the engine-control room there was nothing to sit on. There should have been half a dozen chairs on castors. Their absence was a cause of some potent regret too, for she remembered with a good deal of fondness rolling from one work station to the other across the metal of the deck. If you kicked off hard enough and kept your feet working, you could build up quite a speed. She could have done with some of the simple sense of purpose and power the youthfully exuberant action used to give her.

But first things first. While Richard had been extolling the presence of all the fire-fighting equipment in preparation for getting hot flushes over the RB211 motors, Robin herself had seen something of much more practical use. A heater. She pulled it over to the generator and connected it to the last vacant power point. It purred into life immediately, spewing out warm air that rapidly heated further as the internal elements warmed up. The heater and the generator taken together produced about as much noise as a pair of contented cats. German machines, she thought with awed amusement.

When her nose twitched almost automatically, Robin realized that she was searching the warm air for the stench of burning dust that normally came with such things. But it didn't come and she smiled at herself. Of course. This was a largely dust-free environment. She had forgotten that about ships. No dust. No flies. Or spiders, come to that. Precious little in the way of airborne infection, filth or life. Food going rotten before it went mouldy, unless the ship's rats got to it first.

With these inconsequential thoughts running through her mind, Robin continued to examine the purring jenny. Her wise eyes told her which connection governed which set of lights and she saw at once that she could switch them off by throwing little levers here rather than by disconnecting them. A few more minutes of experimenting returned much of the engineering area to darkness. She ventured out and about briefly before she closed down each arm of light, checking in case there was anything that it might be useful to have with her in her little central hideaway. Then, step by step, she reduced the light she was emitting until only the little room with the generator in it was lit. That and the passage out to the companionway, though she removed every other bulb along the way. She could not bring herself to cut off her eyrie completely, but both well-lit areas at least could be closed off effectively with solid wood and metal doors.

With the beginnings of comfort, Robin found access to a burst of energy and decisiveness. She put all of it for the moment into nest-building. There weren't any chairs down here – well, she knew where to get one. And now that things were beginning to run to plan, her first patrol of the night was called for. One that would not only check up on whether there was any sign of Richard, but would allow her to assess whether her well-lit little hideaway was at all visible from the outside. She was pretty sure it wasn't audible. As always at sea she was preparing for the worst case. Expecting Richard. Getting ready for the men who had chased her from Izba to Snezhok.

Taking her three torches, but leaving her hat and handbag beside the generator, Robin exited the little engineering room and followed the dull light along the short corridor towards the stairs. She opened the door, stepped out swiftly and closed it behind her at once, then she stood in the darkness one deck down, immediately beneath the galley until she was certain that her eyes were fully adjusted to the darkness once again. As she waited, effectively blind, so she found her other senses overactive once again. The stench here seemed to be worse; so strong that she poignantly regretted ever having seen any

film in all her life that involved people being pursued by
rotting corpses. There was also a distant whispering moaning
sound she found particularly unsettling. So much so that she
switched on the big torch long before she was certain her eyes
were properly adjusted, though she had sufficient presence of
mind to shade the beam before she switched it on. Then, her
mind still full of zombies, dogs, pursuers and nameless terrors
born of the darkness, she shone the beam around. Ahead of
her, only the corridor, empty and still, stretching towards the
stairwell that was her primary destination; behind her, only
the corridor reaching back into the fast-shut engineering areas.
Above her, only the corridor deck-head. But here there was
a panel missing and, in the black gape, a further hole. That
explained the sobbing sound at least, she thought. Someone
had ripped out a whole slew of wiring. From behind the equipment in the galley. From behind the freezers there, perhaps.
Behind or beneath, certainly, for the damage had been invisible when she had shown the ship breakers round this afternoon. And whoever scavenged the wiring had left the conduits
empty and gaping to attract the whistling of the wind under
the great brushed-steel boxes. Like the reeds of a church organ
or a fairground calliope.

Robin thought nothing more of the matter but proceeded
with her plan. She paused before she took the first upward
step and looked back one last time. Torch on: no zombies
close behind her after all. Torch off: no light that she could
see escaping from her little hideaway. The darkness was so
utter that she found herself flashing her guarded beam back
there after a moment to make assurance double-sure. The
doorways were defined by the long beam for the instant that
she pointed it there. But there was not the least suspicion of
light when she swung it back again and climbed back up
towards the shelf that held its companions. Here she paused,
deep in the grip of paranoia. After a moment longer she
switched the torch off altogether and put it back on the shelf.
She reached into her coat pocket and pulled out the credit-
card torch. Even then, she shaded the light before she
proceeded further.

Robin followed the little beam carefully along the 'A' deck
corridor towards the ship's library. She could have chosen
the officers' lounge because they had light but comfortable

tub-backed chairs there too. She could even have gone into the dining area if she had wanted something lighter but less comfortable. But somewhere deep in her subconscious she associated libraries with calm, quiet and security. All the things she craved most at the moment, in fact. She opened the door and flashed the fragile beam around at knee level and below. That way she got a clear idea of the obstacles without running the danger of anyone seeing the light. Or so she thought.

Robin was not here to explore. She had no thought of sitting down there reading. In any case, all the books here seemed to have been reduced to papier-mâché by time and dampness. She went for the nearest chair, therefore, swung it round until the arms were facing her and prepared to lift it.

Robin had chosen to use the credit-card torch for a reason – she rarely did anything in an uncalculated manner. She put the tiny thing into her mouth and gently pressed her teeth down. She remembered at the last moment to look down as she bit gently into the plastic. The torch-beam reignited and lit up the seat of the chair. And the book that was lying on it.

Surprised, Robin hesitated. Her mouth began to salivate around the little torch and she took it out and wiped it in the darkness. She was not really surprised at finding a book in a library, of course. It was simply that it was in an unexpected place. And in an unexpected state of preservation. Without further thought, she picked it up and stepped out into the corridor, her interest piqued. One flash of the torch, swift as the blink of an eye, revealed what it was: a copy of the Koran. Robin flicked through it as best she could, putting the flat torch back between her teeth in the end. Remembering to keep one eye closed so as not to compromise her night vision. An old watch-keeper's trick if ever there was one. She could make nothing of the script in which it was written except that it was Arabic and beautiful. She shrugged.

Robin opened the library door, flashed the torch for an instant and put the book on the nearest table. Then she bent to reach for the chair once again. Bent, and froze. She only saw it because at least one of her eyes was so well adjusted to the darkness. She only registered that it might be impor- tant because she was so attuned to everything going on around her. She only reacted to it because of a heady combination of hope and paranoia.

It was a flash of headlights across the forward deck. A car or truck was coming in through the security gates at the far end of the pier.

Using the credit-card torch with almost reckless abandon she ran back to the lading office and looked out of the little side window. Sure enough, the security gates were open and some kind of vehicle was waiting there. The headlights dazzled her but still she could see the hulking shape of the security guard looming beside the driver's door. The black air behind the vehicle showed a brief cloud of exhaust fumes. *It must be Richard!* Robin thought. Richard had come to get her after all.

And yet, something held her back, made her double-check what she was seeing. The vehicle rolled forward, the beams of its headlights bouncing up and down, flashing faintly across the deck in the telltale sign that had first alerted her. Behind the car, the watchman waved and gestured, lit up vividly red by its tail-lights. He put something to his mouth. Robin could not hear the bat-shriek at this distance but she knew just what it was. And sure enough, the dogs came padding out of the shadows and reluctantly gathered around their master as the car rolled on towards his bright-lit hut.

But just as it drew level with the hut itself, the headlights seemed to give an extra flash. Then they died. Robin stopped breathing. As soon as the car was halfway down the pier, the driver had switched the headlights off. Silently, almost invisibly, the car rolled on towards *Prometheus*.

Robin was just able to make out enough under the pallid gleam of the security lights to be sure that she had never seen this car before. It was not one of the Mercedes saloons they had ridden in this afternoon. It was not the car that followed her cab from Izba to Snezhok. It had none of the signs that denoted taxis in Archangel. Robin supposed it still might be Richard, coming to get her along with whoever he had gone off with when he left her in the restaurant, but she couldn't quite convince herself of that either, somehow.

The car stopped just short of the gangplank, right at the very edge of her vision. The doors opened, front and back. Four large figures got out. The instant they did so, one of the dogs burst out of the shadows. It came charging towards the men at full tilt. Its action was so unexpected, fierce and threatening that Robin almost shouted a warning to the newcomers. They didn't need any help at all. In silence, almost in slow motion, one of the figures whirled. He pointed at the dog. The dog fell down. Robin had never seen anything like it. One moment the dog was charging forward like a hungry wolf, the next it was lying on its side like a lapdog on a hearthrug.

The watchman came running up, his inarticulate shouting added the faintest of distant soundtracks to the silent film of the strange situation. The man who had pointed at the dog pointed at the watchman. The watchman stopped. Held out his hands. Everything went quiet once again. Absolutely silent in fact: even the wind seemed to drop. Still pointing, the big stranger walked slowly over to the watchman. One of his colleagues slammed his car door and the sound was just like a gunshot. He walked forward a step or two and looked up at the ship. Robin could see his eyes. It was as though his gaze actually locked with her own. As though he knew she was there.

Robin turned and ran.

Thirteen

'What in Heaven's name is going on?' demanded Richard the moment that Fedor Gulin and he were alone.

Gulin shrugged his ignorance, making a great show of being preoccupied. He was folding up the sheets on the autopsy table with thoughtful care, stroking each crease into place as though it was a favourite shirt he was preparing to put away instead of the *Prometheus* schematics. Though Richard thought it was highly unlikely that Fedor did his own washing and ironing. 'Have you no idea at all, Fedor?' he persisted more quietly.

Fedor shrugged again and looked meaningfully around the room. It was no coincidence that they had been left alone. They were being taped. Put on disk more likely. Certainly audio, probably video. Fedor Gulin was an easy man to under-estimate. The frog-like face masked an acute and insightful intelligence. And, as Richard suspected but had yet to see, considerable resolve. Bravery, in fact.

Richard knew that they were being watched. He could see no other reason for Elena Onega to call Repin and Voroshilov out into the corridor an instant or two after having let Repin reveal the true scale of the slaughter. But he was utterly inno-cent of any involvement in the killing or concealing of the corpses on board his vessel, and assumed his colleagues in the Sevmash Consortium were too. In fact, following his reasoning of a little earlier, he could not readily see any way in which Felix, Fedor or the others could be involved. Not in the actual brutal murders or their immediate aftermath at least.

Richard's main priority, therefore, was not to keep his igno-rance concealed from the authorities but to replace it with knowledge and insight that might help him work out what on earth was going on. Ignorance equalled innocence in this equa-tion, he reckoned. But knowledge was power.

'Did they at least tell you how many bodies they believe to be aboard?' he resumed, gently but insistently.

Fedor hesitated and frowned. But a moment's reflection showed him nothing incriminating in discussing what the customs and immigrations officers had told him.

'Officer Repin mentioned five,' he replied carefully.

'Five more or five in all?' Richard asked the question automatically. He was still trying to work out the implications of having any dead bodies at all aboard *Prometheus*.

'Five more, I believe. But that is just what I remember from Officer Repin's observations.'

'My God.'

'Though I think they will be looking through the ship in some detail when the federal prosecutor arrives. Officer Repin suggested that the federal prosecutor may even bring his own team of investigators, pathologists, forensics and so forth. That's why they have moved only one of the bodies so far, Officer Repin mentioned to me.' Fedor was warming to this strange little game.

'I see.' Richard dragged his mind away from the wider implications of his situation and concentrated on this. Either Repin was unusually communicative or he had let slip the information calculatedly, hoping to frighten Gulin. And perhaps, through Gulin, Richard. Richard did not like being manipulated, but he was more than willing to put up with it if he thought he could turn it to his advantage and manipulate his manipulators a little.

'Did Officer Repin give you any more information about this federal prosecutor they're expecting?'

Gulin shrugged. Shivered a little, but that might have been for the benefit of any camera that happened to be pointing their way. Richard did not actually believe that Fedor was scared at all. 'Apparently he is a man with a fearsome reputation,' the Russian answered slowly. 'One of the Prosecutor General's inner circle. Very close to the President himself, therefore. And at a time like this, so close to the presidential elections, that makes him a man of truly immense power, of course. It seems that he was promoted from the provinces when the new team went in after Chaika succeeded Ustinov, though that's a while ago now. A bear of a man. Absolutely ruthless. Never failed to solve a case. That's why he's on the

Federal team, I suppose. Only the most outstanding regional and state prosecutors get promoted like that.'

There was a slight emphasis on *outstanding* that warned Richard Gulin might well mean *politically connected*. He nodded, impressed. 'Any names mentioned?'

'No.' The extra shake of the head said to Richard *pointedly not*. Gulin was good at this game.

'Right.' Richard breathed through his nose and frowned in deep thought. 'So. The situation as I see it is this. Repin and his men found six bodies and brought one here. Though I'm not absolutely clear about why they went aboard in the first place. *Prometheus* had gone through a standard customs inspection already. Put that on one side for the moment. When they found the bodies, of course they contacted their own superiors. Who would have contacted a wider range of local authorities. And Investigator Onega was assigned from the local Prosecutor's Office in Archangel. They were acting pretty quickly, I should say. And so did she. She put her team together and came to question us in record time.

'In the meantime, however, the Prosecutor General's Office was also alerted and decided almost immediately to send in a senior team. And if Officer Repin – and presumably the others – know who has been appointed to come out here, then the Prosecutor General's Office is moving pretty quickly into the bargain. So far so logical. There must be a great number of implications for the authorities to consider after all. If the men are all Chechens, then someone at Counter-Terrorism in the FSB will have to become involved, for a start.'

Richard stopped there and considered other implications that he did not want to share with Gulin under the eye of the Investigator's camera. As part of his preparation for this deal he had spent a good while with the Intelligence section of Heritage Mariner. Staffed by people culled from Naval Intelligence and MI6 – ex-doomwatchers as well as ex-handlers and retired field personnel, it was well able to keep its finger on the pulse of events and probable events worldwide. It was they who had brought him up to speed with the changes in both the security services and the Prosecutor's Office whose implications he was facing now. Especially if the six dead men were all Chechens and were found to have any link to the separatist groups, the Moscow Theatre siege, the Beslan school massacre or the more recent incidents in Ingushetia, Nalchick and Moscow itself. Or, of course, to al-Qa'eda. The counter-terrorist arm of the FSB's Service for the Protection of the Constitutional System would be involved pretty quickly. Their leader Aleksandr Bragin was almost as close to the President as General Prosecutor Chaika. And his right hand, General Yury Sapunov, head of the Internal Terrorism Directorate, was by all accounts almost as powerful and influential. If the man Chaika was sending up here was also one of Bragin's boys, or had been briefed by General Sapunov, then he would indeed be formidable. But Richard and Fedor would have to wait and see with that one. Repin had probably only planted the idea of Federal Prosecutor Bogeyman to frighten Gulin. No sense Richard frightening himself into the bargain. Certainly not by wild speculation into areas that weren't really supposed to be common knowledge in the first place.

'So, they found these people in the refrigerator?' Richard continued smoothly. Only moments had passed since their last conversation had faltered into his thoughtful silence.

'Yes.' Fedor's frog-eyes were narrow, his dark lids heavy with speculation as he tried to keep up with Richard's train of thought.

'Did Officer Repin mention how they did so?'

'As a matter of fact, he did. Dogs found them. That's what Officer Repin said.'

That made sense. They had all noted this afternoon how perished the seals round the refrigerator doors in the galley had become. And the place had certainly smelt foul enough. Noses more sensitive than theirs might well have been able to discriminate the stench of human putrefaction from all the other stenches soiling the atmosphere there. Thank God none of them had thought to open the doors for a closer look at the damage.

Or on the other hand, perhaps, *if only they had* opened the doors . . .

But then, as ever, Richard's mind was questing further ahead. 'Did Officer Repin say which body they brought out?'

'No. I don't think so. Why? Is it important?' Fedor was taken off guard. The question was genuine. They would discuss the answer and its implications later and in a more private environment if by chance the opportunity arose.

'Might be. Just a thought . . .' Richard was almost theatric-
ally dismissive in the face of Fedor's surprise.

Richard fell into silence once again. He put aside the thought
about where in the fridge the man next door had been lying,
and re-examined some of his earlier thinking in the light of
the sudden arrival of the five friends sharing the freezer with
him.

The Archangel option became immediately much more
problematic, it seemed to him. As with almost any city in
England, Richard could imagine that in Archangel there might
be thugs racist enough to beat a man of Arabic appearance to
death for no reason other than his ethnicity. With the current
climate, it was possible in a wide range of cities throughout
America and the European Union. That thugs such as these
might then be able to smuggle the body aboard *Prometheus*
was, as he had calculated, a problem. But not, he also calculated, an insurmountable problem. Even given the watchman
and his guard dogs.

But *half a dozen* dead men?

That was another kettle of fish. As the authorities here and
in Moscow had already recognized by starting a Federal investigation more powerful than a local one. By sending in a top
man, whether or not he was an ogre. Six men killed and smuggled aboard *Prometheus* could only mean an organization of
enormous power and influence. The Mafia or the Government
were the only two that sprang to mind. And neither of these
organizations was likely to have allowed the Archangel investigation to get this far. The Mafia would in all likelihood have
started adding to the tally of the dead. The Government would
certainly not be sending out a well-connected specialist. Unless
of course they wanted to ensure a public cover-up of some
kind. But Richard only entertained that thought for an instant.
That way lay the darkest of paranoid terrors.

The alternative, however, seemed to mean that the bodies
had been aboard since Wilhelmshaven and the towing watch
had not discovered them during the days and nights they were
on duty aboard. Why should they? Who would want to go
poking around in ancient, disconnected freezers? But if the
dead men were put aboard in Wilhelmshaven, what in Heaven's
name did that mean?

The implications there were simply too enormous and

simply too complicated to consider at this moment. Because, like the tip of an iceberg sitting above some very murky waters indeed, the same basic logic held true. These men had either been killed by some enormously powerful Neo-Nazi Mafia or by some secret arm of the German government. The Federal Crime Office – equivalent to the Service for the Protection of the Constitutional System here.

Which in turn might explain why the usually super-efficient German civil service had been so happy to get rid of a vessel that was still full of such eminently saleable items . . .

'Where's Felix?' he asked suddenly.

Gulin looked up, taken a little off-guard. 'What?'

'Felix. Did Officer Repin or someone else from customs, the Militsia or the Prosecutor's Office pick Felix up as well? Is he somewhere here or at Militsia headquarters, wherever that is?'

'Oh no.' Gulin shook his head earnestly. 'I thought you were aware of the plans. Felix went to Moscow this afternoon. The idea was for him to go straight on to Talagi Airport immediately after he dropped you at your hotel. There is an afternoon flight to Moscow. It takes about three hours when it's running to time. He should be there now. I think.' He glanced at his watch. 'He had another meeting or two this evening. I expect he will be back tomorrow.'

Richard was just beginning to consider the implications of that tit-bit of information when the door opened and Investigator Onega re-entered the room, bristling with abrupt efficiency. The corridor behind her was empty, Richard noticed. The other Militsia men dismissed and Voroshilov and Repin with them, about some other duties, or in the video room double-checking the tapes or discs they had just made of his conversation with Fedor Gulin. 'The pathologist wishes to discuss some matters with you,' she informed Richard brusquely. 'Please return to Pathology Laboratory Number One.'

'May my colleague come too?' Richard gestured to Fedor Gulin.

'Of course,' agreed Onega, narrow eyed and clearly not too happy to be robbed of the initiative, even in something as insignificant as this. 'Though it is not his expertise that is required, I believe. It is yours. *Such as it is*,' she added with a sudden excess of catty humanity which Richard, for one, found almost endearing.

So, thought Richard. My expertise is required. In what area, I wonder.

In the least likely area of all, as it turned out. He and Gulin entered the path lab side by side to find only Dr Kashin there. The body on the table was now covered with a stained white cloth whose outlines showed all too clearly that the flesh and bone beneath it were not quite in the places they had been when they went through next door with Investigator Onega. And that was independently of the heart that had already popped out to show its fatal weakness to the pathologist. Richard noted with an interest born of his slight but memorable acquaintance with such places that the gutter at the end of the table and the drain in the floor beneath it were surprisingly clean. Hardly a drop of blood there at all. And yet, at one degree Celsius, it shouldn't have frozen. Could it have set? He wondered.

'What can you tell me of the internal arrangements of the galley on board *Prometheus*?' demanded Dr Kashin.

'The galley? Ah let me see . . .' Richard dragged himself back from more sanguinary speculation as to where the corpse's blood had gone. He closed his eyes, as he often did when trying to dredge something out of the nether recesses of his capacious memory. He had a photographic memory that had been razor sharp in his youth but was becoming occasionally fuzzy now. He described to the pathologist the manner in which the galleys were laid out aboard the *Prometheus* series. Half a dozen ships and more, only one kitchen design.

'The work areas and sink units are in the middle of the galley with a great deal of the necessary hardware on hooks above or in drawers or cupboards below,' he began. 'On one side of this, the forward side, in fact, there is the serving area with access through to the dining area. There are some hot plates and steam ovens here designed to keep food at optimum before serving. On the other sides of the main work area, aft and starboard, there are the ranges, griddles, ovens and hot plates where the food is actually cooked. There are not an excessive amount of these for the crew rarely numbers more than forty and it is almost unknown for them all to eat together because there is someone always on watch. Even at Christmas. Even in harbour. Aft of the cooking areas are the kitchen storage areas. These are the dry-goods store which is a small walk-in area furthest aft of all, the fridges and the freezers. These are very much bigger. Although there are walk-in refrigeration rooms, meat lockers and cold stores further down below on the upper engineering decks, nevertheless it is traditional to keep a great deal of food to hand in the galley area itself. Chef might only be cooking for forty at a sitting, but he needs to keep supplies available for up to three months continuous work at sea. And hard work breeds hungry appetites. There are two massive refrigerators as well as the dry-goods store and the cold room for fruit and green vegetables. But there are also two large freezers, which I suspect are what you want to know about in most detail.'

Richard paused here and waited until Pathologist Kashin gave a curt nod. She did not enjoy being manipulated any more than Elena Onega did. At this point also, by apparent coincidence, Repin and Voroshilov reappeared. So they had been in the video room after all, thought Richard. And clearly Lab Two wasn't the only lab wired for sound.

'The freezers are the largest commercial capacity. They are each nearly two metres deep and about the same wide and high, allowing for the motors and the lining of course. They have double doors, sealed with rubber strips using the magnetic system of closure. But the doors have big double handles too so that they can, if necessary, be almost unbreakably secured.'

Richard looked up at that and saw Voroshilov and Repin exchange looks. Repin grimaced in a gesture of wry agreement with his words and Voroshilov grinned showing no sympathy at all with the customs man. So. The doors had been secured. They may even have had to break them open. The dogs must have been pretty bloody certain.

And if not the dogs, then the men who had brought them aboard.

'Each freezer has adjustable shelving which is not dissimilar to domestic freezers except that in the *Prometheus* vessels the shelves were not flap-fronted or of basket design. They slide straight out and in, allowing easy access to whatever is stored right at the back. The shelves were made of strong stainless-steel wiring. They may have been covered with plastic coating, I really can't remember.'

At this point, Pathologist Kashin lifted the cover off the body on the table. The edges of the huge Y had been folded in again over a suspiciously hollow-looking torso and abdomen. And the fact that the lines no longer met made the scales fall from Richard's eyes. And he understood almost everything that the Investigator and the pathologist were just about to ask him.

Fourteen

'Let me try and answer the next few questions before you get round to asking them,' said Richard, suddenly grasping the initiative with both hands. 'Yes, I believe it would be possible to put a body on one of the freezer shelves. And, from memory, you could fit four in there without too much trouble. Three would be easy. Three in each or two in one and four in the other. Especially if you put the bottom-most body on the shelf that was in the lowest set of grooves. Face down or face up equally easily. But of course, storing the body face down might mean that the corpse's hands and what-nots might actually hang down further.' He looked across at Onega. 'They would easily fit through the wire rack,' he emphasized. 'Fingers and genitals and what-have you.'

He transferred his cold gaze back to the pathologist. 'Yes. From what I recall, the wire rack is almost identical in form to the pattern on the corpse's chest, stomach and legs. The twisting of his toes is consonant with his feet having been pushed up against the back of the freezer. Though I noted at once, as did you, that the body is less than two metres tall.'

Richard crossed to the table and pulled the cover back still further, revealing the dead man's hands. 'Yes,' he said. "The missing fingers. Like you at first I supposed this damage was part of the torture. But it wasn't, was it? The wounds are too ragged. The stumps of bone have been scraped. I believe the same will be true of the damage to his genitals.'

He looked round at Repin. 'He was on the bottom shelf, wasn't he? Face down as I said?'

Repin nodded his reply.

'The dogs must have gone mad,' Richard probed.

'They did,' confirmed Repin.

'And you thought it was just the smell of the corpses?'

'What else were we supposed to think? Once we got the

door open, nothing else even occurred to us. Until Dr Kashin here explained she wanted to speak to you – and why.'

'Well, Dr Kashin here or whatever pathologist the federal prosecutor brings with him from Moscow will be able to be more precise when they examine the inside of the freezer itself. I've never seen it but I'm not hugely surprised. There must be just enough space where the two doors join at the bottom, where the rubber is thickest and the stainless steel bends back into the individual wings of the double doors. And I guess, that's where it perished first. And in all honesty if you think about it, there was probably a good deal of outward pressure from the inside unless whoever was involved took a great deal of care to prepare the bodies before they started storing them.'

'I don't think they did.' Repin shuddered at the memory of the insides of the freezers.

'But then,' added Richard suddenly upon a thought, 'the bottom shelf, with those poor chaps lying on it, can't have been quite at its lowest setting, can it? Fingers and genitals are one thing, but the rest seems pretty well preserved. And the others. They're OK? Fingers, toes and what-nots so to speak?'

Repin nodded again. Elena Onega was frowning and even Voroshilov looked grudgingly impressed.

'And, just to dot the last "I" and cross the last "T",' said Richard, well in his stride now, 'and just so I can sleep relatively easy tonight, always assuming that sleep is on the agenda, it *was* only men, was it? You're sure there were no women in the freezers at all?'

There was a kind of stunned silence that he should ever have even entertained such a thought. Then Repin's eyes slid away towards Onega's and his face went pale in the green-white light.

'Right,' said Richard heartily. 'Glad to hear it. Though I guessed that you'd have mentioned it if you had noticed. That's it. For this section of things at any rate. Unless Dr Kashin has anything else she wants to check with me?'

Dr Kashin was still shaking her head when Voroshilov closed the door behind them and shoved them down to Lab Two once again. Although he slammed it pretty quickly he wasn't quite fast enough to obscure the sight of Onega swinging round on Repin who was already shrugging apologetically. That last one would put the cat amongst the pigeons, thought Richard. Unless someone was going to get back aboard again and double-check in triple-quick time so that they could have their initial report all straight and accurate for the federal prosecutor when he arrived. And of course if it was the federal prosecutor who had ordered everything to be marked off-limits and left, then he'd be equally upset if anyone went back aboard *Prometheus* for any reason whatsoever.

'I didn't understand any of that,' said Gulin. 'My English is very good, but you might as well have been speaking Greek. Can you translate a bit for me?'

'You followed the last bit well enough?' said Richard. 'I don't think Officer Repin actually checked on the gender of the corpses. I can't blame him. It must have taken him aback more than a little to find freezers full of dead people instead of frozen meat. But it'll be one of the first things the federal prosecutor will ask. Next after ethnicity, I should think. But ethnicity is the crucial element, I believe, which is why they brought out a representative sample for Dr Kashin to check.'

'But if they knew he was representative in terms of race . . . '

'Of skin colour, of hair type. You could do that with a fairly careful look, especially if they were all naked. My bet is they were told to touch as little as possible. And if the bodies were all stored face down, head nearest the door, you'd have to do a fair bit of moving and checking to be absolutely sure of gender as well, wouldn't you?'

Gulin nodded. 'OK, I get that. But what about the rest of it?'

'This body at least appears to have been stored face down because the marks of the rack were in the front. You got that?'

'Yeah. That wasn't rocket science.'

'Neither was the rest of it, once you know a bit about ships.'

'That's why they called you through. Because you know more about ships than they do. Though I guess they already had their suspicions. So?'

'The body we had to look at was stored face down in a freezer that was old and unconnected. It had been out of use so long that the rubber seals round the doors were perishing at the very least.'

'OK, I get that.'

'The bodies would have leaked. Bodies do.'

'Yeah. I have friends in the army who have served at the front. They tell me things when they're drunk. Bodies leak big-time. I was in Admin myself.'

'I know. And highly regarded. I've seen bits of your file. But that being said, the bodies leaked. The seals were perished . . .'

'Especially where the doors join. At the bottom. I get that.'

'So that's where the stuff that leaked, leaked *out*.'

'What the dogs found first, I get it . . .'

'What the dogs found second, Fedor.'

'What do you mean? Second?'

'I mean something else found it first. That's where ship-knowledge comes in handy, you see? Ships are special places. Hardly any flies or any other kind of bugs, all far away from land and so forth. Food sometimes doesn't even go mouldy like it does here. I've seen bits of bread that have just shrivelled to a kind of pale toast where they would have housed colonies of mould ashore.'

'Right.' Gulin drew out the word. 'I get it . . .' though all too clearly he still did not.

'So on ships there aren't any flies or moths or mosquitoes or moulds unless you're very near to shore. You get that. But, and this is the important part, there's something else.'

'There's what?'

'There's rats, Fedor. Rats. Rats went up into the galley. I bet they were eating the rubber seal. They must have been hungry enough, God knows. But then there was something more nutritious. They burrowed in through the join at the bottom of the door and they ate what they could reach by sitting up on their haunches. They can't have got more than a nibble. Fingers, what-not. But they couldn't have got a proper grip with teeth or claws or they'd have climbed up and eaten everything. And they must have tried. Because there's very little in God's creation as cunning as a hungry rat.'

'Jeez,' said Fedor Gulin, much the same colour as Repin had gone just a little earlier. 'I'd have been happier leaving it all in Greek. I'm sorry I asked for a translation now . . .'

*   *   *

No sooner had Fedor Gulin delivered himself of this heart-felt speech, than a brief bustling outside prefaced the throwing open of the door once again. Voroshilov and Elena Onega re-entered, but this time the atmosphere they brought with them was subtly different. Chillier. More threatening. Something in the situation had slipped yet further out of their control. And that seemed to Richard to be a bad thing. They could stand insultingly clever foreigners giving them lectures in deduction. They could accept the arrival of Ogres from Moscow disguised as federal prosecutors. But something had really upset them now. They had also brought a stranger who looked suspiciously as though he had just been in a car-crash.

'This is Militsia Sergeant Paznak,' snapped Onega.

'Nice to meet you, Sergeant. Do you need to have a seat? That leg looks pretty battered . . .' Richard was playing for time rather than being flippant. But Sergeant Paznak simply growled and came for him as though he planned to punch his lights out there and then, bandaged face, arm in a sling and all. Though, from the way he was moving, the bandages and the sling may have been a bit of window dressing to impress the Investigator. To awaken her sympathy, at least.

Suddenly Voroshilov was between them. The rifle-barrel eyes were just about all that separated his frowning brows from his bristling moustache. 'The sergeant has some questions, *Angliski*,' he grated. 'His English is not so fluid as mine so I will translate questions and answers. But I warn you this is serious situation and Sergeant Paznak was champion fighter in his unit.'

'What sort of fighting?' asked Richard, still playing for time in the face of Paznak's blazing outrage, trying to work out what on earth this was all about.

'Every sort,' spat Voroshilov.

Paznak started speaking then, in short hoarse sentences punctuated by the kind of wheezing that warned of broken ribs. As he spoke he glared at Richard over Voroshilov's shoulder. When he stopped speaking, he continued breathing with great tearing agonized breaths and he continued glaring with an intensity that reminded Richard irresistibly of Hannibal Lecter.

'Where is your wife?' demanded Voroshilov on Paznak's behalf.

'What?' Of all the questions Richard might have been

expecting, this was absolutely the last. It threw him off balance more effectively than one of Paznak's punches would have.

Richard's reply didn't need translating. His shock, confusion and concern were all too clear.

Paznak spat his question again.

'Do you know the current whereabouts of your wife?' Voroshilov extrapolated more formally.

'Isn't she in our hotel? What's it called? Zelyony! She's at Zelyony, isn't she?'

Again, there was no need for Voroshilov to translate Richard's answer.

But he had to translate Paznak's response, for it was long, laboured and borderline hysterical. 'No! She is not at your hotel. As Sergeant Paznak is sure you are well aware. She vanished from the Izba restaurant in a manner suggesting special services training. Familiarity with British and American intelligence and security undercover techniques. She was able to throw off a well-trained Militsia unit. She was tracked, however, because of the good citizenship of a taxi driver. She was tracked to Snezhok, where she may well have been making some kind of clandestine contact. And she vanished once again, after having assaulted this officer and causing a multi-vehicle pile-up which may in turn lead to several deaths. So he asks again. Do you know where your wife is?'

Richard. I'm safe . . .

Richard replayed the interrupted message in his head. Clearly it didn't mean what it had said at all. Clearly there was more. A hell of a lot more, in fact. And the extra section reversed the impression of security given by the opening phrase. *Hell's teeth . . .*

But the simple fact was that he did not know where she was. And that was all he could deal with at the present moment in the current circumstances. 'No.' He put all of his considerable power and intensity into the word. His gaze switched from Paznak to Voroshilov to Elena Onega as the word lingered. 'I have no idea where my wife is.'

Fifteen

There was the briefest of pauses, then Richard's whole manner changed, from assurance to accusation. His face darkened and his voice rose as he spoke. And he spoke very clearly indeed. Here was something that he definitely did want to go on their record of conversations and events in these rooms.

'I had believed from what I had been told by the Investigator that my wife was safe in our hotel. I am very disturbed to hear that this is not so. And very disturbed and enraged to hear that Sergeant Paznak and his team have been pursuing her when Investigator Onega had assured me she was safe and sound. And now you tell me you've been running and driving after her? And she's *gone*? You've been hunting her through a city she doesn't know, chasing her into places she has never been before and she's suddenly *vanished*?'

Richard could feel rage and frustration building dangerously in his breast. He would be as severely out of control as Paznak in a moment. The red mist was really coming down. Voroshilov saw this and stepped back, pushing the crippled fighting champion back with him. Seeing for the first time, perhaps, what Richard himself was capable of.

And it was precisely at this moment that the Investigator's personal phone went off. She answered it at once and something about her demeanour defused the situation slightly. Certainly, they all stopped staring each other down like a bunch of schoolyard bullies and looked at her instead. She spat half a dozen syllables singly into a very one-sided conversation that lasted less than fifteen seconds, then she closed her phone and looked up, frowning. She seemed more than a little shaken herself, all of a sudden. 'The federal prosecutor will arrive at Talagi Airport within the hour,' she snapped breathlessly. 'He wants to see us there as soon as he deplanes into the arrivals area. Which he will of course do immediately after touch down. And his invitation includes you, Captain Mariner.'

'I'm not going anywhere until I find out where my wife is,' grated Richard, stepping forward once again. Voroshilov didn't move this time and he was actually sandwiched between the two still-raging men.

Elena Onega took control. 'Sergeant Paznak will find your wife and take her to your hotel,' she said, stepping forward to join Voroshilov, shoulder to shoulder. Her dark eyes bored into Richard's with an intensity that could not be denied. 'You have my absolute word on that. Voroshilov, go with Paznak. Find Captain Mariner's wife and don't return either here or to headquarters, go off duty, sleep or eat until you have her safe.'

She drew a deep breath and continued no less forcefully but less intensely, perhaps. 'I'm sorry, Captain Mariner, but the federal prosecutor's requirements are absolutely clear. If you refuse to accompany us at once then I will have you arrested and taken to Talagi under restraint. Under sedation if I have to.'

Her tone became more intimate and desperate, almost pleading. This was as close as she could ever come to begging, he realized with something of a shock. She must indeed be desperate. And on the verge of being terrified. 'No one in Archangel is better qualified than these two men to find her and bring her safely home,' she insisted earnestly. 'They are certainly ready, willing and able to do far more than you could ever do yourself. And far more swiftly and effectively. You, on the other hand, have been summoned by the federal prosecutor. Summoned personally. It is a summons I cannot allow you to ignore. Make up your mind, please. We have no more time for hesitation.'

They all but ran out of the front of the building past the bustle of the Internet cafe. There were several cars parked on the road. The Investigator paused by one, a battered little vehicle that resembled nothing more than a Morris Minor. But she whirled past it and led them to a much more solid, powerful and official-looking car. Richard inconsequentially recognized it as one of the vehicles that he had seen at the security gates this afternoon. Of course. It would be. It must be Repin's squad car.

'Keys!' she snapped.

Repin tossed them to her, robbed of any desire to remonstrate by the tone she used. He didn't even shrug as she opened up and gestured for them all to get in.

Investigator Onega drove, with Repin beside her in the front, with his hands on the dashboard and his arms rigid. Richard and Gulin filled the back seat. Richard would have deduced that this was a car from the Militsia pound rather than the Investigator's own vehicle almost immediately, even had he not recognized it. They were right at the far end of Prospekt Obvodny Kanal and on the northern outskirts of town before she stopped grating the gears and making the customs officer wince. Then she settled down and proved to be a very competent, very fast driver indeed. The other thing that made Richard assume this was a Militsia car was that none of the GAI patrols they passed at velocities that shattered speed limits gave them a second look or even dreamed of flagging them down.

But Richard's observations were all made on automatic pilot, for he was fearsomely focused on Robin and her whereabouts.

Richard, I'm safe, she'd said.

But she hadn't meant it. Logic already exercised told him there must have been more to the message. So the first thing Richard did was to interrogate his phone. He called her cellphone number time and time again but there was no reply. He left half a dozen messages with the automated voice of the service that explained her number was unobtainable. He went into his own cellphone's memory, but the clever little machine let him down – it had not recorded what she had said. Though, to be fair, he had not asked it to do so. In the end, he put his head back on the plastic of the moulded headrest and closed his eyes.

Richard, I'm safe . . .

He replayed it over and over again in his memory. Just the next word might make all the difference. The next syllable. The next letter, even. If only he could call it to mind. If only he had heard it.

Richard, I'm safe, but . . .

Richard, I'm safe, however . . .

Richard, I'm safe for the moment, but . . .

But there was a distracting amount going on around him. Not least the conversation in the front and the fact that Gulin whispered a translation of the Russian words into Richard's ear, clearly trying to be helpful. Actually being an increasing distraction. Especially as the information was of increasing interest to Richard, who had to make some kind of preparation if he could, for his interview with the God-like federal prosecutor.

'You'd better hope the federal prosecutor's a pretty small man,' said Repin, clearly out for revenge after the commandeering of his squad car. 'You'll never fit him in the back seat.'

'*You'd* better pray he is,' snapped Elena. 'If he wants a lift in this pile of junk then likely as not you'll be the one left at Talagi whistling for a taxi home.' Then she relented. 'But don't worry. The likes of the federal prosecutor would never be seen in a mere squad car like this one. There's no question of it. Regional Prosecutor Bakatin will be there himself, of course. He couldn't ever miss an opportunity like this. At the very least he can do some brown-nosing and if he's lucky he might even do himself some good. And Bakatin will have his Zil and his driver. Though even a Zil will be slumming it a bit, I should imagine. What do you think federal prosecutors drive around Moscow in?'

'Whatever the hell they want,' answered Repin cynically.

'Got it in one,' agreed Elena Onega bitterly.

Richard was still running through the possibilities when the lights of the airport reared into view and a jet settled through the lower air towards the single runway ahead, passing so low over the speeding car that it seemed about to graze it with its undercarriage.

'Shit!' spat Elena Onega and really trod on the gas.

Repin's arms went rigid once again and his whole body seemed to lift a little out of the passenger seat.

It was well after 10 p.m. local time, and the airport should have been closed, but it was still busy. Onega's wisdom in taking an official vehicle was further emphasized by the fact that she was able to ignore the No Parking signs on the apron by the main doors. The squad car screamed to a halt with her front bumper mere centimetres behind the rear bumper of a Zil that sat behind a Mercedes saloon. They had their motors running. Onega killed hers, then leaped from the vehicle and vanished into the Arrivals Hall, slamming the door behind her.

Repin got out of the front seat stiffly and followed more slowly, chivvying his reluctant companions along with him. Neither of them bothered with locking it up. No one in their right mind would hot-wire a squad car, even here.

Richard looked at Repin's slow, stiff-legged walk. 'Nearly put your foot through the floor?' he asked, though levity and, indeed, sympathy could hardly have been further from his mood.

Repin gave a grim laugh. 'My breaking foot,' he acknowledged. 'I may have broken it. I think I felt both bone and metal begin to give when the Moscow flight came in over the top of us and the fair Elena took the revs up past the red.'

'She certainly is a woman in a hurry,' Richard acknowledged.

Repin laughed again and led them through the doors. 'In all sorts of ways,' he answered.

Elena Onega was almost on tiptoe, like a passionate maiden awaiting the arrival of her lover. Beside her stood a plump little man wearing a bulky black overcoat and, of all things, a bowler hat. Richard didn't need Repin to tell him that this was Regional Prosecutor Bakatin. But after a glance at him, Richard focused once again on her.

All around her, weary staff were closing up shops and kiosks. Departures was empty, the departures screens blank and dark. The arrivals area was not quite bustling. Only the Moscow flight still showed up on the screen. Its late arrival explained why the airport was still open. Exhausted men and women waited to complete admissions checks, baggage handling. Equally exhausted colleagues, friends and relatives waited for the passengers from Moscow to come through the gates. In the middle of all of them, Onega shone like a candle flame in a chapel.

Richard felt his heart twist within him like a trout on a hook. Normally, only Robin could light up a place like that.

Richard, I'm safe ab . . .

The memory came out of nowhere and it stopped him dead in his tracks. But it came at the worst of all possible moments.

For just as he hesitated, his mind full of Robin's words and the implications of that extra syllable, so the arrivals doors opened and Elena Onega was in motion, dragging the bowler-hatted Bakatin with her. Repin pushed Richard and Fedor Gulin forward as well. Figures loomed in the shadows of the baggage hall behind the gaping doors. But the kind of people they were waiting for would not concern themselves with mundanities such as baggage. Or anything else that tested mere mortals at airports. They strode straight through as they had strode first off the plane without having to queue, as they had strode first and unquestioned through immigration and as they had passed first and unchecked through customs.

Felix Makarov came through first, his fawn British Warm open, his jacket buttoned but seemingly recently pressed, his gold silk Fabergé-patterned tie gleaming against the snowy perfection of his shirt. As he entered the arrivals hall he looked back, not forward, and hesitated for an instant mid-stride. And Richard, already surprised to see his business associate instead of the federal prosecutor, was simply and utterly shocked to see who was following in Felix's footsteps.

Gobsmacked, as his irreverent son was fond of saying. *Banjaxed*. Simply bloody horrified. And aware at the same instant that a lot that had been puzzling him during the last hour or so now made complete and utter sense. In the least pleasant possible way.

Behind Felix Makarov, like a monstrous shadow cast by a footlight on a stage, came his giant double. The overcoat was the darkest possible slate grey, but obviously a cashmere and angora compound, with that slight patina of white that comes with the most expensive of wools. The suit beneath it was one shade lighter, the faintest of conservative pinstripes emphasizing the perfection of the tailoring. The tie was blood red and marked with gold stars while the shirt was striped white on French grey. Where Felix's head gleamed like a billiard ball, his shadow's was hidden by an Astrakhan hat. On the one hand it was unbelievable that such a man should have access to such perfect tailoring. On the other it was almost inevitable, given the circumstances. For the man behind Makarov dwarfed him. He stood six foot nine in his socks. His chest was the size of a barrel and his arms would have made a good pair of legs for a lesser mortal.

But it was his face that claimed attention. The face of a battered prize-fighter. A face that made Voroshilov look like the most effeminate of Greek gods. Overhanging brows that seemed as much scar tissue as flesh, with ragged eyebrows better fitted for a bull or a bear. His nose was flat, the bridge non-existent, the nostrils as wide as that of a Hottentot. The mouth little more than a scar, a shark's mouth. But when it opened to address a word or two to the anxious Makarov, great ivory tombstones of teeth flashed. Only the passionate intelligence of the piercing eyes gave the lie to the brutish appearance of that gargoyle countenance.

Richard said, horrified, '*Yagula!*'

And Repin whispered, awe-struck, 'You *know* the federal prosecutor?'

Sixteen

Richard lowered his head automatically under the lintel as he entered the little room that was all Talagi Airport currently offered by way of corporate amenities. Felix Makarov did the same. They were both big men. They would have banged their heads if they had not stooped a little. Federal Prosecutor Yagula seemed to bend almost double. When he straightened, the tiles of the suspended ceiling seemed at risk. When he threw his Astrakhan hat on the circular table in the centre it looked like a sleeping bear cub. And it completely concealed the little grey suede briefcase he put down there first.

The room seemed too small to hold the three of them, and yet Elena Onega, Officer Repin, Fedor Gulin and District Prosecutor Bakatin all needed to squeeze in too. But they made it. More, they all managed to sit around the table like knights at King Arthur's court. Or rather, thought Richard, King Yagula's court. And King Yagula did indeed briefly hold court there as the chair creaked dangerously beneath his massive frame and the lights went out in all the other airport areas around them. There was no question of their lights going out, of course. The airport's manager himself would await the federal prosecutor's leisure. And if the federal prosecutor's chair actually collapsed he would likely lose his job.

'So,' he rumbled in the *basso profundo* that Richard remembered so well. 'Once again we have trouble with your ships, eh, Richard?'

Both men affected not to hear the stir that went round the table – round the Archangel section of it at any rate – at the unheard-of familiarity.

'It looks like it, Federal Prosecutor.'

Yagula's long dark eyes crinkled infinitesimally at their outer corners. It was the closest Yagula usually came to a smile. And Richard, from old acquaintance, read the wicked challenge there. That he should use Yagula's first name and patronymic as airily as Yagula had used his own.

Maybe later. An ace up his sleeve, he thought. Well, a deuce up his sleeve, perhaps.

Yagula continued, 'But last time it was no one aboard your vessel when there should have been a full crew. And this time it is six dead men when there should have been no one at all.'

'Last time you were the District Prosecutor for Murmansk. Now you are Prosecutor General Chaika's right hand, so I am told. You have come a long way in a short time.' Richard countered with appearance of ease while his mind raced almost out of control.

Richard, I'm safe ab . . .

What did it mean? What *could* it mean?

Whatever, it had to go on the back burner now, thought Richard grimly. Only a total fool would face Lavrenty Michaelovitch Yagula with anything less than his full attention. That had been true when he had been a lowly being, the equivalent of poor bowler-hatted Bakatin. How much more true was it now!

'I have come a little further than from Murmansk to Moscow, you mean? Perhaps. Perhaps. But we are an old team, Richard, and a good team. We will sort out this affair together, as we settled matters so satisfactorily aboard your *Titan 10*. You know the lovely ex-Investigator Maria Ivanova is still in Butyrka? I visit from time to time now that we live so close together, so to speak. Not, of course, that I live anywhere near Novoslobodskaya Street. I look in to see whether her case is anywhere near ready to come to court yet. Apparently not, sadly . . .'

Richard was not at all put off his guard by Yagula's massive bonhomie. His *Let's talk over the old times* approach. Especially as he knew as well as anyone at the table what a terrible threat was held in the apparently off-the-cuff reference to Butyrka prison. The unfortunate Maria Ivanova would be one of the few women there, held in a cell with twenty others if she was lucky, as she waited hopelessly for the Russian justice system to get her to trial and sentence her. But the Russian justice system could make the Mills of God seem like an Aston Martin in comparison. The poor woman was likely to have TB or Aids and with a fair chance of dying before her case ever came to trial, if what Yagula said was true. Richard felt a prickle of guilt at having saved her life and condemned her to this where Yagula would have left her to die in the end. That might have been a kindness after all, perhaps . . .

There might be an element of mutual respect between the two men, born of their adventures on the submarine *Titan 10*, but it was reluctant to put it mildly, and there was no warmth. Richard remembered all too clearly how ruthless Yagula was when last they met and it seemed to him that the meteoric rise to the offices in the Kremlin and the ear of the President, even at one remove, could hardly have come if the man had become less ruthless. His reference to Maria Ivanova, the one survivor of the criminal conspiracy on *Titan 10*, drove that message home with a vengeance.

But this was a different Yagula without a doubt. Smoother. More emollient, on the surface at least. The most obvious difference was above his ears. When last they had met, Yagula had been as bald as Felix was now, his great head shaved daily in a never-ending battle against the vigorous stubble springing there. Now he had let his hair grow, obviously undeterred by the narrowness of the band of skin between his wild eyebrows and his widow's peak. And the short but luxuriant brown locks themselves seemed specifically designed to demonstrate that a man powerful enough to be this perfectly tailored could be perfectly barbered into the bargain.

His cuffs, when he shot them, were laden with cuff-links that looked like nuggets which had just been dug up, welded to the shanks and given a shine. The watch was by Patek, wafer thin and on a gold band that would have made a decent belt for Elena Onega. And on the pinkie of his left hand, there gleamed that most fashionable accessory of all, a golden signet ring. Which must, thought Richard, have been the thumb-ring of some late and self-indulgent Tsar.

'But, to business,' Yagula rumbled like a restless volcano. 'Time spent renewing old friendships may never be wasted, but time is important to us here. Regional Prosecutor Bakatin, your report, please.'

Bakatin had put his bowler on his lap, too nervous to allow it on the table with Yagula's Astrakhan. Now he half-rose as the federal prosecutor addressed him and squashed it between his thighs and the table edge with a sound like a cardboard box being crushed. 'Federal Prosecutor,' he answered, labouring with the English that everyone else seemed to be speaking so fluently, 'it is for Investigator Onega to report. She has reported to me of course but I feel she should update you more fully herself . . .'

The edges of Yagula's eyes crinkled ever so slightly again. His attention switched to the Investigator, as intense as that of a starving wolf eyeing a lost lamb. 'So, Investigator,' he rumbled. 'Update me. Fully.' As he had with the unfortunate Maria Ivanova, and as he did with all his pretty underlings, Richard suspected, Yagula made the suggestion sound vaguely indecent.

Elena Onega obliged, coolly unfazed by the federal prosecutor's flirtatiousness. And Richard was mildly surprised to note that she neither hogged Repin's glory nor hung him out to dry for his little errors. Furthermore she freely admitted her own fault in the matter of requiring the customs officer to return before he had checked the gender as well as the ethnicity of the bodies. And it was her responsibility into the bargain that, having assigned Sergeant Panzak to apprehend Mrs Mariner as Sergeant Voroshilov had brought in Captain Mariner himself, Panzak seemed to have lost sight of her.

Much of what Elena Onega was saying was familiar to Richard and he found it increasingly difficult to control his thoughts.

Richard, I'm safe ab . . .

Ab . . . What could that mean? What words began with ab . . . ?

As methodically as when he was seeking a crossword answer, Richard began to go through the alphabet, fitting in words in order, certain to find one that would make some kind of sense to him.

Richard, I'm safe aback . . . No, that wouldn't do at all.

Richard, I'm, safe abaft . . . Better. It was the sort of word Robin might use . . .

But Elena Onega's clear words soon distracted him back to the matter in hand once again. Her summation of what they had discovered so far was detailed, authoritative and simply masterly. And it added several details of procedure that Richard had been unaware of. The site had been photographed, though only one of the bodies had been moved. The body that had been moved had also been photographed in great detail and the photographs all forwarded to Moscow over the Internet. This was automatic procedure in such cases, apparently, but would have been done in any case as soon as it became obvious to Elena Onega and the team from the Regional Prosecutor's Office that the pictures did not match the ID papers of any local men, which were, of course, all held on computer at the Militsia headquarters.

And they hadn't just sent photographs. They had taken and sent on a series of DNA samples for the rapid allele-specific typing and the longer, more accurate RFLP typing. The samples, in fact, had gone to Moscow on the same flight that had taken Felix Makarov this afternoon. They were hoping for a DNA profile of their mysterious corpse at the earliest possible moment.

'And it may be that your first clue has returned as swiftly as Mr Makarov here,' boomed Yagula. He moved his hat with slow theatricality and revealed his briefcase like a magician producing a rabbit. He snapped the locks open and raised the lid. From inside, he extracted a piece of A4 paper in a plastic see-through folder. He held it up for all of them to see. It was a full-face ID photograph of the dead man at the Medical Academy, with an impenetrable column of printing filling the page beneath it.

'His name is Mu'hmud Kamyshev. Or it was. Those who know about such things believe he was one of the up-and-coming Chechen warlords getting ready to replace Khattab and the others we have killed during the last few years of the anti-terrorist campaign in Chechnya. There is very little doubt that he had links to worldwide terrorist movements and Saudi-sponsored Islamic militant groups. And to al-Qa'eda.'

Richard used the pause in Yagula's speech to carry on with his crossword clues.

Richard, I'm safe abduct . . . Tempting, but it still didn't make sense.

Richard, I'm safe abeam . . . Another word Robin might use. File it away for later examination perhaps. In the meantime, Yagula was talking once again.

'The Terrorism Control Directorate, Operations and Co-ordination for the Caucasus and Regional Anti-Terrorism all seem to agree with this. And so, for a wonder, do the CIA and British Intelligence. Even the German Federal Crime Office got in on the act, according to our records. Well, FSB records, which are of course the old KGB records supplemented and updated.

'Though I must observe that so much certainty and agreement is usually the kiss of death to truth. Consider everyone's absolute certainty that Saddam Hussein was in possession of immediately deployable weapons of mass destruction in Iraq . . .'

Yagula waited for the appreciative chuckles to circulate around the table.

Richard thought, *Richard, I'm safe ablaze . . .* A little silence distracted him almost at once, however. Yagula was watching him narrow-eyed. He smiled and nodded once to show he was still listening. The federal prosecutor resumed.

'Kamyshev had travelled widely, however. And quite legitimately. Contrary to popular opinion, we do not keep all our Chechen Muslims chained to their own front doors. Though of course we do keep an eye on potential trouble-makers. He was a student and spent time at several madrassas in various locations worldwide. I won't bore you with the details, but that is certainly why he was so widely recognized. More to the point, he vanished from Baku nearly a year ago, apparently on his way to Pakistan.'

Richard leaned forward, frowning. '*Vanished*, Federal Prosecutor?'

'You have put your finger on it, of course, Richard. Yes indeed. Vanished. One moment he was there, under precisely the sort of surveillance your wife seems to have been under. The next, *Pouf!* As the French say. He was gone.'

Richard, I'm safe above . . .

'And you never discovered where he went?'

Richard, I'm safe about . . . He had lost the thread of his crossword reasoning. Damn!

'As I say,' resumed Yagula, 'it was assumed he would turn up in Pakistan. But he didn't. He turned up in your freezer, Richard. And there are people from here to heaven knows where who want to know how, when and why.'

'And where he was in the meantime, as well as who his companions are, into the bargain, I'd say.'

'Richard! Richard! It is always such a pleasure working with you. Your finger is always on the nub . . . Is that the right word? Nub? Always on the nub of the problem.' Yagula glanced almost roguishly at Elena Onega. His gaze rested briefly on her face and then moved down. 'Though Richard has discovered two nubs to this problem, I should say.'

'And of course,' inserted Felix smoothly, breaking his unusual silence at last. 'Whether the friends in the freezers are the only friends the late Mr Kamyshev has aboard *Prometheus* . . .'

Richard, I'm safe aboard Prometheus . . .

It hit him like a freight train. It rang so true. How could he have taken so long to work it out. He was halfway to his feet before he realized it. And they were all frozen, looking at him, open mouthed.

He played the deuce he had up his sleeve for all it was worth. 'Well, Lavrenty Michaelovitch, let's go aboard *Prometheus* at once and take a look. What do you say?'

Yagula laughed. It was a very unsettling sound indeed. 'Richard! Richard! Ever the man of action. Yes, indeed. That is just what we must do. But I'm afraid Felix and I took action even more quickly than you would have us do. We do not have the facilities to perform a proper search of *Prometheus* here in Archangel. So we have arranged to have her moved at once to Severodvinsk where we can do what you planned and take her apart bit by bit. But do it under the proper control of the Prosecutor's Office.'

Richard sat down, shaken if not stunned. 'You're planning to move *Prometheus*?'

'More than planning, old friend. Felix here called the ship-yards before we boarded the plane at Moscow. *Prometheus* will be under way by now.'

Seventeen

You can't just move a supertanker on a whim. The captain of the tug *Dvina* knew that. Like turning one or stopping one, moving one takes time. But under the right circumstances you can get it ready for sea in a couple of minutes flat. The captain knew that as well.

But the captain knew that *Prometheus* had been brought here after a long tow and had been left ready for another one. Even to the extent of having main tow ropes already anchored on deck and attached to buoys in the water ready to be picked up, winched home and pulled. So he and his colleagues in the other three tugs that Felix Makarov had alerted reckoned on getting her back under way in record time. They discussed the best way to do this as they came nosing four abreast up beside her silent forecastle, appearing almost silently out of the darkness beyond the security lighting on Komsomolskaya Pier.

And what they planned was pretty fast indeed. Fast enough to catch even an experienced tanker captain off her guard, in fact. Though the captain of the *Dvina* and his three colleagues could not be expected to know that.

Robin ran almost wildly down the dark companionway to the ill-lit but telltale engineering section. She had no idea at all who was coming aboard but they had shot a dog and probably a watchman so some unexpected woman in the wrong place at the wrong time was hardly going to be a problem for them. But if she could cover her tracks, then she would almost certainly be able to hide away and probably be able to get back on to the pier without anyone even noticing. Except the watchman and the dogs, if any of them were left alive.

These thoughts were enough to take her down the central stairwell, into engineering and through to the dim little corridor with every other light-bulb missing. She calmed herself by an effort of will and walked more carefully through into her little hideaway. Next after the light, she felt the warmth upon the air. Would that be a giveaway strong enough to spark off a search? Probably not, even if anyone thought to come down here in the first place. Was she overreacting? She hesitated, wondering. But then she moved forwards. Better safe than sorry, she thought.

Better looking stupid than being dead.

She hit the off-switch on the generator and silence surged back with the darkness. Damn! She thought. If she had been as serenely on top of things as she had supposed she was, she wouldn't have forgotten to pick up a proper torch on the way down here! Had she time to go back up for one? Time to take the batteries from the others, ensuring she had light while the strangers could not rely on it unless they had brought their own? It was certainly worth a try. She had no idea why the men were here or where they were likely to go, but she was quite confident that, with care, she could avoid them. With time she could find out what was going on. With luck she could get everything sorted out.

She felt in her coat pocket for her credit-card torch. It wasn't there. She froze, simply horrified. A booming, rhythmical thudding suddenly echoed through the suffocating, stygian silence. It took her a moment to realize that this was the thudding of her heart sending blood pulsing through her ears with shock.

The torch must have fallen out of her pocket somewhere along the wild route here. The chances were that it would be up on 'A' deck corridor, lying there like a kind of reverse trap, waiting to be trodden on. Waiting to give her away. She was hardly going to remain secret and unsuspected if someone did tread on it. Even if they brought torches of their own, it was almost certain that someone treading on the credit card and sending out a beam of light from underneath his foot would notice it. And if they noticed that, then they would almost certainly begin to wonder where it had come from. And wondering would lead to speculating.

And speculating would inevitably lead to searching . . .

Blessedly, in the deepest recess of the pocket, weighed down by the car key, was the key torch. She took it out and pushed the button at once. How tiny and feeble the light seemed now!

But thank God she still had it. There were tears of relief welling up in her eyes and tickling her eyelids and cheeks. The first place she shone it was on the top of the generator, where her hat and hand-bag still lay safely side by side. Simply finding them brought a swelling of relief that steadied her pounding heart. So that the thudding in her ears began to lessen blessedly. Someone less decisive would have wasted light and time double-checking the hand bag just in case. But Robin knew where she had last used the credit-card torch. She knew therefore roughly where it must be lying.

She knew how utterly vital it was that she should go and get it. And then, if she got the chance, take the other torches as well. The fright had emphasized with brutal force just how vital any kind of light would be. She picked up her hat and pulled it down on her head as far as it would go. She zipped her bag shut, slung it over her shoulder and squeezed it under her arm as though she was planning to play it like a bagpipe.

She followed the key ring's fragile luminescence through the massive blackness all around her as swiftly as she dared and as silently as she could. The doors whispered open under her hand. She tiptoed up the stairs, though she knew that she would certainly see the beam of any torches they brought aboard metres in front of them, and long before they even began to suspect that she was there. It would be like seeing car head-lights in the distance on a night road long before the vehicle presented any danger. Even so, she switched off the key-ring light as she turned the corner, and stuck out her head at ankle level into the utter blackness of the corridor. At this level also, she shone her torch along the corridor, knowing that her credit card would show up clearly if she caught it in the beam. But there was nothing. The key ring's tiny beam was weak and beginning to fade. Torn, she glanced back at the bigger torches. And, decisive as ever, decided to risk it. She ran back down the stairwell, following the dying beam of the key-ring torch with every bit as much empathy as if it had been a dying friend. And good friend it proved, for with its dying glimmer it guided her to the nearest big torch. She snatched it down with her left hand even as she put the key ring back with her right. Then she ran back up the steps unerringly in the dark, counting under her breath. Down on her knees. Head around the corner at ankle height, torch ready, finger on the switch.

And the big door at the end of the 'A' deck corridor swung open. The inward wash of brightness showed her exactly where the credit-card torch was lying, just in the doorway of the first officer's work room. Anyone coming along the corridor itself might just miss it, she thought wildly. Anyone going into the lading area would almost certainly tread on it. But that was all the time she had for thinking. Men with torches were stepping in over the raised foot of the doorway and coming towards her down the corridor.

Only superhuman self-control stopped her jerking her head back as the first torch-beam swept over her. As any hunted thing knows with life-preserving instinct, it is movement that will give you away. She stayed still as a rabbit in the brief flash of torchlight, therefore, and slid back into the welcome darkness as soon as it flashed away. Had they not come upon her so swiftly and unexpectedly, she would have taken all the torches at the turning of the stairs. But even though the noise they made became almost overwhelmingly loud as they crowded into the corridor, she did not dare pause to do it now. Or to run the risk of knocking one over or dropping one in case the noise might give her away. Her hands, she discovered, were shaking as though she had palsy.

She ran to the foot of the stairs and froze on the uppermost engineering deck with the angle of the wall running down the valley of her spine. Her straining eyes saw the way the brightness came and went in the stairwell up above. Though it seemed to her that the brightness remained relatively distant. As though they had not ventured much further in than the doorway to the lading areas. Or perhaps the doorway to the galley opposite and a little further in.

Robin was breathing through wide-stretched mouth and nostrils as she waited for the thudding of her heart to settle and the noise in her ears to clear. Even so, it was a moment or two more before she realized that the men who had just come aboard were speaking in English.

'In here?'

'Yeah.'

'You sure?'

'I told you.'

'In the kitchen? Are you kidding me? I mean, that's pretty fucking bizarre.'

'Freezers seemed most convenient, I guess.'

'But the freezers weren't even on. Jesus.'

'They weren't supposed to be frozen, for Christ's sake. It was just for the storage . . .'

None of this made any sense to Robin. Nor would it have even if she could distinguish the speakers and work out who was saying what. All she was sure of was that all except one had vaguely American accents. Which meant very little these days, of course. One of them might actually have been American. She thought she detected a New England accent, and she had been to Boston often enough to recognize one. Another sounded more German to her. But that could have placed the speaker anywhere from Bremerhaven to Budapest as far as she was concerned.

But one of them sounded English. Really English. Plain, blunt Northern, bold as brass.

The conversation faded. The light died. She ran back up the stairwell, certain that they hadn't looked down here yet. She risked one flash of her big torch to establish everything in her retinal memory and then she reached out through the darkness and gathered all the torches to her. Two fitted in each coat pocket and the last one went in her left hand. Then, like a well-armed trainee Jedi, she tiptoed back down into the engineering corridor ready to awaken her light sabres at the merest flick of a switch. Feeling the Force for all she was worth, and hoping the hell it was with her.

Down here the strange conversation was clearer, eerily so, until a strange flickering overhead luminescence reminded her about the hole in the deck-head above. She was drawn to it as surely as any moth.

'Shit! This is really weird! Would you look at this?'

'What could have done that?'

'If the locals have worked it out, it'll be in the next report. You still got the stuff they put on the Web about Kamyshev?'

'Here on my phone. Look.'

'Shit. You'd think they'd be more careful about Internet security . . .'

'This is the Prosecutor's Office. This isn't the FSB or the KGB or whatever. It's just cops and robbers to them.'

'At the moment it is. This is where he was, huh?'

'Kamyshev? Yeah. I guess . . .'

'You don't know?'

'I don't remember. OK? And anyway, it wasn't me that put the sorry fuckers . . .'

'HEY! What's that?'

'What?'

'Didn't you feel that?'

'What the fuck . . .'

And the lights and sounds faded over a pounding that this time was not Robin's heart beating in her ears. She had felt it as clearly as the profane men in the galley immediately above her. And she knew what she had felt, too. *Prometheus* was coming under the direction of some other vessel.

Robin ran up the companionway into the relative darkness of the 'A' deck corridor. The darkness was only relative now because the port-side door leading out towards the Komsomolskaya Pier was wide. Security lighting was just about strong enough to creep in here like a yellow mist. Robin ran across the corridor into lading, too focused on this latest crisis to stop and retrieve her credit-card torch. She looked out of the lading office. There were four men running down the foredeck towards the distant forecastle head. They were focused exclusively forward and their shouting was beginning to fade away.

Robin ran back into the corridor then out through the door. She had seen more than four fleeing figures. She knew what was going on, in ship-handling terms at least. And she knew what her next priority must be.

Prometheus was under tow. Great hawsers stretched from their anchor-points midships and on the forecastle head itself. Four hawsers. Each secured to the stern of one of a pattern of distant tugs. She could see a name she understood because of its familiar shape – *Dvina*. The tanker was beginning to move away from the pier head and if she didn't get off immediately and down on to the pier, dogs or no dogs, then she was going to be stuck aboard like the four men running uselessly down the deck.

Robin could hardly believe it. The tugs that had brought *Prometheus* here must have left the tow ropes ready in place, anchored on the deck ready to be picked up at a moment's notice by the next set of tugs that would take her to the breaker's yard.

The massive hawsers must have been lying across the deck, hanging down over the side, moored to buoys on the water, ready to be taken aboard the next set of tugs. And she hadn't even noticed. But then, she hadn't been anywhere on the deck in the daylight. And hadn't been out of the bridge house in the darkness since.

She ran to the opening in the deck-rail that had married with the head of the gangplank but the gangplank itself was retracted, clear of *Prometheus*'s side, and crouching back on the outer edge of the pier head now. A jump of three metres, ten feet at most, but only if she was very quick indeed. Three metres across the black water of the harbour and about two metres down on to the leading edge of the gangplank. Which was itself the better part of three metres wide.

Without a second thought, Robin threw her handbag. It landed safely on the broad lip of the slowly receding gangplank. She ran back across the deck, turned and sprinted for the edge with all the speed and might at her command.

But the puddle of oil that had made her lose her footing on the way aboard performed the same savage office once again. Her right foot skidded out from under her just as she was gathering herself to leap. She hit the deck hard and rolled across it helplessly, badly out of control and in a fair way towards simply sliding overboard. She was simply too shaken and winded to stop herself as she rolled helplessly onwards. Knees and elbows took the brunt as she tried to bring herself under some kind of control. Only the greatest of control, but control of another kind, stopped her screaming with rage and frustration – and fear. Until a stanchion of the safety rail stopped her just short of going over the forty-metre drop to the icy water by smacking her across the forehead with stunning force. It would have knocked her cold had it not been for her hat. As it was, she pulled herself erect and stood there for a moment, swaying on the edge of the abyss. She put her hand to her head and as she traced the tender line of the swelling welt, her hat came off altogether. She made a half-hearted attempt to catch it but it tumbled away.

Robin turned, defeated for the moment, but still undiscovered. She staggered blindly back into the deck-house and straight on down the stairwell. Some timeless instinct from an animal ancestor countless generations back in history came dream-like out of her deepest cortex and drove her down and down and down. She did not stop running until there was nowhere left for her to run.

Then she sank to her knees, toppled forward like a falling tree and let the utter darkness claim her.

Eighteen

The Mercedes saloon was built for comfort but it was still capable of speeds in excess of 200 kph, according to the clock. The one parked outside Talagi Airport belonged to Felix Makarov as Richard would have realized on his way in if he hadn't been so preoccupied. He recognized it soon enough on the way out, however, even before Felix crossed towards it and the chauffeur leaped out to hold the door for Felix and his guests.

Yagula squeezed in first, of course, then Richard. As he climbed in Richard heard Felix say to the driver, 'Komsomolskaya Pier. As quickly as you can.' As Felix spoke Russian, he understood the first part of the order and assumed the second.

Felix himself felt they would be too late no matter how fast they got there, and *Prometheus* would be long gone. But, with Yagula's grimly cheerful prompting, he was willing to try. Especially as his driver was ex-Special Forces and had trained at the Militsia's Moscow School of Advanced Driving Techniques.

On the way down from the corporate hospitality suite, Yagula had cheerily suggested to the horrified Bakatin that it was essential that he and his colleagues in the Zil and the Militsia squad car should keep up no matter what the cost. As soon as they hit the pavement, therefore, Bakatin had thrown his battered bowler on to the Zil's back seat and followed it like a terrier chasing a rat.

Repin had reclaimed the keys from Elena Onega, who was happy to surrender them – Yagula wanted her in the warm, fragrant, leather-upholstered intimacy of the saloon with him. She got in last, however, with her cell glued to her ear. What she spat into it was in Russian and far beyond

Richard's competence but Felix obliged, leaning forward conspiratorially.

'She is speaking to Militsia Central Despatch, Richard. It appears that she is trying to contact two men called Voroshilov and Paznak. Militsia sergeants currently under her command in this investigation. Their phones are switched off, which is apparently against procedure except in an emergency. She has also ordered that a patrol should be sent to the Komsomolskaya Pier at the earliest possible moment; and ordered another to find Voroshilov and Paznak and also to get them there. Her language is very forceful. It is as well there are no young children listening.' He gave that ghost of a conspiratorial wink that had so disturbed Robin earlier this afternoon.

As the Mercedes surged into motion, Elena Onega broke off her connection and sat back, shuddering slightly. Suffering the inadequacies of her foot soldiers in silence, clearly, and looking a little like Joan of Arc at the stake.

Richard leaned forward, looking urgently at the massive federal prosecutor and the slight Investigator sitting beside him. It was doubly vital that he get some kind of a handle on what they thought was going on aboard *Prometheus* if Robin was actually aboard her as well. Whether or not Robin really believed she was *safely* there. 'So, this Mu'hmud Kamyshev, character, he was a Chechen separatist leader . . .'

'Terrorist,' insisted Yagula, a little less smoothly. 'Let us be clear, Richard. A terrorist in contact with al-Qa'eda. A man determined on another Moscow theatre siege. Another Beslan school . . .' He shuddered like Elena Onega. It didn't look so good on him. He looked more like the Grand Inquisitor.

'Very well,' allowed Richard. 'But what in God's name was he doing aboard my ship? And if he has five other corpses with him, then who the hell are they? And what are *they* doing aboard my ship?'

There was a little silence as the Mercedes whispered at breakneck speed through the thinning traffic towards the outskirts of Archangel. Then Richard approached the heart of his current horror. 'And what will their presence there actually mean for anyone trapped aboard with them?'

'Clearly,' said Elena Onega, forthrightly and bracingly, 'the existence of five corpses in a couple of freezers will have no effect on anyone aboard at all. And if you mean that Mrs Mariner might somehow be aboard, she almost certainly has no idea of their existence.'

'None of us had the slightest idea they were there when Mrs Mariner showed us around the bridge house this afternoon,' added Felix.

'So there is no reason to assume that she will have even the faintest suspicion that they are there,' emphasized Yagula.

'Fine,' said Richard. 'But what about the people who put them there? I mean, six corpses didn't just find their own way aboard like something out of Zombies R Us, did they? Somebody put those corpses there. What about them?'

There was another little silence. The Mercedes was proceeding exactly like a modern super-train now, hissing forwards in air-pressured silence, slicing through the night at hair-raising velocities.

'I don't quite follow the line of your reasoning there, Richard,' rumbled Yagula.

'*I* didn't put six dead bodies aboard *Prometheus*,' snapped Richard. 'You don't think I put them there either. If you thought that for a moment, I would be somewhere slightly less luxurious than this. I know you play mind-games, Lavrenty Michaelovitch, but you would have changed beyond all recognition if the leather involved in them is wrapped around a car seat instead of a cosh. So, if I didn't put them there, then who did?'

As nobody seemed keen to vouchsafe their thoughts on the matter, Richard ploughed on. 'At first I thought maybe it might have been some local thugs from here in Archangel. That was conceivable when there was only one body, maybe. But six is too many, isn't it? And the fact that one of them is a terrorist simply adds to the certainty that this is some kind of institutional thing doesn't it?'

Again he paused, as though asking two questions on the trot would stand a better chance of guaranteeing a reply. But they all just watched him as the car whispered though the night and the first lights of Archangel itself flicked shadows across their faces. 'Some government or government agency put them there, therefore,' Richard persisted at last, unable to bear the sibilant silence. 'Your government, possibly. Just

possibly. FBS or whoever could have slipped them on board
in the forty hours between *Prometheus*'s arrival and Officer
Repin's big discovery. But again, if you put them there, then
why are you making all this fuss? That would be one hell of
a mind game. And, although I know Felix here likes James
Bond films, we're not living through the middle of one!

'So. *I* didn't put them aboard. *You* didn't put them aboard.
But *somebody* put them aboard. But who?'

Richard knew better than to pause for a reply now. He just
pushed on regardless, his voice shaking with concern and
mounting anger. 'At the moment, my money's on the Germans.
And of course my worry is that they'll want to send someone
aboard to recover the bodies or to get rid of them. Someone
who might also want to get rid of Robin if she gets in the
way.' He looked around the sceptical faces framed with
perfectly fashioned black-leather Mercedes upholstery. The
flickering shadows. The glittering eyes.

'Look,' he continued earnestly. 'Not everything in Germany
works with the same precision as their motor cars. This has
all the hallmarks of a government screw-up. One arm of the
government thinks, *Oh! There is a supertanker anchored off
Wilhelmshaven. What a good place to hide a few of the
Counter-Terrorism Department's little mistakes for a while . . .*
While another arm, quite independently, thinks, *Oh! There is
a supertanker anchored off Wilhelmshaven. Let's sell it back
to the original owners and please the Department of the
Exchequer . . .*'

Yagula's laugh bore all the hallmarks of a volcano on Saturn
– a distant rumbling eruption of almost interstellar iciness.
'You should be on the stage, Richard. Or, perhaps, writing
spy thrillers yourself.'

'But, Lavrenty Michaelovitch,' said Felix smoothly. 'You
must allow that it is at least possible. The Germans are as
worried about international terrorism as we are ourselves.
Though they have had few home-grown cells or cadres,
perhaps, since the Baader-Meinhof group. But the BKA have
been worried about Islamic extremists for five years and more.
There were the bombs on the trains in 2006 . . .'

'Not just the BKA Federal Crimes Office,' emphasized
Richard. 'The BfV Federal Office for the Protection of the
Constitution, equivalent to your own, also has an anti-terrorist

brief. So does the LfV State Office. So do the BND Chancellor's office, the ANBw Army Intelligence. And, of course, the MAD Army security . . .'

'You know a lot about German security matters, Richard,' said Yagula, suspiciously, sounding like the old Yagula at last.

'I get briefed, Lavrenty Michaelovitch. My company has an intelligence section staffed by ex-intelligence people. Before I go into a deal or a country I get briefed. Though all that information could just as easily have come straight off the Internet.'

'Ah yes. The Internet. Information without limit. Access without control.'

'But Kamyshev was one of ours,' interrupted Elena Onega. 'He was a Chechen. Why would the Germans be holding him?' Her interest seemed genuinely caught by the conundrum at last.

'Perhaps he was allied to something larger,' allowed Yagula. 'If he did have links to al-Qa'eda, then who knows who might be interested in him? Alive or dead?'

'At the very least,' added Felix, 'we can agree that for some extremist elements the whole of the West is a legitimate target and anywhere within the European Union is therefore as legitimate as anywhere else.'

'Your IRA taught us that many years ago, Richard,' added Yagula, back on form. 'Belfast might be more relevant. But Brighton is much more *spectacular*.'

'And anyway,' added Richard tartly, 'there'll be a good number of officers and men in the MAD who at least remember the Stasi from the days before German Reunification and the old alliance with the KGB.'

'Past history.' Yagula waved a dismissive hand as large as a black bear's paw. 'It's all past history now.'

'But, history or not,' persisted Richard, 'you'll agree that someone might well have put those bodies aboard at Wilhelmshaven. Someone who might stop at nothing to get them back now.'

The Mercedes swung right out of the Obvodny Kanal Avenue and on to Komsomolskaya Street. Richard strained to see the pier, which was about a kilometre straight ahead. But all he could see clearly was the galaxy of flashing lights gathered around the security gate. 'Hey!' he said. "What in the name of God . . .'

And Elena Onega's cellphone began to ring. She hadn't even begun to reach for it before Yagula's was ringing too.

Nineteen

Sergeant Voroshilov believed he was more sensitive and empathic than Sergeant Paznak. Voroshilov also believed, firstly, that this was because Cossacks had more soul than Slavs and, secondly, that it made him a better detective. Certainly, it was Voroshilov who worked out where Captain Mariner's missing wife must be. Even before Central Despatch got through with the Investigator's message.

And long before the shit really hit the fan.

Of course they started at Snezhok. If Elena Onega had given it a moment's thought, she would have realized they would. And, because it was important to trace the missing woman's footsteps, they were forced to go into the auditorium itself. Even though the show was still on, the lights were down and it was almost impossible to see anything. Anything except what was going on onstage. Because it was official business they flashed their cards and didn't even have to pay. But they did agree to switch off their cellphones.

'You must turn them off, officers. You will be right down by the stage and should they ring it might be disastrous. These girls are artists,' insisted the manager, still mopping a face made pale by the shock of suspecting a raid. 'Some of the things they do could be extremely painful if their concentration was broken. Perhaps even dangerous.'

'That looks pretty fucking painful in any case,' whispered Paznak as he and Voroshilov lingered in the area immediately in front of the stage making a pantomime of looking for clues. 'I mean look at the simple size of that thing.'

'It is certainly a credit to local salad farmers,' agreed Voroshilov. 'Though I expect it was grown to be pickled.'

'Perhaps they'll pickle it later,' suggested Paznak. 'When they have finished with it here.'

'Perhaps that what's happening now,' countered Voroshilov. 'An entirely new method of pickling.'

'Wow,' said Paznak, awed. 'You think it'll ever catch on?'

There was a brief silence while Paznak considered this. And Voroshilov considered the mission they had actually been sent upon.

'Paznak,' said Voroshilov eventually. 'How many women can you count in here?'

'Well, there's the ones on the stage . . .'

'Not them.'

'And the whores with the punters.' Paznak dragged his eyes reluctantly away from the show and looked up at the audience. 'Not many of them though and they're looking pretty green. I mean, the *ideas* they'll have to talk people *out of* later tonight . . .'

'Not the whores. Women. Wives and mothers. *Women.*'

'Oh. There aren't any *women* in here.'

'Precisely. Why did *she* come in here, then?'

'Who?'

'Mariner's wife. The woman you lost. The one we're supposed to be finding, you moron!'

'Oh. You don't think she might have come in to see the show? I mean, some of these Western women are supposed to be pretty well advanced, if you know what I mean.'

'Yes, I know what you mean. What we used to call decadent. And they aren't. They're like our women. Our wives and mothers. So she didn't come in to see the show. Then why did she come in, Vladimir? And why did she leave?'

'Because she saw what was happening on stage?'

'Excellent. Precisely. And, furthermore, we can assume she wasn't meeting anyone here either. Or she would have stayed in spite of the show. But she left. How did she come out?'

'She came out,' said Paznak with a great deal of feeling, 'full-throttle. Like the Trans-Siberian Express.'

'Upset? Offended? Outraged?'

'All of the above. But mostly outraged. And that's putting it very mildly indeed.'

'She came out like a train. Through the doors.'

'Slammed them open right into my face. I went arse over tit into Pavel my driver and we both went down like ninepins.'

'*Then* what did she do? After she ran you and Pavel down like elks on the Vladivostok line?'

'She went straight across the road. Lights were with her. Lucky for her. We leaped into the squad car. Pavel pulled out and *whammo!* A tram. Can you believe that? Only a fucking *tram*!'

'Did Pavel check his mirror?' Voroshilov had to ask.

'Does Pavel ever check his mirror?' answered Paznak mournfully.

'He will in future,' said Voroshilov. 'If he's ever allowed to drive again, that is.' He took Paznak by the undamaged arm and led him out into the vestibule as though he was blind. It took a moment or two for Paznak to readjust his focus forward. Then he blinked, as though surprised to find himself out here.

The pair of them crossed to the ticket desk. 'Hey,' Voroshilov called to the pustular youth behind the screen. 'Did you see a foreign woman in here earlier this evening?'

'Unh. Yeah.' He might be at the cutting edge of the Archangel service industry but he hadn't forgotten he was a teenager.

'What did she want?'

'Unh. Ticket.'

'I don't think so, Ivan,' Voroshilov read the name tag on the office window. 'I think she wanted something else.'

'Unh. Ivan's on Thursdays,' said the youth. 'I put his name up early. My shift's almost over.'

Paznak leaned over Voroshilov's shoulder. 'Listen, Ivan,' he snarled. His breath fogged up the window. 'Just answer the fucking questions or by the time you get out of prison they'll be calling you Catherine the Great! Understand?'

'Yes, sir. Sir. I think she wanted the phone.' The kid held up a fist with his little finger pointing to his ear and his thumb towards his mouth. The fist was trembling as though he was being electrocuted somewhere under the metal ticket dispenser. Paznak could have that effect on impressionable people. Something secretly Slavic, in all probability, thought Voroshilov.

'And you told her exactly where the phone was, did you, Ivan?' snarled Paznak. The window fogged further. Seemed to consider melting.

'No, sir. I sold her a ticket, sir.' The boy had gone from surliness to pathetic whining. 'I'm on commission here. Piece work. I have my studies; my place at the Institute. It doesn't come free . . . I sold her a ticket and sent her in. One more punter, one more kopek. Sir.'

Voroshilov took Paznak by his undamaged arm and led him out. 'Why was she looking for a phone, Vladimir?' he asked gently.

'Let me sort out that kid, Voroshilov. Please. I swear to God, if he'd just told her where the fucking phone was none of this would have happened. None of it! I'd be up for a commendation for bringing her in. Pavel wouldn't be in traction. Our car wouldn't be written off. And the tram people wouldn't be threatening to sue! It's all that spotty little shit's fault. Let me sort him out. *Please*, Voroshilov . . .'

'Maybe later. But tell me about the phone first, Vladimir. Why did she need a phone?'

'The guy at Izba said hers wasn't working properly. Her personal cell. The taxi driver said he thought she tried it in his cab too. No joy.'

'That was it? She went in there because she couldn't get a signal on her *phone*?'

'Looks like it, I guess. But I can't see why she would choose a strip joint . . .'

Voroshilov took Paznak's undamaged arm and turned the pair of them round to look up at the massive posters on either side of the door. *Alexander Nevsky* said one and *Ivan the Terrible Parts One and Two* said the other one. 'See?' said Voroshilov. 'It says Eisenstein. It doesn't mention awesome Olga and her amazing *aguret*.'

'I see that.'

'So, Vladimir. Empathize. You are a frightened woman. You have been left alone in a strange restaurant in a foreign city and then pursued by terrifying-looking men. And you can look terrifying, can't you? Look what you just did to the kid. So, pursued by terrifying men you rush into a cinema looking for a phone and find something else that offends you terribly instead.'

'The amazing Olga and her awesome *aguret*.'

'Precisely. Or whatever was onstage then. You are offended. Every sensibility wounded, like it used to say in books. Out-fucking-raged in short. You run out and – *whammo!* as you so cleverly put it – there are your terrifying pursuers! You evade them. You run wildly across the road, seeking escape at any price. And, behind you, *whammo! Whammo!* Indeed.'

Voroshilov had used this speech to lead Paznak across the junction and into the final section of Komsomolskaya Street. They stood side by side, looking straight ahead, towards the Pier, with its security gates and its dim yellow lighting and the massive darkness beyond.

'But you are not just *any* frightened foreign woman,' whispered Voroshilov, almost awed by his own deductive powers. 'You are a business woman. You own things. As a matter of fact, you own something that happens to be just at the end of the pier down there . . .'

Not to be outdone, Paznak said, 'Hey, did you remember to switch on your phone again when we came out of the strip show?'

'No,' said Voroshilov. 'But don't disturb me with irrelevancies. I think I'm on a roll here.'

Voroshilov was so confident that they didn't bother to check as they went forward. Paznak would have liked to have rung a few bells and hammered on a few doors just on the off-chance of finding an amazing Olga lookalike wearing a see-through nightie. Or less. But Voroshilov wouldn't let him.

In Voroshilov's experience the only women who answered the door to Militsia at night looked like Nikita Khruschev. And they never wore see-through nighties. Which, on balance, was probably just as well.

With gathering pace, Voroshilov led Paznak down the street until they were as close to a run as the limping sergeant could manage. Then, right at the very crossroads, immediately opposite the tall security gates, he stopped. Paznak stood gasping at his side. 'Thanks a bunch,' he wheezed, 'that near as dammit put me back in casualty with poor old Pavel.'

'Stop playacting. Save the performance for the delicious Investigator. Two questions, Vladimir,' said Voroshilov curtly. 'One: do you have your pistol with you? Two: can you use it with your arm like that?'

The answer to both questions was yes. 'But why?' asked Paznak, reaching gingerly into the depths of his clothing.

'Something doesn't feel right, Vladimir. There should be tape on the gates. Repin said he'd taped them up himself. They shouldn't be open, even a little way. And the side entry shouldn't be open either.'

'Come on, Voroshilov. There's supposed to be a security guard. How's a man with half a dozen dogs going to get in if he doesn't mess up Repin's pretty tape?'

'But then, is a man with half a dozen guard dogs going to leave the gates open? I mean those would be really well-trained guard dogs not to make a break for freedom through three half-open gates, now, wouldn't they?'

'There is that, Sergeant Voroshilov. Let us check our weapons and proceed with utmost caution. At the very least there's half a dozen attack-trained guard dogs on that pier . . .'

'Or someone who could take out half a dozen attack-trained guard dogs and who might just be keen to do the same for us.'

'Oh, that's nice. Cheer me up. I should have stayed with the amazing Olga . . .'

Both men got out their elderly standard-issue 9mm x 18 semi-automatic side arms and checked them carefully as they talked. Checking the loads and easing the mechanisms before any potential action got under way. Knowing how cranky and unreliable the weapons could occasionally be. Knowing that they would be outgunned by anyone hiding behind the gates armed with anything more powerful than slingshots.

Then, holding the guns low, they crossed the quiet road, still deep in their whispered conversation. They stopped, side by side at the side gate, guns, high now, Paznak's in his damaged hand, the sling round his neck like the Lone Ranger's bandanna. 'Go in hard? Kick ass?'

'The Slav way, you mean? And get torn to shreds by six angry Dobermanns? No, we do this the Cossack way.'

'Tiptoe in and run screaming for Mummy at the first sign of any trouble?'

'Too bloody true, Vladimir. If we knew who your mummy was. Or your daddy come to that . . .'

If Paznak was offended by that last crack, he did not get a chance to say so, for just as they tensed themselves to creep through the small side gate, so the big main gates burst wide. They slammed wide with amazing force, literally driven outward on their hinges by the front bumper of a big black saloon. The vehicle must have crept down the pier in low gear, almost silently, the purring of its motor lost beneath the wind, the rain and the whispered conversation. Then it accelerated through the gates, out into the street and away. It showed no lights. It had tinted glass so that it was impossible to see inside. The driver was so careful with the impact that although the gates slammed wide with jarring force and thunderous noise, there seemed no damage to the car itself. The lights remained dark because the driver left them off, not because he had smashed them. Because the lights were off, the little bulbs above the license plate remained dark. All the stunned detectives saw was a black saloon exploding out of the pier-foot and swerving away down the road like a drunken bat out of hell. It was simply a matter of good luck that there were no cars or trams coming by, or the saloon would have caused a massive pile-up.

'Shit!' whispered Paznak, simply awed. 'Now that's what I call driving! If only poor Pavel had been here to see that!'

They went in like Cossacks, side by side and silently.

There were no dogs in evidence. The security lights paced almost uselessly down the length of the pier to a vast and slowly moving darkness at the end. A square-built, dark-windowed lemony pallidity the size of a block of flats seemed passing with ghostly silence through the misty rain and away into the night down there. Right at the end of the pier near the side of the slowly moving supertanker squatted a half-retracted gang plank and just this side of its inner end, a bundled shape which might have been that of a sleeping child or a resting dog.

Halfway between the detectives and the departing ship was the watchman's hut. It was the only thing on the whole massive expanse of the benighted pier that looked in any way real, substantial, warm or inviting. Side by side they ran for it as fast as Paznak's leg would allow. Paznak would have kicked the door wide and run on in, if only to escape the drizzling dark. But Voroshilov stopped him. Instead they peeped through the windows.

And there sat the watchman, sound asleep with his head on the table and his watchdogs also sleeping at his feet. A fire burned in a pot-bellied stove giving off a bright, ruddy light as well as a warmth they could feel even out here. Everything in the room seemed bathed in that light, as though there was a sunset shining in through the windows. Or the frostiest of winter dawns. The watchman's head and shoulders were red.

The table under his sleeping face, around his folded arms, was red. The dogs looked red and the floor upon which they were lying all looked red as well. Red and warm and inviting.

'What the fuck,' said Paznak and hit the door.

'Vladimir!' called Voroshilov. 'Stop!'

Too late. 'Hey Voroshilov!' called Paznak from inside the hut. 'There's a funny smell in here. And the floor's all sticky. Oh, shit! OH SHIT!'

Voroshilov was running on past the hut by this time, heading for the end of the pier to see what there was to see down there. One more dog, curled on its side. At least the big pool of its blood looked less like a sunset under the yellow security lights. Through the middle of it and over the body of the dead dog ran a geometric pattern of tyre tracks that showed where the car had turned. Voroshilov knelt and looked more closely, though there was little more that he could tell. Except that these were definitely tyre tracks. And the dog was just about as dead as a dog could get. And finally, as a matter of fact, Paznak was right. Its blood looked like shit. And Voroshilov could almost hear the merry splatter of it hitting fan after fan after fan.

He ran on, along the side of the crouching gangplank and out to the end of the pier. The supertanker was well out in the Dvina Bay by now, and he could see one pair of the tugs that were pulling her across towards Severodvinsk. The rain gusted more thickly and someone somewhere hit a fog-horn. As the mournful sound echoed out of the night, Voroshilov wearily put his gun away. He turned. Returned.

Paznak was standing outside the hut being sick. 'It's delayed shock from the crash,' Voroshilov assured him, although he was personally certain that it was something to do with seeing so many dead dogs. Something Slavic. 'Come down to the end of the pier. Get a breath of air. We need to talk. Then we'll switch on our phones together and call this whole sorry mess in.'

A ferry heading in towards the Krasnaya Pristan Pier passed close enough to brighten up the tanker's sluggish wake and cast a little light on the end of the Komsomolskaya Pier itself. The detectives stood there side by side, trying to get their story straight for Elena Onega, chewing on the cardboard ends of cheap cigarettes, sucking in the bitter smoke like gall. And there, turning over in the water ten metres or so below, was a woman's hat. 'Hey, look at that,' said Voroshilov, the cloud of his smoky breath adding to the fog around them as the fog-horn sounded again. 'That looks like sable to me, but I don't know much about such things. Perhaps we should make a note, though, because you don't see many sable hats floating in the harbour like that.'

'I should make a fucking careful note if I were you,' growled Paznak, sounding as depressed as hell and utterly pissed off. 'Because it's *hers*. It's the hat she was wearing when she went over the top of me like the Trans-Siberian Express coming out of Snezhok.'

Then he turned and saw on the ground beside his foot something that looked exactly like a woman's handbag. 'And that's her bag as well,' he added gloomily. He stooped and picked it up. He slung it over his shoulder, wincing at the pain. When it hung safely beside the big bandanna of his sling, he reached into his pocket and switched on his cellphone and it began to shrill like a dentist's drill.

'I doesn't take much of a fucking detective to work out what's happened to her, then!' concluded Voroshilov. He flicked the stub of his cigarette away into the water like a falling star and switched on his cellphone also with a grimace of the purest agony. He knew trouble when he heard it, and this was going to be very bad trouble indeed.

Twenty

Komsomolskaya Pier was bedlam. Militsia officers stopped the Mercedes at the sagging main gate, and it was only when Elena Onega leaped out and identified herself, and then identified Federal Prosecutor Lavrenty Michaelovitch Yagula himself in no uncertain terms, that there was any question of them proceeding. Having done this, Elena Onega vanished down the pier looking for the two detectives who she fiercely characterised as *Dumb and Dumber*. Even so, the Mercedes had to worm its way through two overlapping squad cars which were, in all but name, a roadblock.

Like Yagula, Elena Onega had enjoyed a brief, mono-syllabic cellphone conversation during the final five hundred metres of Komsomolskaya road itself, and was grimly up to date with what Voroshilov and Paznak had found.

In the matter of violently deceased night-watchmen and dead dogs, at least.

'Well, identifying the watchman shouldn't be a problem anyway,' announced Yagula as they all climbed out of the Mercedes after it had pulled on to the main pier and parked. 'Felix. He was your watchman. What was his name?'

Felix Makarov's eyebrows rose as though they would slide up off the top of his head. He straightened slowly, his face oriental, angular and aristocratic under the yellow light, like the mask of a Manchu emperor. His expression suggested strongly that it was about as likely that he would know the man's name as the Tsar would know the under-footman's. Yagula might as well have asked him the names of the dead dogs.

'Gulin will know,' he said.

Gulin was with Repin in the squad car and they arrived next, snaking between the squad cars unchallenged. It took Gulin a moment or two to recover from the excitement of the officer's speed-driving techniques. To steady himself on his feet, to overcome the nausea and get his head round the question Felix barked at him.

But then he supplied, 'Fort Knox . . .'

'That will be the company name, of course,' prompted Felix, oozing the scary kind of patience Yagula specialised in. 'What was the dead man's name?'

'Stolypin. Fort Knox is run by the Stolypin brothers. Bela and Boris. I don't know which brother this dead one is . . .' Felix turned on his heel and walked off as though disgusted by the lack of factual precision.

'No. But the other brother will, won't he?' snapped Yagula, growing as bored with the game as Felix, but more hesitant to let his victim go. 'The one that *isn't* the dead brother. Now, do you have the number for Fort Knox, or must I enlist the help of the Regional Prosecutor, now that, I observe, he has joined us? *At long last . . .*'

Richard hadn't even become involved with these games. As soon as he came out of the back of the Mercedes into the blustering drizzle on the pier hard on the angry Investigator's heels, he was off. He followed in Elena Onega's determined footsteps, pushing through the Militsia men as though it were he, not the giant emerging from the car, who was the federal prosecutor. As she veered off towards the watch-keeper's hut, however, he walked purposefully straight along the pier, his eager pace only slowing from the edge of a flat run when it became clear that the pier-head berth was empty.

Prometheus and Robin, safe aboard her or not, were gone.

Richard ended up standing, deep in thought, with his left arm along the outer edge of the crouching, half-retracted gangplank, staring out into the misty darkness that at last succeeded in concealing the massive bulk of *Prometheus* altogether. Far behind him, out of earshot, Gulin was just finishing his explanation of who the watch-keeping brothers were, and Bakatin was on his cellphone trying to get their number.

'She's sailing without lights,' he said, disapprovingly, as Felix joined him.

'Special dispensation of the harbourmaster and so forth. It's not all that unusual. She's only going across the bay. She'll be in Severodvinsk by daybreak.'

'I've got to get aboard her, Felix. You do know that,' said Richard, determinedly. 'And the sooner the better.'

'Ah . . .' temporized Felix.

Richard swung round. 'You didn't think I'd leave my wife all alone on a powerless hulk being towed across the Dvina Bay?' he demanded stormily. 'Even if the freezers weren't stuffed with the dead bodies of Chechen terrorists, I'd still want to get her off PDQ.'

'Of course . . .' temporized Felix, more defensively.

'And this mess here.' The sweep of his hand took in the dead dog, the bloody tyre tracks, the hut, the bustle of uniformed bodies that seemed to be multiplying as they watched, like ants pouring out of a nest. The roadblock. Elena Onega yelling at her two very sheepish investigators . . . 'What if the people who caused all this have somehow got themselves on board along with her?'

'Is that likely?' temporized Felix almost terminally. 'I understand that a car seems to have made off at great speed. Just as the two detective sergeants came on to the pier a while ago. The men who killed the watchman and his dogs were probably all in that. I mean, is it at all likely that anyone even went aboard, let alone remained there?'

'Of course it is!' Richard reposted, at his most forceful. Desperate. 'It's almost inevitable, I'd say. If they aren't still on board her now, then they certainly were a while ago, weren't they? I mean why else would anyone be on this pier at this moment in time and at this hour of night in any case? Anyone desperate, or ruthless, or *well armed* enough to kill a watchman and six dogs? I mean it's not a coincidence, is it? I have to say I don't know what Yagula's thinking on this is, but if I were in his shoes I'd have the nearest Spetsnaz unit up and out and aboard her within the hour!'

'Would you?' rumbled a massive voice behind them, and Richard turned, remembering how good Yagula was at appearing where you least expected to find him. And how expert at getting there in utter silence, like a hunting bear. 'Would you indeed?' Yagula paused. Then he continued, focusing all his massive attention on Richard as though there was no one else nearby at all. 'In fact, Naval Delfin or FSB OSNAS units would be better,' the federal prosecutor corrected him, like a teacher with a wayward pupil. 'And there are half a dozen units in the district as well as those assigned to the local Fleet HQ.

'But they are Special Forces, remember. They would want to go aboard in their big attack Kamov and Hind gunship helicopters, armed to the teeth with their AKSU special assault rifles, their Dragunov sniper weapons and their RPG 7 anti-armour missiles. Not to mention their various grenades, their mines and their flame-throwers.' He paused, so that Richard could envisage what a Special Forces assault was likely to do to *Prometheus*, and anyone trapped aboard her.

Then he continued, smoothly, 'After what Alpha Group's involvement at the Beslan school massacre revealed about their anti-terrorist techniques, I am a little hesitant to risk such a firefight in such a place, I must confess. I would have thought that you, too, would have been hesitant. I know that Felix would be very hesitant indeed, and he wouldn't even be the unfortunate individual who actually *owned* whatever was left of the vessel after our brave boys had finished with it. If there was, actually, anything much left of the vessel. So, on behalf of the Prosecutor's Department, and with the best interests of international economic relations, I repeat. I am extremely hesitant to send in Special Forces.'

He turned and, with apparent surprise, discovered Elena Onega standing close behind him. 'Especially when I have several fine Militsia trained ex-army personnel here now. At my command so to speak. Men who are fully conversant with the situation, honed to perfection, straining at the bit, ready, willing and able to go aboard at once.'

'I will go with them of course,' said Richard, into the cavernous silence that greeted the federal prosecutor's words. He looked around as he spoke and saw that Yagula hadn't been exaggerating. A lot of the new men were of Repin's stamp. A good long step above the lowly Militsia and GAI at the gate. He turned back to his companions, his mouth open to emphasize to them just how crucial he thought it was that he should get aboard immediately, even if he had to go alone.

Suddenly everyone was speaking Russian and no one was obliging with a translation. Richard had no idea what they were saying and this made him very suspicious and not a little worried. But he remained in ignorance for the moment.

'If he wants to go and find his wife he's too late,' said Elena Onega at her most rapid. 'Paznak and Voroshilov say she is dead. They have her handbag and her hat is somewhere in the harbour. They say they have seen it. They are certain that she is somewhere in there also. And not taking a healthy little swim.'

'This is worrying,' interposed Makarov. 'The Captain and his wife were very close. If she is in fact dead then he is likely to pick up his marbles and go home, as the Americans say. This would be a very bad thing indeed.'

'Especially as the marbles in this case are *Prometheus*,' added Yagula thoughtfully but no less rapidly. 'We cannot allow this. But the man is no fool. We cannot lie to him. He will see any lies we tell at once. Decide now. Do we want him on board the ship or do we not? Everything else must stem from that.'

'If I send Voroshilov, Repin and Paznak aboard, will he be of help to them or not?' demanded Elena Onega. 'They are extremely hesitant and will at least want more up-to-date weaponry if it can be supplied. Would the Englishman be an asset I could sell to them?'

'He could well be of inestimable help,' answered Felix. 'He knows every nook and cranny of the ship. They would be lucky to get round it unscathed without a guide like him.'

'But he has a soft heart,' warned Yagula. 'Remember the woman presently in the Butyrka facility waiting formal arraignment about whom we talked earlier this evening. She would be dead but for him – and justly dead at my hand. He went back and rescued her although she was guilty of deception, fraud and murder. And he himself was wounded in the rescue.'

'Then we must stiffen his resolve,' said Elena Onega brutally. 'And the best way to do that is to let Voroshilov tell him the truth before we send them all aboard. And then give him also the best gun we can get our hands on.'

'You stiffen his resolve, Investigator. I'll see about scaring up some firepower,' said Felix. 'And Lavrenty Michaelovitch, could you please work out a way of getting four men on to a supertanker without alerting too many people?'

'What was that all about?' demanded Richard suspiciously as Elena Onega came past Yagula to stand at his side.

'We were discussing you, Captain Mariner.'

'So I guessed. What were you saying?'

'We have a situation I need to talk over with you. Could you come with me to the watchman's hut, please?'

'Of course. But we need to be quick. I need to get after my wife. She's aboard—'

'It is about Mrs Mariner I need to talk, Captain.' As she interrupted him, the Investigator took his arm firmly and guided him across the bleak pier.

'Why do we need to go to the hut?' he demanded uneasily.

'I have something to show you, and Sergeant Voroshilov wants to describe to you something that he and Sergeant Paznak saw just before we arrived tonight.'

She pushed open the door and led him into the warm stench of the place. 'Watch your feet, Captain. We are going across to the sideboard here . . .' Richard stopped, turned, closed the door in a kind of mindless slow motion.

She took his elbow once again and led him round the massive bloodstain on the floor where the dead man's fluids mixed with his dogs'. Here the two sergeants stood side by side with their backs to him, sorting through something on the wooden top in front of them.

Elena Onega continued speaking gently as they walked slowly towards the two men and all at once he realized that her tone was the special one used by people getting ready to break bad news. He had heard it in hospitals. Used it himself. No matter what the words said, they meant *Get ready for the worst possible news.*

'The sergeants are just checking to make double sure,' she was saying, 'but we are certain that this is your wife's handbag. Do you recognize it Captain Mariner?'

As though the words were some kind of signal, Voroshilov stood aside and there, neatly arranged on the sideboard, were the contents of Robin's handbag with the bag itself standing open behind them as empty as a gutted fish. He moved forward in a daze, reached out and touched them, then jerked his fingers back a little, shocked by how cold they all were. Her purse. Her credit-card wallet with a picture of the twins as children framed on one side. Her chequebook in its little leather case with the golden ballpoint in the spine. Her little bottle of Chanel. Her calculator. Her little electronic address book.

Her lace handkerchief with RM embroidered on the corner. The twins had teased her when he gave it to her. She was as good as a granny already, they had said. Her house keys. The key to their hotel room. Her phone.

Her useless bloody phone.

'Where did you find this?' he asked. His voice sounded strange and hoarse to him.

'It was on the very edge of the pier, Captain. Beyond the end of the gangplank,' answered Sergeant Voroshilov. His eyes no longer looked quite so much like gun barrels poking from a hunter's hide.

'Right at the end?'

'We were lucky we noticed it, Captain. It nearly got kicked into the harbour alongside . . .' Voroshilov stopped and looked questioningly at Elena Onega.

'What?' Richard asked. 'What else was there?'

'There was a hat in the water,' said Voroshilov quietly. 'Sergeant Paznak identified it as the hat your wife was wearing. It was sable I believe . . .'

'It looks like sable,' Richard said dully. 'I think they call it faux-fur. She doesn't approve of killing things for fashion . . .' He looked at Paznak with a truly piercing gaze. A glare that had only just enough sanity in it to keep him under some control. 'It was hers,' he said. 'You are certain?'

'Hers,' said Paznak. 'In water. Is sunken now. Gone.'

'I have to get aboard,' said Richard, his voice shaking as though he were somehow caught alone in an earthquake here. He swung that strange gaze back to Elena Onega. Took her by the shoulders as though she could keep him upright at the centre of this suddenly reeling world. 'I have to be certain.'

'Of course,' said Elena Onega, gently, but still with that soft funereal tone. She squared her shoulders beneath his crushing grip. 'But you said yourself that there might be armed men aboard. Men who did this . . .' She looked over her shoulder at the reeking carnage in the hut. 'Men who might have . . .' She stopped, as though shocked by her own idea.

'What?' asked Richard, still trapped at the heart of his terrible, lonely earthquake. He asked, though he suspected the full horror of what she was about to say and he really did not want to hear her say it. 'Men who might have what?'

'Done the same to her,' she whispered, her eyes fathomless pools of liquid sympathy. 'Then dumped her body overboard.'

Richard looked into those bottomless eyes with such intensity that he could see himself reflected as though in the surfaces of two black wells. 'I must get on board,' he rasped. 'Even if there's a regiment of terrorists waiting there.'

A door opened. It seemed to Richard to be a very far-off door indeed, although it was in fact only the door to the hut. And when Felix spoke, he might almost have been calling in from another solar system. Until Richard grasped the full meaning of his distant words.

'I think I've solved the problem of getting you some decent guns,' said Felix. 'Now we just have to hope that Lavrenty Michaelovitch has worked out how to get you aboard.'

Twenty-One

Robin awoke. *Came to* might be more accurate, for she had been unconscious, not asleep. Returning consciousness made her groggily aware of several unpleasant facts. She was deeply disorientated, acutely uncomfortable and only partially aware of where she was and how she got there. When she first looked up, there was no improvement in her vision. She went from absolute blackness to absolute blackness with only the sensation of eyelids sliding apart and blinking to tell her that her eyes were open. She sensed her body in the utter gloom. It was battered, bruised and in some vague, general pain. It was lying slumped on its right side, curled in an almost foetal position. It was lying on something hard that was vibrating almost infinitesimally with a familiar kind of movement.

She licked her lips and swallowed. Her mouth was dry. The unpleasant taste was a function of the disgusting smell. There was none of the iron flavour that warned of blood; none of the acidity that said sickness. Maybe she wasn't too badly hurt after all.

Robin raised her head. A bar of pain slammed across her forehead as though she had been hit with a bat. The pain was accompanied by an illusory wall of fire, which faded at once, and merely served to emphasize both the darkness and the terrible cold. She put her head back down on the gently vibrating floor and began to summon up the energy she needed in order to move. She counted to three, then rolled on to her back with a massive effort. Then she lay, exhausted, sprawled like a starfish on the bottom of some Stygian abyss. Her head span. Her stomach heaved. 'This won't bloody do at all,' she said, aloud.

The sound of her voice echoed dangerously in the cavernous darkness and the whispering silence. It electrified her in a way that no drug or medicine could have done. It reminded her that there was danger here. Danger that might well be coming after her. She sat up at once, dismissing the waves of nausea. Her first calculated action was to check the time, but she could not see her watch and when she pushed the button on its side it remained stubbornly dark. She ran her fingers over its glass and felt a spider's web of cracks and glass-dust. It was obviously a casualty of her crash up on the deck, she thought grimly. And if she had managed to smash her watch, God only knew what else was broken or lost entirely. She put her hands on the deck beneath her and tensed herself to rise. But her right hand encountered a solid, slightly rubbery column that she recognized immediately as a torch. She brought it close to her face, almost breathless with anticipation, shaded the front, narrowed her eyes and depressed the switch. Nothing happened.

Robin put the torch between her legs, resting against her tummy where she wouldn't lose it, then she began to feel around, for she remembered that there were others. Please God she hadn't lost or broken them all. She started in her pockets, gathering the spread of her coat around herself in an attempt to bring back vital warmth lost to shock and inactivity in the damp and icy atmosphere. There was one torch in each pocket, and another on the deck close by. That made four. But she was sure there had been six. She put the four she had found so far all in her lap together and then began to test them carefully, one by one. The last one gave a solid beam of light. The instant that it flashed on she switched it off again, all too well aware that light might give her away as surely as sound, if the four strange men were anywhere nearby.

It did not occur to her at that point that there might be other, more secret enemies aboard as well, to whom darkness and silence were dangerously close allies.

The functioning torch replaced the first one immediately against her belly. She began to unscrew the others with the blind assurance of a Special Forces soldier stripping and reassembling his gun with his eyes closed. The batteries came out and went into her pockets. She reassembled the empty barrels with fastidious neatness, deep in thought. Her fingers re-checked the glass fronts and the bulbs – most at least cracked. Some smashed. The story of her poor watch over and over again. Still, she thought bracingly, remembering the wild dash, the failed leap for safety the battering pain of rolling head over heels across the deck, nothing ventured nothing gained. And you can't make an omelette without breaking eggs . . .

Robin at first decided she would put the broken torches back if she could and hope that the strangers had not noticed they were missing already and would not notice their return therefore. But then, on second thoughts, she reckoned maybe she could hide them somewhere. That might be better. Hiding them safely away couldn't possibly alert men who didn't know that they existed in the first place. Even so, she stuffed the empty barrels back into her pockets on top of the vital batteries. She would decide exactly what to do with them later. When she had made a survey of her position here and established where the sinister strangers were.

Lost in thought, Robin got up, holding the good torch carefully in her right hand. At once she felt the lack of something vital. She froze, wondering what could possibly be missing now. She couldn't work out just what it was to begin with, but she was concerned enough to risk flashing the torch around. And she had established it was nowhere near even before she remembered what it was. Her handbag. The shock of realizing her bag was gone hit her almost as hard as the stanchion that had come so close to braining her.

Robin was so preoccupied with the enormity of her loss that her eyes flooded with tears and the whole bright passage around her seemed to take on a strange, illusory motion of its own. So that she really did not register the flash of genuine movement at the outermost edge of the long bright beam.

Shading the beam with her left hand so that only the thinnest possible blade of light escaped the blood-red glow between her fingers, she explored the stairwell ahead of her and took the first step on the long climb upward.

Behind her, the darkness surged back, so solidly and absolutely that it seemed to have mass, and a sound of its own. A kind of rushing, whispering squeal so quiet that it was almost subliminal, like the throbbing of the deck brought by the movement of the massive but powerless vessel through the restless water of the bay.

The next torch she found, the fifth, was at the first corner of the stairwell. A careful test revealed that it too was still working. She eased her hands under the folds of her coat and jacket and slipped the cold column down the front of her trousers as though it were a gun, settling the broader section at the front above the buckle of her belt. The column underneath it dug into her quite intimately and reminded her a little prosaically that, on top of everything else, it would soon be time for a brief visit to the toilet. The sixth torch was with her hat at the bottom of the harbour. She would never find it, of course, and it would play no more part in the night's adventures. Unlike the little credit-card torch that still lay undiscovered in the doorway of the lading office up on 'A' deck far above.

The four men up in the bridge house had no idea that Robin was aboard. They were not hunting her, therefore. Nor were they taking any precautions to conceal their whereabouts – nor their considerable outrage. Robin caught up with them again as she came creeping along the upper engineering corridor immediately below the 'A' deck corridor and the work areas, offices and other facilities opening off it. The ghostly glimmer coming through the hole in the deck-head persisted, showing that they had returned to the ship's galley for the moment. But they had no plans to stay there, any more than they planned to be aboard for one moment longer than was absolutely necessary. She listened to the interweaving accents and voices, unable to put a face or identity to any of them yet. Aware that there were four of them, and of little more than that. Except that, unlike her own dead phone at the bottom of her lost handbag, they had all too efficient contact with the outside world. And people giving them information. People from far and near.

'If the worst comes to the worst they'll take us off at Severodvinsk. We'll be there at dawn.'

'You're sure? They'll take us off at Severodvinsk?'

'It's what they say. If the worst come to the worst. But they have plans. And they have to move fast. The shit's hit the fan on the Komsomolskaya Pier . . .'

'The shit hit the fan long before this tub ever got to Archangel, Mac.'

'Maybe. But it hadn't hit the Russian fan. And it's the Russians we need to worry about at the moment.'

'I guess . . .'

'OK. That's all water under a very old bridge now. What do they want us to do with the cargo? I mean they've one up at the Institute now and we know they know it's Kamyshev. And they've the dead guy on the pier and his dogs. We can't just heave the rest overboard, can we? I mean we're here to cover this up, not get it primetime on Fox News.'

'We just got to sit tight for the moment. It's all in hand. We'll get more specific orders soon . . .'

'Listen. I will not just sit tight on anyone's say-so. Especially when the fucker texted it in. Especially not in shit as deep as this. And certainly not after watching you work on the Pier. I want at least some sketch of a game plan before I sit back and wait for anything.'

'OK. I prefer *need to know* but if you want to take the risk, I'm game. Anything to foster international camaraderie.' A big sigh. Then the gentle American accent continued, 'In a little while from now a team from Archangel will come aboard. They'll come aboard all secret like some kind of undercover unit of marines. But they'll be cops. Just cops. They will be well armed and fully equipped. But they won't have trained together, prepared their plans, zeroed their weapons. Nothing. They're just a bunch of amateurs winging it. One of them may even be some English guy. They're just a random bunch, I promise you. And better still, they don't know that we know they're on the way. We will give them a hot reception and they will not retake the vessel. They will not, in fact, survive.'

It hit Robin then in a kind of delayed shock. Very much a part of the strange, distanced horror of the evening so far.

One of them may be some English guy . . .

Richard. Richard was coming aboard looking for her and these madmen seemed to be planning to kill him. For no reason at all that Robin could begin to understand.

Like the gentle American professor's voice just said. *Randomly.*

'I can see you want to ask a question but hold it for a second and consider a few things.'

The gentle Boston tones were addressed to one of the others in the galley, of course. But he could just as well have been talking to Robin. Yes, she wanted to ask a question. She wanted to scream it. To take him by the lapels and howl it into his face. Except for the fact, of course, that she didn't even know what he looked like. And for the fact that, except for that one overwhelming detail, she really hadn't the faintest idea what he was talking about.

'First, these guys only suspect we are aboard.' He resumed as though addressing a class at Harvard. 'They don't know for certain. That gives us one hell of a fucking edge. Secondly, just as they don't know we're here, they don't know how we are armed. I may have seen off an old guy and a couple of dogs on the pier but I didn't use anything like my full armoury in doing so. Seven taps with a suppressed Special. And none of you used anything you're *packing*, as we used to say. That's another edge that will let us get some pretty effective booby traps and whatnot in place, eh? We'll be advised on that any time now.

'Thirdly, and lastly, the team will comprise all the people most closely involved with the Kamyshev case so far. Their decease will be really bloody neat, therefore. Doubly so. Enough to give you a headache it's so neat. Because once all the guys that really have a handle on this so far have joined the cargo in the freezers, so to speak, we will slip quietly overboard and the outraged authorities will send in almost all the Special Forces up here in northern Russia. And you just *know* what they are going to do!'

'OK. I see your point. Spetsnaz or whatever will come in here like gangbusters and leave nothing to check up on at all. Now that really is fucking neat! And if anything goes wrong . . .'

'We still have safe haven in Severodvinsk and there'll just be yet another accident arising out of old-fashioned equipment, personnel and work practices. Or, more likely, another terrible al-Qa'eda atrocity which will explain why there are half a dozen terrorist bodies in the unlikely event that there is anything left in that scenario either. It's a win-win situation. No matter how you look at it this sorry stinking tub and everything aboard it except us is halfway between *history* and *toast*! And we are in the clear and squeaky clean.'

What shook Robin most was the calm assumption that *anything going wrong* would still leave these madmen able to slip safely away. What would happen, she wondered, if Richard and his team were actually able to overcome them? Capture them or kill them. What then? Nobody asked, so she never knew the answer.

'OK. Where do we start?' demanded the plain broad northern English tones.

'Apparently there's light and heat in engineering,' the gentle Boston tones replied. 'A nice efficient German generator left by some of our predecessors aboard. We can check our equipment and make our plans down there.'

'Good enough. Let's go!'

Twenty-Two

A rmed with nothing more than two functioning torches,
six batteries and a great deal more knowledge than she
understood, Robin began to draw her plans at once.

First, she watched for a frozen instant as the dark returned
to that strange gaping area in the deck-head up above her.
Then she withdrew to the far end of the corridor as the torch-
beams came shining with gathering intensity down the turns
of the stairwell. Then she moved at a flat run, spinning to her
right and hurling herself forward on tiptoe and throwing herself
almost bodily into the first engineer's office that sat exactly
beneath the lading office of his opposite number on the deck
immediately above.

She stood there in the shadows just inside the door, mouth
wide and breasts heaving painfully against the constriction of
her all-in-one, and as she gasped so she became aware that
the bloody thing was creaking quietly as it accommodated
her. The all-in-one was a piece of clothing she was beginning
to regret. It was designed to keep her firm and warm. It was
not designed for running, tumbling, deep breathing and moving
silently. She waited as silently as possible, therefore, while
she watched the wavering beams of their torches flash up and
down the passage and heard them discover the door into the
engineering area. The light died a little as they swung their
torch-beams in there and passed on down towards the little
passageway that would be dimly lit with one bulb for every
two sockets when they pushed the starter on the generator in
the room beyond.

Darkness returned as they followed their torch-beams down,
but it was no longer the total, blinding darkness of earlier that
night. The men seemed only able to move within a great ball
of light, and at the centre of a considerable sphere of sound.
Then it was in any case replaced by a dull glimmering, a

duller muttering. And the gentle grumble of the generator as though Felix Makarov's Mercedes was parked nearby with its engine just turning over.

'Hey, for fuck's sake would you look at this? Someone's taken half the bulbs out of this string. Who'd have done that?' called someone suddenly with utterly unnerving clarity.

'Locals, probably,' answered another. 'Light bulbs are worth a hell of a lot in Russia. There's a ready market in used ones. At least there was the last time I was here . . .'

Then, more distantly, a third voice added, 'Come on in here you two and stop chattering like old women. Someone's fixed up a heater in here. It's bright, you can see what the hell you're doing and it'll get warm pretty quickly. If you would be kind enough to shut the fucking door . . .' Light, heat, sound diminished considerably with the slam-snap of the closing door.

They didn't bother closing doors except for that one. Or taking care. Or whispering. Why should they? Even had they known Robin was there they would hardly have feared her any more than they feared the watch-keeper on the pier and his dogs. It began to occur to her then, though it did not become a fully fledged idea until later on, that they might also be spreading all that light and sound around themselves because they were also nervous of the terrible atmosphere aboard the stricken ship.

But their ignorance of her presence aboard gave Robin the one thing she needed most for the moment. It gave her freedom. She crept out into the corridor and turned left. Pressing herself against the forward wall, as far away from them as she could get, she oozed past the open door down to the dull corridor and the closed door protecting the bright, warm room beyond. Then she ran for the stairs and tiptoed upwards, holding her breath like a child playing hide-and-seek.

Robin might understand almost nothing of what was going on around her but she certainly understood that for some reason these four strangers had come aboard to check the freezers in the galley. That was the place she decided to start. If she understood about the freezers, then she would be one step nearer to understanding how, step by step, their reasoning could possibly lead to the unbelievably insane plan of killing Richard when he came aboard looking for her. And then calling down the Russian Special Forces to destroy the ship altogether.

Robin tiptoed across the galley, following the daringly naked, unshaded beam of her torch. She remembered where the freezers were. She flashed the torch more widely as she went, checking that everything was just the same. And so it was. She went around the central station with the sinks and chopping boards with the equipment hanging from the hooked racks above it. She passed the cold and silent ranges and gas hobs with the huge hoods of the extractors above – extractor motors torn away to leave great hollow air-con ducts gaping vacantly in the walls.

Robin realized that she was standing, hesitating just in front of the freezers. Her torch-beam was resting on the great steel doors. Four doors. Two pairs, side by side, fronting the two huge freezers. Each door two metres high and one metre across. Big ornate chrome handles stood bright against the brushed steel, as though they had been stolen from 1950s Cadillac saloons and stuck here willy-nilly. She reached out and watched the fingers of her left hand fold down on the nearest, pressing the hardness of the chrome into her palm, feeling the icy coldness soaking through the palm of her glove as her thumb folded up towards her curling index finger and her fist closed. She tugged. The handle swung out and the door followed it. There should have been a gasp and hiss but there was nothing, for the seals were perished. And worse.

Robin had automatically expected an interior light to come on. She had never opened a fridge or freezer in all her life that had stayed so dark within. But this one did. It looked like the mouth of an abandoned coal mine. She shone her torch in. Because one hand was already busy, she had no opportunity to shade the beam, to soften what it lit up with shadows.

The unforgiving starkness of the beam lit up a naked shoulder. The top of a bare black-haired head. There was a naked man in there, Robin realized, her perceptions made almost dream-like by simple shock. He was lying on his face. His skin was the strangest colour, a kind of mottled browny greeny grey. More like the trunk of a fallen silver-birch tree than anything human, really. As though the torch had a life of its own, the beam moved up. And there, on the shelf above, also lying face-down, was another naked form. The angle of the relentless shaft of light lit up the underside of the shoulder and the right side of the hairless breast that was sagging through the wire rack the body was lying upon. It was impossible to tell whether the little hammocks of dark flesh were the breasts of a plump man or those of a slim woman.

The torch moved up again and revealed shoulder, right breast, right arm wedged with its fingers seeming to clutch at the shelf like those of a prisoner trying to shake his prison bars. And the face of their owner above. The puffy face of an ill-shaven man whose eyes and mouth were wide, seemingly just on the very point of shrieking in outrage or pain, or calling for help or vengeance. Then everything went dark. There was a *thump!* on the deck by her toes.

Robin looked down in stricken horror. The torch had slid out of her horrified fingers and dropped to the floor at her feet. It rolled away from her under the freezer's cabinet, sending its bright beam into the hole in the rear deck area where the wires once had been.

'Hey,' came a voice from below, so loudly the speaker could have been standing in the shadows at her back. 'What the fuck is that? You see that light in the ceiling of the corridor down there? Just what the fuck *is* that?'

Robin had closed the freezer door and was down on her knees in an instant. The torch was easy to reach, but, all too aware of how suspicious it would look if the light suddenly vanished, she invested precious seconds in rolling it around so that it would seem to fade. Then she was up, again, looking around wildly. They would be up here to check the moment they worked out which room was above the bright hole in the ceiling, even if she had managed to make the returning dark-ness look fairly unremarkable. They would be coming up the stairwell and along the corridor. Or they might just cut in through the dining area. They would, if they thought things through. She daren't risk either escape route.

Decisive as always, inspired by simple fear, Robin ran towards the cooker. As she moved, she was pulling off her coat and bundling it up in answer to the desperate plan that was forming in her mind. Both doors into the galley were closed. They would not see her light until they opened them, so she dared to keep it on an instant longer, as she scrambled up on to the gas hob, flashing it up into the maw of the extractor. The whole system consisted of a square steel tube bolted securely to the wall and deck-head. Its mouth and throat were a metre wide and high. Standing on the gas hob, she was forced to bend at the waist anyway, for her head and shoulders were already within it. She pushed her coat right in, flashed the torch once more and switched it off. Then she kicked off from the hob, pulling her hips in by wedging her elbows in the lower corners and dragging her kicking legs up after her. Once her knees had purchase on the metal floor she could slide forward much more swiftly, easing herself round a corner with a silent prayer of thanks for all those Pilates sessions that had kept her fit and supple. But the movement was only achieved at the cost of a whispering sound that seemed dangerously loud to her.

Then she heard running footsteps. No, not running – hurrying. They seemed to come directly towards her as though two midgets were walking determinedly down the steel-sided tunnel in front of her. It took a moment to realize that this was the sound of the suspicious men coming up out of the stairwell and along the 'A' deck corridor. The acoustics in the air-con system were astonishing, she thought. But when she heard the door which seemed to be immediately below her open she stopped moving, stopped breathing, stopped thinking, and concentrated on stillness and silence with all her shaking being.

'See?' said a voice that seemed to come from her shoulder as though a devil sat there like in the old books. 'It was nothing. What did you think? Maybe it was a ghost or something?'

'*Yeahhh* . . .' The word was drawn out into a sceptical growl, dismissing both the ideas of '*nothing*' and '*ghost*' at once. And Robin could imagine the bright torch-beam probing the shadows she had only just vacated. Silence returned and lingered. It stretched out until Robin really believed the men had gone and it was safe for her to move again. But she was just tensing herself, uncertain whether to retreat into the galley or proceed along the network of pipes to seek another, secret outlet, when that quiet voice, like the devil on her shoulder said, 'I guess it was nothing after all. Let's get back to the others.' And the door closed firmly once again.

The only things that Robin knew about crawling around in

maintenance shafts, heating systems and air-conditioning ducts came from films like *Alien* and *Die Hard*, neither of which seemed like a particularly effective guide either for real life or for her current situation. And if the thought of worming secretly around the ship, crawling from place to place listening in to conversations and popping in and out of unexpected places was tempting – it was only in a mad kind of fantasy manner.

It seemed to Robin far more likely that she would get wedged somewhere, fall down some unsuspected shaft that plunged directly into the engine areas beneath the funnel. Or simply fall out through a weaker panel and land sprawling helplessly at the feet of the murderous men.

Having given herself this determined reality check, Robin began to worm her way backwards, returning to the opening above the gas hob. She noticed at once something she had not appreciated before, however. The ducting was wider than she realized. She could feel little sub-tunnels running off through the wall into the dining area. That explained some of the interesting acoustics, she thought. She noticed also that the metal all around her seemed unexpectedly clean. There should have been some cooking fat accumulated up here. The extractor fan above her stove at home certainly got gunged up with fat quickly enough, but this almost seemed to have been licked clean. Weird.

The idea of the ducting remained at the forefront of Robin's mind, however, especially as her experience just now had shown how easily the conduits seemed to carry conversations. And things were different out of the main work and accom- modation sections. The ducting was far more substantial down below in engineering. It might offer opportunities that did not involve behaving like a worm, especially if it led from room to room through walls, like this did up here. With these thoughts in mind, she let her legs fall silently out of the gaping hole above the cookers and eased her weight out of the ducting and down on to her feet. Pulling her coat back after her, she squatted, sat uncomfortably, then stepped silently down on to the floor.

All too well aware that the adventure in the ducting had probably used up all the good luck she had coming for the rest of the night at least, Robin switched on her torch and flashed it around with breathless care. Practical as always, she was well aware that if she was going to make any use of any of the pipework or ducting down below she would need a screwdriver at least. She knew well enough that there would be screwdrivers down in engineering itself of course, especially as so little equipment down there seemed to have been stolen. But she needed something now. Something to take down with her at once that would allow her immediate access until she had the leisure or the opportunity to get the right kit.

And it was this, a practical requirement rather than fear or thoughts of self-defence or even of attack, which led Robin to look at the chef's knives. But no sooner had she decided which ones might make satisfactory tools than she saw at once what effective weapons the huge steel carving knives would make. And that thought in turn put it into her mind that it would at least be some kind of insurance to go out capable of inflicting a little damage if things came to close combat anytime in the near future. When she stepped silently back into the 'A' deck corridor, therefore, with her coat back on but still unbuttoned and her fingers closed across the face of her torch, there were two strong paring knives tucked into her belt like guns at her hips. And, in its plastic safety-sheath to stop it carving any bits of her, the largest, longest and sharpest of the cook's knives lay vertically blade-down across the centre of her hips and deep into the cleft between her buttocks.

Robin flashed the thinnest blade of light along the deck-head above. A surprisingly short way ahead, just at the corner of the stair well, the ducting she was following seemed to split. There was a vertical shaft there. She closed her eyes, trying to remember the layout of the system. That shaft went down into engineering. In engineering the air-con system was bigger, far more robust. And it mostly ran along the decks, tucked into the corners at knee height instead of hidden away on the deck-head up in the air. Mostly but not entirely. The duct into which the generator's exhaust was secured for instance, ran at deck-head height, high above the men who sat beside the gently humming machine, quietly drawing their plans. Immediately beneath the sick-room floor.

But, most importantly, thought Robin as she tiptoed forward, because the big square tubes were conduits for wiring, pipework and circuitry of all sorts down there, there were regular cross-overs, side to side and up and down, through walls, partitions, decks and deck-heads. Like the ones she had sensed in the conduit in the galley. On top of that, there were maintenance panels which were designed to snap on and off for ease of access. These were solid and airtight, of course, because of the air-con functions of the system, but they had small glass panels in them.

And hence the need for screwdrivers, actual or improvised. If Robin did go back into the steel-walled little tunnels for any reason, she would at least be able to check before she decided which exit to use. Her adventure in the ducting had made her aware of something else, however. And that awareness came off the back burner and into the forefront of her mind now as she came along the long dark shadowy corridor. The men were afraid of the ship. In the same way as she was. They kept their noise and their brightness close around them like armour against the darkness. And when light glimmered unexpectedly at the far ends of long dark corridors, they talked uneasily of ghosts.

Such men, it seemed to Robin, were not going to wander about quietly exploring. They would come and go noisily at least in pairs up and down passageways and companionways. If she stuck to cold and unexplored places, she was likely to avoid them. At least until they had drawn up their plans to meet the upcoming invasion by Richard and his team. Though of course it was only her intrepid, heroic, stupid, stupid, stupid man she really cared about. Just returning to the thought of the men's plans for Richard terrified her even more than the thought of freezers full of corpses. And drove her onwards. For, now she knew how desperate the situation was and how many dead people it involved already, she knew that only superior intelligence would help the pair of them survive.

Twenty-Three

R obin's silent, thoughtful footsteps did not take her to engineering at once. Instead she followed her torch-beam past the vacant gape of the companionway and into the sick room. Almost as though the torch and not the woman who held it had intelligence and will, the bright beam guided her across the sick room and over to the bunk built out from the port-side wall. Here she sank to her knees and folded herself forward until the torch down the front of her belt made it too painful to go further and the knife between her buttocks threatened to tear itself free of the seat of her pants. She shrugged off her coat, emptied her belt, front and back, right hip and left, and lay flat out on the floor.

Inured to small dark spaces now, Robin wormed her way under the bunk with her torch and the two paring knives. The bunk was built out above a conduit. In its square side there was a panel held in place by two big screws. Heritage Mariner ships were carefully maintained, but it was often the case that the vessels were hardly maintained at all after they were sold on. This was obviously the case with *Prometheus*. And it worked to Robin's advantage now. The screws had never been painted over. When Heritage Mariner owned the vessel, they had always been removed during painting and replaced afterwards. And no one had painted this panel since the last Heritage Mariner spring-clean. The screws were rusty, but they were not solidly stuck. They yielded to the insistent twisting of the knife blade. After ten minutes or so, the panel came loose. Robin lifted it free and laid it silently on the filthy, rotting linoleum of the deck. The hole it revealed was large. Robin might even have been able to get in and out through it, if that had been her intention but it was not. She did nothing, in fact, but stop everything and listen.

'No matter how they come aboard,' said a voice distinctly, echoing up the pipe through the deck from below, 'they'll be coming in along the corridors. If they get on to the main deck in front of the bridge house here, then they'll have to come in through these doors at either end of that corridor up above our heads. The one outside here, where Mac saw the ghost in the ceiling, hasn't got doors. It doesn't open at the ends, see? But the one up above does. Opens on to the main deck like I say. Those doors are the choke points. We set up fields of fire there and the job's done.'

Robin was having trouble breathing. Not just because of the shock of hearing these men so coldly planning to kill Richard, but genuinely. Her chest was hurting, her vision clouding. She flashed her torch into the hole.

And came face to face with a rat. The rat was huge. It was black and lean, brindled and bony but disturbingly powerful looking. It had long yellow teeth fringed with incredibly long whiskers, bright button eyes, ears folded back like those of an angry cat and a long tail that looked to be the same colour as the dead men in the freezer. Robin had banged her head on the underside of the bunk twice in the uncontrolled panic of her reaction before she realized the thing was dead.

Robin felt an overpowering desire to vomit. She tore herself back out of the box space beneath the bed and rolled across the sick-room floor. There was a tiny toilet in behind here and she made for that with all the speed that silence allowed. On her knees over the bowl, she heaved and heaved. Testing her iron self-control to the uttermost limit, she emptied her stomach silently, praying that the liquid sound going down the dry bowl would be lost among the sea-sounds and the wind sounds that still occasionally battered against the ship.

But as Robin emptied her stomach and her lungs, so her mind also began to clear. And she realized why the rat had died. It had been gassed by the fumes from the generator. They had been pumping exhaust gases like those of a car or lorry into the air-con ducts, but without the engines running to circulate the air, the gas had simply built up in here. If she wanted to hear more of the men's plans she would have to work out some way of overcoming the build-up. She crept back as soon as she felt she could trust herself and, holding her breath, she managed to move the body of the dead rat and slip her head and shoulders into the opening. Her eyes burned and watered, but remained clear enough to give her an object lesson in taking care. The light from below shone through the sides of the plastic pipe and showed her very clearly where and how it had been thrust up into the pipe that led downwards into the engineering room below. She could see clouds of elephant tape grasping the edges of the strengthened plastic tube, holding it solidly. But the tube itself was like the venting tube from a tumble-drier. Circular bands of strengthening supported almost transparent plastic – made more flimsy by the heat of the exhaust fumes.

The light also showed Robin quite plainly where the pipe was against the wall, and where it was open to the room. A few silent slices with her makeshift screwdriver and she had cut a section raggedly free. Then, inspired almost to the point of madness, she pulled herself free, took another gulping breath, and returned to wedge the body of the rat into the hole. No more fumes came out into the system. They all started pumping back into the room, unsuspected, silent and deadly enough to kill more than rats, given time. For another thing had changed during the last few sickening moments. She now thought of these men as her enemies. And she was no longer merely avoiding them. She was beginning her own little campaign to incapacitate them before they hurt Richard if she could. Incapacitate them, trick them, distract them, attack them if need be. She might have considered the possibility of killing them but that seemed so remote a possibility at the moment that there was almost a kind of safety there. Until Richard arrived at any rate.

And Robin had been using her ears as well as everything else as she worked. The first thing she had heard on returning from the little toilet was, 'OK. So even if they come in over the back . . .'

'The stern . . .'

'OK, the stern. But we're not in the fucking navy now. If they come in from behind, the side doors up on this what do you call it – "A" Deck – are still high percentages of entry. What are their main objectives after all? What will they be planning to do? Check to see if there's anyone aboard after what went on on the Pier. Check on the stiffs in the freezers. They have to do either or both of those things in this immediate area, don't they? They could come up from the *stern* and still come in the doors I told you about earlier. Or they could go up the stairs outside. There are doors that come in on every deck up to the bridge or whatever they call it.'

'The navigation bridge.'

'OK. You want to do this? I mean if you know so much about fucking goddamn boats and all . . .'

'Nope. I'm cool. You lead on this.'

'What I'm saying is, whatever way they come in they got to come down the stairs. The lift isn't working because the power's off. Main objective's likely to be the freezers in the kitchen at any rate like we said. So they either come in the doors on the main corridor here and we have them covered. Or they come in some other way and down the stairs beside the lifts. And we have them covered. That's it. Cover the stairs as well as those doors and we have them dead to rights.'

Robin breathed, got her knife, returned to cut the pipe and began to make use of the rat.

'What kind of guns are they going to have?' the conversation was continuing. 'Well, I guess my answer to that would be: Russian service issue. Solid. Reliable if it's modern. Underpowered, inaccurate and not a lot of use if it's not. 9mm load either way. 9mm parabellum, maybe armour-piercing if their stuff is new. 9mm x18, more or less useless, if it's old. Might as well spit at us unless they get in real close.'

'Assume they got Graches with nine-mil armour piercing. Prepare for the worst. Then if they have anything else we'll be fine.'

'Good thinking. And we'll be fine in any case. I mean we've got, what, a couple of SIGs, two nice big 226s, a Heckler P7, watch your accuracy with that, Mac, and a Glock 17. We got red-dot sights. We got enough 9mm parabellum armour-piercing loads to stop an army. Very nice. Gentlemen, I do believe we have them outgunned.'

'They'll come in with body armour.'

'*May* come in with body armour. *Might*. But it'll be that Russian home-made stuff again. Not Faust manufacture or anything like that. No Kevlar in all probability. Tin hats if

they're lucky. Either too light to be any good or too bulky
to work in, and not a whole helluva lot of good either. Not
against armour-piercing.'

'At least they'll have it. Mine's at home hanging in the
bedroom closet.'

'Mine too.'

'Unless your wife's popped it on to entertain her soldier
friends while you're away.'

'Oh ha bloody ha.'

'So if you're worried about armour then we simply make
double sure we take them out before it gets to a close-quarters
firefight. Like I said, all we have to do is lay down our primary
field of fire to cover the doors off the "A" deck and then have
a secondary field ready to go up the stairwell if that's needed.
Remember, we got the element of surprise. They're coming
aboard on a fishing expedition. They don't know for certain
we're here.'

'And we got your friend on the end of the cellphone.'

'Right. So while we're waiting for him to call back why
don't we look at our preferred war zones, pace out some
angles, lay down some concealment if we don't have any
protection and put up some markers.'

'Sort out the barrels and wait for the ducks to arrive.'

'I thought it was fish. Easy as shooting fish in a barrel.
Isn't that right?'

They came up slowly, generating light and noise as Robin
knew they would. By the time they reached the 'A' deck
corridor she was outside the port-side door on the main deck
tiptoeing aft along the side of the bridge house in the tempo-
rary shelter of the bridge wing. Although she had taken the
time to retrieve her torches, her knives and her coat, she had
not stopped to button up and make herself comfortable before
running out through the doorway. Now she paused as the
great iron roof four decks above her head cut the worst of
the rain. Lost in thought, while her hands were busy, she
settled everything she was carrying to her satisfaction before
she did up her buttons and pulled up the soft warmth of her
faux-fur collar almost to the level of her ears and eyes. She
felt safe in the assumption that for the time being at least
her enemies would remain inside, preparing their fields of

fire, their defensive positions, their barrels or whatever. And what their leader had said about Richard's possible methods of coming aboard had set her to thinking literally outside the box. If she dared not run the risk of being discovered inside the bridge house then she could get much more freedom of movement out here. The only downside to it was that she would lose contact with the men for a while and perhaps miss some vital piece of intelligence. But if she climbed the outer companionways and got up on to the top of the bridge wing she was currently lingering under then she would in so many ways command the high ground. She could creep down the stairwells until she saw and heard what plans they were making down there. And by the same token she could at the drop of a hat run out on to the observation platforms with which the bridge wings ended. Observe what was going on. Perhaps even be able to see when Richard was coming aboard. Be able to signal to him. She had two torches, after all.

But it wasn't enough. It was a practical minimum. The sort of thing any little *hausfrau* might attempt in the face of a threat to her lord and master. Hide away, sneak around, stay out of danger and flash a torch out of a safe hideaway. Robin thought more of herself than that. And she had been running away from bloody men all night. Somewhere in her veins there flowed the blood of Boudicca scourge of the Romans, Joan of Arc the Warrior Maid of Orleans, Ann Bonney the Pirate Queen.

Robin turned on her heel and strode down the deck to the starboard after companionway. She swung herself round it and began to march up it, her footsteps so determined that they almost made a noise on the steps. As she climbed forward once again, mounting the side of the bridge house and heading forward towards the aft edge of the bridge wing only two decks above her now, she went through her strengths and her determination in her mind. She knew this rotting tub from the rusty hawseholes for the rusty anchor at the stem to the stubby little stick with the red duster drooping off it at the stern. She knew it from the foul keel below to the bird-spattered excrescence of the useless radio mast which was as near to a crow's nest as she possessed above. Every plate and every rivet. Inside and out. And she knew where her enemies were and what they were planning to do. And she knew that they didn't care that the men in the freezers were dead, even if they hadn't killed them; that they didn't care that the man on the pier was dead and that any one of them could have killed him. That they would kill her if they caught her. And that they were planning to kill Richard.

She paused on the little platform outside the 'B' deck doorway. 'Enough,' she said aloud, 'is enough.'

No sooner had Robin spoken than the door she had stepped out of less than five minutes ago burst open almost immediately beneath her feet.

'HEY!' shouted one of the faceless voices, the German-sounding one. 'HEY, LADY!' He was calling out to *her*. They must know she was aboard!

She stood. Riven. So shocked that it was four full heartbeats before she thought to turn off her torch.

The volume dropped and the man who had just called to her continued a conversation with someone close behind him. 'You're sure he says there's a woman on board here somewhere?'

'Yeah,' the American answered with utter certainty. He had been talking to his informant. 'It's why the English guy is coming. The woman is his wife. The others think she fell in the harbour and drowned but this guy's sure she's still alive and somewhere on the ship.'

'That's the only reason he's coming? To look for his wife and she's dead?' Another voice.

'Well, I haven't seen any woman. Have you?' Another. They were all there, just below her boot-soles, scant metres away, discussing Richard. Discussing her.

'Unless she was the strange glowing at the end of the passage there . . .'

'Like her ghost or something, you mean? She's in the fucking harbour like the Russians say. Forget her.'

'Naaahhhh . . .' said the American, suddenly very distinctive indeed. He drew it out as he had drawn out his sceptical *Yeahhh* . . . when they had so nearly discovered her in the galley. 'I think maybe the husband could be right. I got a feeling, you know? Had it all night.'

'Well, one way or another, he's making a big mistake

coming looking for her. Whichever way you look at it he's just about to have a very bad day indeed.'

'*Yeahhh* . . .' came that sceptical drawl again. 'In fact I'd say they both are.'

Twenty-Four

Robin had spent her working life trying to stop people killing or injuring themselves aboard her vessels. Beyond the workaday health and safety aspect, she had never before considered a supertanker, its contents and equipment as an array of deadly devices, an arsenal of lethal weapons. Never imagined in her wildest dreams that she would ever have to do so. But she started to do so now, in no uncertain terms.

Because Robin had decided to go up on to the navigation bridge, she continued her climb, but with every step now, she went through an itinerary of what she had seen aboard that afternoon, what she had found this evening and what she had learned tonight. What was there that she could get to easily, manage quickly and deploy effectively that would kill or incapacitate her enemies below? The first things that sprang to mind were the fire extinguishers. Richard had made a song and a dance about how many there were down in engineering, but there had been a fair few up here as well. They would make useful smoke bombs at the very least if she sent them foaming down the companionways at decisive moments. Then there was the possibility of fire itself. There was stuff up here that would burn. The surprisingly well-preserved bedding in the officers' quarters. But she would need to look around carefully to find fire that she could rain down on them without gassing herself with smoke as effectively as the generator had gassed the rat.

Mind you, Robin thought to herself as she stepped up on to the port wing outside the navigation bridge and paused, if I just set fire to all this lot, it would sure as hell warn someone that something wasn't right. But then, if bad luck dictated that she set it all ablaze at the wrong moment, it could all too easily become a fatal distraction for the men she was trying to protect, and a potent warning to their enemies that she was aboard and active. God! It was a bugger balancing the odds!

Robin began to wonder how much time she had actually to get this all organized, whatever it was she was going to do. Not long if the double agent, whoever it was, had had the opportunity to warn her enemies that Richard thought she was still here. The assault team must be getting kitted up, she guessed. Discussing their reasons for coming aboard. Passing on to the double agent the fact that Richard at least was coming after her and allowing him or her the opportunity to warn their confederates aboard. Did that mean the double agent was a member of the team or just one of the people getting them ready? Her money was on Felix Makarov. She really did not trust that man. Or Fido Gerkin, of course. She really did not like him at all.

With her head full of dangerous distractions, Robin opened the door and stepped on to the bridge. This was where her guided tour had started in the early afternoon. She really didn't have time to retrace every footstep that Richard, she and the ship breakers had taken. 'Think,' she said to herself fiercely. *'Think!'*

But in fact she was almost too busy acting. She had felt so constrained for so long. Mentally constrained by darkness and fear, physically constrained by tight places and small hideaways. Now it was her enemies who were likely to be staying in the same small sections of the same two decks. And she had the whole of a massive supertanker at her beck. Her mood lightened, and as it did so the clouds parted, allowing a full fat moon to flood the ship with surprisingly strong white light. Robin laughed out loud. The four men below had condemned themselves to moonless areas. Another edge that she had over them. A temporary one, fair enough, but a significant one in the meantime.

These impressions, scarcely thoughts at all, were enough to take Robin's free and purposeful strides across the bridge to the radio shack. Richard and she had both remarked on the old-fashioned nature of the equipment in there, but that could be an advantage under these strange circumstances. For an old-fashioned radio operator, sparks, would double as ship's electrician. And in a drawer immediately underneath the shelf of the radio desk he would likely keep some tools. Robin flashed her torch around and there, ready to hand, she discovered another unpilfered little gem. A complete set of screwdrivers, electrical pliers, fuses and wire all in their own little work case. That came out and the strap slung over her shoulder. Beneath it, a real treasure-trove. Again ancient but priceless now, like the eggs made by the man whose mark was on Makarov's Fabergé tie. Also in a secure little box, also with a shoulder strap, was a complete set of distress flares. This is very good indeed, thought Robin. This was *cooking with gas* as the man said. The knowledge that the man who said it was Tony Hancock the long-dead British comedian really didn't dent her mood at all.

Robin put the straps of the cases over her head so that they crossed like bandoliers front and back. The cases themselves sat firmly on her hips. She pulled the knives free and chopped off two lengths of wiring from behind the radio to make lanyards for the torches. These went round her neck as well, leaving her hands free. The knives themselves slid through the stitching on the equipment case and that black cloth with its foam-rubber padding became a convenient sheath for them. Very nicely kitted out indeed, she thought, as she left the bridge almost at a run.

Robin crossed to the lift. Her enemies had dismissed it, for the lift car was stuck now that the power was off. Robin had other ideas. Beside the fast-closed door there was a small box on the wall. 'IN CASE OF EMERGENCY, BREAK GLASS' it said. Behind the glass was a big Allen key. She put her elbow against the glass and leaned in with all her weight. There was a very muffled *crack* then she was able to pull out a shard or two and take the key. The Allen key fitted in a lock at the top of the door. She turned it and heard the mechanism inside slide open. She pulled the door back thirty centimetres or so, and was confronted by a black shaft. The air in it was particularly rank and foetid. If she held her breath and listened hard there were scurryings and whisperings. She flashed in her torch-beam and revealed nothing but the iron rungs in the shaft wall and the ropes of the winch mechanism holding the car. The central rope was taut. The brakes would have disengaged with the switching-off of power. That was good to know. Now she just had to hope that the car itself wasn't stopped at a place that would be inconvenient to her. But the chances were on her side. The shaft led right to the lowest decks of

the ship and the car could be at any of the eight storeys it
was designed to serve. The stench on the dead air was no
doubt issuing from the lowest decks of all.

These decks were traditionally the domain of the rats. On
a ship like this, which had been at anchor for a couple of
years with almost no humans to supply their wants, a truly
fearsome breed would have evolved, she suspected. If the dead
one in the generator tube was anything to go by. They would
have turned cannibal long ago. The babies would have gone
first. The old, the weak. The slow to adapt. The unintelligent.
She was surprised they hadn't worked out some way to get
at the bodies in the freezers. She was surprised they hadn't
come for her while she lay unconscious on the lower deck.

Robin was going to use the lift shaft to get her up and
down through the decks and past the men as they prepared
their traps for Richard and his team. But she had no intention of wasting time or effort climbing further than she
needed to. She would have to be careful passing up and
down through 'A' deck corridor, even concealed by a solid
metal door. But, apart from that, she could risk opening the
doors two decks down and stepping out again on the second
engineering deck.

Two decks down, one deck above the muttering men with
their lights, their guns and their murderous plans. Robin went
to work. She placed the two nearest fire extinguishers at the
very head of the staircase, hoses unclipped, pressure buttons
up and ready to go. Then with a swift final check around,
she crossed to the lift door, slid it half open and swung
herself in on to the metal rungs. Her torch, hanging round
her neck showed the shaft reaching down below her feet to
the top of the lift car. She swung back, put the Allen key on
the inside of the mechanism and slid the door silently shut
behind her. Then she was off, hand over hand and grateful
that she had kept her gloves on. Grateful too for her stout
boots and practical trousers. She had kept her coat on in
spite of some misgivings. It was not all that practical for
climbing, working and – if push came to shove – fighting.
But it kept her warm, it worked well as black camouflage
in the darkness and it was another layer of protection. Six
of one . . . she thought.

As she went past 'A' deck she paused.

'It'll have to be a chopper,' someone was saying. 'I can't see them coming any other way. There's a helipad on the main deck. I saw it when we went down earlier. We keep an eye on that and we'll get good warning.'

Robin tended to agree about the chopper. There were very few other ways of getting on to a half-laden supertanker whose deck sat more than ten metres above water level. And all of them involved help from the crew. But she knew other places aboard where it could land and so did Richard. Places on top of or even behind the bridge house, where their arrival would be much less obvious if they were careful.

These thoughts took Robin on down to the second engineering deck, the level below the little room with the generator, the warmth and the light. Her good luck held. The lift car was stopped on engineering deck three, immediately below. She was able to stand on its roof and open the door with the Allen key. But she paid a double price to do so. Firstly in terms of hearing the mechanism groan as her weight added to the strain on the cable. And secondly in a near-heart-attack as the whole thing settled downwards infinitesimally under her and she thought for an instant that it was going to fall there and then. But she stepped safely out on to the engineering deck and flashed the torch around.

Robin had come here because this was where the best equipment was. Richard had been like a little boy showing Felix all the fire-fighting stuff down here and Robin was keen to make use of it if she could. Most of it was fire-fighting equipment, but she reckoned that in the right hands it could be turned to uses other than those its designers had in mind. And those hands were her hands.

Most of the equipment was on trolleys for ease and speed of movement. Metal bottles and canisters like oxygen tanks the better part of a metre and a half high stood on two-wheeled trolleys. Drums like oil drums lay on their side on four-wheel trolleys. They contained everything from foam like the ones at the head of the stairs three decks above to inert gas at huge pressures and special powder designed to melt into oxygen-excluding blisters over stubborn incendiary flames. Everything was stored at enormous pressure, designed to foam or spray. Or, if you hit them hard enough, to explode.

Robin began by wheeling the trolleys that were easiest to

move across to the lift. Then, with infinite care, she rolled
them on to the top of the lift car, squeezing them in like a
three-dimensional jigsaw. The single cable accepted the strain
in silence. But with a tension that quivered more and more
dangerously.

When Robin was satisfied she could cram nothing more on
to the roof of the lift car, she went back across the cavernous
darkness of the half-open engineering deck. She was following
the conduits that she had briefly considered worming her way
inside. Because she wanted to go where they led to. She wanted
to get into the funnel.

The funnel was another shaft that led from the highest sections
of the ship to some of the lowest. It was not the massive open
well it seemed to be from the outside. Instead, it was for the
most part packed with lesser shafts, all bound together like a
stand of cut corn. There was room to move between most of
them, and up and down at will. And, as with the lift shaft, there
were rungs to facilitate this. But Robin did not plan to go inside.
She found the maintenance panel that she was seeking and
sparks's largest screwdriver came into its own. When the panel
was open, Robin was able to stick her head and shoulders right
in. Here, as with the lift shaft, the still, stale column of air was
heavy with rat smells, full of the rustling whisper of their inquisitive movement. Robin shone the torch-beam down, but it was
gulped into the darkness before she could see any details down
there. She could imagine the secret glitter of their eyes, however.
And the gleam of their cannibals' teeth. Almost without thinking,
she was picking up anything nearby that looked as though it
would burn. It was engineering, so much of what she found
was oily rags left mouldering where they were dropped by the
last watch afloat or the last shift at the fitters' in dock. There
weren't many, but there were enough for her needs. It took her
perhaps five minutes to gather enough and bundle them down
through the hole.

Robin had just finished pushing the rags into the shaft of
the cold dead funnel when the torch-beam stabbed through
the darkness like an accusing finger. By the grace of God, she
had shone her own torch into the funnel shaft itself to see
how far the rags had fallen. But had she not been looking
downwards, she might have seen the flash of light he caused
as he came out of the generator room.

The instant Robin saw the beam flashing through the shadows she had the presence of mind to switch off her torch. But then she froze, heart pounding, like a rabbit caught in headlights. She knew at once who it was. The one enemy who was not convinced she was dead at the bottom of the harbour. The man she assumed had killed the watchman on the pier and his dogs. He was up on the upper engineering deck and he had done what Robin had assumed they would not do. He had come through into the darkness behind the generator room. Into the areas that had been lit by octopus arms of cables hung with bulbs. Thank God she had disconnected them. Because there was not a doubt in her mind that he had come through searching for her. He had no real idea of the vastness of the space he was trying to illuminate, she thought, trying to stiffen her resolve. He was up there on a steel balcony on the edge of a three-deck-deep hole. The lift shaft was at his side, but the open door and the well-packed lift car some five metres beneath his feet, invisible beneath the metal decking of the balcony he stood on now. Ahead of him, a vastness big enough to contain three RB 211 motors, their gear housings and their shafts. And all he had to explore the hugeness of this silent, lightless place was the puny finger of his torch-beam. But still, as he shone it around, Robin shrank back against the outer wall of the funnel, as though she believed he would be able to see her.

Then, horrifyingly, even as she waited, literally holding her breath in the silence, so the thudding of her heart seemed to spread out from her chest. To fill the column of still air beside her. Until the whole of the funnel seemed to be reverberating with her terrified heartbeat like something out of a story by Edgar Allan Poe.

But then the door behind the man with the torch opened, framing him abruptly against the light from the generator. 'I hear a chopper,' called a rough voice. 'We have company.'

The pair of men hurried out of the vast chamber and Robin tore herself into action. She opened the case at her right hip and took out a flare. She ripped the little lanyard trigger off the top, closing her eyes against the flare as she shoved it through hole she had just stuffed with oily rags and dropped it.

'It's showtime!' she said, almost exultantly.

Twenty-Five

The little Kamov KA-32 helicopter settled on to *Prometheus* like a rather fat little dragonfly alighting on the largest lily pad on the pond. Its double rotors held it almost aloft while the wheels just touched the square of decking behind the bridge house that in some of the *Prometheus* series covered a swimming pool.

Richard went out first, running round the thrust of the left wheel arch, eyes narrow in the moonlight, hesitant to start flashing torches around as yet. Hs body armour was bulky and made moving difficult. It covered him from throat to thigh both front and back and seemed to have been modelled on the armour of the Roman legions. But it felt like cardboard, it creaked loudly if he moved too suddenly, and the best thing that could be said for it was that it might keep him warm. It would need to do so too, because it replaced both his jacket and his British Warm. He might as well be in braces and shirt sleeves beneath it, for the black pullover Voroshilov lent him was designed for colour not comfort. And, like everything else, was really too small for his big frame.

Voroshilov piled out of the chopper immediately behind him and came up level with his shoulder at once. 'Way in?' Voroshilov was in charge. There was no doubt about that. Paznak was here but hobbling. Repin was currently helping him down from the chopper as Richard and Voroshilov assessed the lie of the land. So to speak.

They had gone over Fedor Gulin's schematics during briefing, of course, in the same way as they had made themselves familiar with the Yarygin PYa MP-443 handguns that for some reason Richard couldn't fathom were called '*Graches*', or crows. The complicated flimsies covered with lines and figures couldn't begin to replace a guide who knew what things actually looked like on the ground. So the

Cossack would be commander but the captain would be point man.

The Kamov lifted off at once and whirled back to wherever Yagula wanted it to wait until it came to collect them later. To collect them or whatever was left of them. 'Here,' gasped Paznak, just as Richard said, 'There!' and they were off. The plan was for them to stick together, work well within earshot of each other and communicate in monosyllabic English. Repin's unit had supplied the handguns that Felix was so proud to have produced. Perhaps because the elderly, second-rate ones Voroshilov and Paznak usually used bore his family name – Makarov. They had a Yarygin PYa Grach each therefore, holstered with the full eighteen-shot load and another shell in the chamber. There were three or four opponents at most, Repin had said. The better part of eighty bullets would surely be sufficient. So they hadn't bothered with extra magazines. Customs and immigration had also supplied the body armour; Repin's own looked lighter and more businesslike as a consequence. But they had drawn the line at their communications equipment, which was newer, more expensive and much harder to replace even than the Graches. Repin had his own, of course. He assured Felix that it would communicate from ship to shore, so he was communications man. Though all four of them had cellphones preprogrammed with all the numbers needed for this little jaunt. Richard, Voroshilov and Paznak had been offered bulky old bricks so Richard had retained his own. He noticed that Repin, too, had kept his own, which was, like the body armour, far better than what was on offer to the others. It was, by a strange little coincidence, the very phone that Richard had bought for the twins to take to university with them. And all of them had torches, selected from a variety on offer and chosen for the ease with which they could be held alongside a handgun. In place of comms equipment, they all wore earmuffs designed to match the body armour. Customs did a lot of gun-work in confined spaces and the earmuffs were designed to allow through monosyllabic whispers but block out any loud noise at all. This would be fine when the gunfire started; crucial, in fact. Richard knew all too well how agonizingly disorientating the noise of a gunfight in an enclosed, steel-sided space could be. He just hoped that no one had to shout anything important at a critical moment.

And that was it. Cellphones, armour, Graches, torches, muffs. They were as well kitted out as time and circumstance allowed.

As they ran forward across the after deck and into the shadow of the bridge house, another thought was added to those already rattling around in Richard's combat-tense head. Not so much a thought as a conundrum, arising from an unexpected observation. *Prometheus* was being towed without power. She had neither lighting or heating beyond the generator in engineering. So why was there smoke coming out of the funnel? There wasn't much of it but it was clear in the moonlight and impossible to mistake. And it looked very worrying indeed as far as Richard was concerned.

The four men went up the outer companionway with Richard and Voroshilov in front, Paznak and Repin behind. The officers had crepe-soled shoes and moved with a sure-footed silence denied Richard in his leather-soled Oxfords, but while he could squeeze into armour at its loosest setting, there was no way his feet would fit into less than a size twelve and they were in short supply. With just a footstep and whisper more noise than they would have liked, they arrived at the port-side balcony exactly opposite the point where Robin had stood listening to the suspicious strangers call to her less than half an hour earlier.

Richard paused here for a second to let Paznak steady his breathing, then, just like Robin had done earlier, he turned and went on up to the wing on this side of the bridge house that mounted up to the wing outside the navigation bridge. It was another long, fast quiet climb, which allowed Richard and Voroshilov to get well ahead of the other two. Commander and point man had no chance to discuss it, of course, but they needed to make a decision about this. For the last few steps, therefore, Richard slowed his pace although to do so ran exactly counter to his instincts and desires. Like any combat unit in the field, they would go at the best pace of the slowest man. Until the slowest man was a handicap dangerous enough to put the rest in danger. Or until the slowest man was dead.

Stepping up on to the outer wing at last, Richard pulled the Grach out of its holster on his belt and held it up for a heartbeat so that the others could see it against the mottled white paint of the bridge house. Then, as the other three gathered behind him, crossed to the door into the bridge itself. He took the handle of the door, pulled it open and swung in, body armour creaking at his movement. With the short, solid Voroshilov as his partner, it was inevitable that he would go high while the Russian went low. Richard held the Grach in standard two-handed firing position, courtesy of a little work with Special Forces some years earlier, standing squarely, on wide-parted, solidly settled feet. He was as confident around guns as any of the others and handled his Grach as well as the other two, almost as well as Repin who used his regularly, and practised weekly in the Militsia shooting range.

Part of the plan in coming in this way was that it allowed Richard to use the moonlight as Robin had done earlier. He was stepping into a relatively bright environment, and one where it would be hard to mount an ambush at the outset.

'Clear,' he said, and Voroshilov echoed the word in confirmation. The pair of them moved on past the open door of the radio room and out of the back of the bridge itself.

The passage ahead of Richard was absolutely dark. So he released his left hand from his right wrist and reached back for the torch at his gun-belt. 'Flashlights,' he said and he felt the others around him reaching for theirs. When he stepped forward, his method of holding the gun had changed for the torch was hard alongside it and he was aiming along the beam. 'Passage,' he said and moved off with Voroshilov immediately behind. And the other two a few more steps back, Paznak bringing up the rear. Four long torch-beams cut through the shadows ahead and already showed the corner that would take them round to the lateral corridor and the central stairwell which was their goal.

Because the flare down the funnel was so far removed from anything her enemies would have any idea of, even if they heard it, Robin was emboldened to run up the skeletal stairway that led from the second engineering deck to the first. Here, where the man who was hunting her had stood flashing his torch around, there was another fire point. It was not supplied with all the advanced canisters of the deck below but it had a fairly wide range. Robin flashed her torch along the row whose position she had known unerringly in the darkness, and she took a water and foam-based one, exactly like the three

standing at the top of the stairwell three decks above. It said in big black letters:
WARNING: WATER BASED FOAM.
DO NOT USE ON ELECTRICAL FIRES.

Robin swung the solid red cylinder out of its place with her left hand and strode silently across to the door whose brightness had framed her hunter and his friend a few moments earlier when they had first heard the sound of the landing helicopter. She eased the door open a fraction and peeked into the brightness, all too well aware of the damage she was doing to the night vision of her left eye. The room was empty, except for the quietly purring generator. The air was thick with fumes, but it was a case of too little too late, she guessed. The best she could have hoped for with the dead rat in the exhaust was to make them a bit slower and a bit wheezier. She stood the canister immediately outside the door and closed its hose securely in the crack, wedging the entire Heath-Robinson contraption with the weight of the extinguisher itself. Then she hit the button. The whole thing seemed to leap as the white foam came flooding out. With unerring accuracy it soared across the room and exploded across the top of the generator.

Robin whirled away, blinking, her left eye streaming, trying to come to terms with the vertical bar of bright green light that lay across everything in front of her. But her dominant eye was her right eye and her brain had dismissed what her left eye told her even before the distraction faded. She ran across to the lift shaft and slid her Allen key into the door. As soon as she swung her head into the shaft she smelt the smoke from the fire she had started in the funnel and heard the restlessness of the increasingly frightened rats. She swung back out and risked her torch again. There on the wall, behind the fire point was a large red-framed, glass-fronted box, big brother to the little one that held the Allen key. It still said:
IN CASE OF EMERGENCY BREAK GLASS,
but this time the glass protected a fire axe and a big pair of red-handled bolt-cutters the better part of a metre long. She switched off the torch but moved unerringly to her objective. This time she broke the glass with her shoulder, glad once again of the thickness of her increasingly battered coat. She pulled the big shards out by careful touch, glad of her leather gloves, and laid them on the deck, then she reached in gingerly

for the bolt-cutters. They were surprisingly heavy. Even so, she held their ungainly weight in her left hand while she shone her torch into the lift shaft again, assessing with all the accuracy she could precisely where the cable was, and how she would get the bolt-cutters round it in the dark. She left the torch on for a few seconds longer than usual, as she crossed to the open lift door and sank to her knees a metre back from the edge. Then she switched off, lay forward and shuffled gingerly into position reaching out with the cutters across the void one deck above the car itself. The weight of the things tore at her shoulders at once, and with unexpectedly agonising force. It came as a great relief when the jaws reached the cable and seemed at least to be taking a little of the weight. She tensed herself to cut the cable.

And a torch-beam lit up everything around her. 'What the hell?' said an English voice from very close at hand. 'I'll be damned if Sam wasn't right! Oh, will he ever want to talk to you! Get up on your knees, whoever you are and put your hands behind your head.'

Robin considered closing the bolt-cutters' jaws. For about a nanosecond. If there had been any kind of chance that she would be able to cut the cable in a flash she might have tried it but there wasn't. He could have shot her a dozen times over before she got even halfway through the braided metal. It would have been pointless.

'Please don't shoot,' she called, making her accent so Home Counties she might have been impersonating the Queen. She had no real idea where he was except that he was close behind her. She slid the bolt-cutters along the deck beside her shins beneath the spread skirts of her coat as she pulled herself up into a kneeling position.

Robin was certain that there had been no flash of light this time. So he hadn't come through the generator room. That was about all she was sure of. He must have been putting in one last quick recce before settling down with his colleagues to spring their murderous trap on Richard. She put her hands behind her neck as he ordered and laced her fingers together obediently. He was surprisingly close and must have come creeping up behind her with truly catlike stealth. She didn't hear his footsteps as he moved round in front of her and came even closer now.

Robin knelt there looking wide-eyed up the torch-beam towards him, hoping for something she might recognize later. If there ever was a *later*. But because of the dazzling torch-light all she could really see clearly was his right hand holding the Glock 17 with its red-dot sight like a tiny drop of luminous blood exactly on her heart.

Twenty-Six

Richard led Voroshilov, Repin and Paznak round the first corner and down into the dark stairwell leading down from the bridge deck to 'C' deck next below. They moved as a stealthy unit, torches raking the still black air ahead of them at four different angles and levels. Six steps down to the little landing then round through a hundred and eighty degrees and down into the 'C' deck corridor.

The first reason they had decided to enter the bridge house at the topmost level was the tactical help afforded by the moonlight through the clearview windows. The second was also tactical. Starting high would allow them to check every deck they passed through so that if there was anyone aboard who wished to harm them, the enemy at least would not hold the high ground. It was tactically efficient, but it was also a lengthy process, Richard thought, especially slowing things down for Paznak. His main priority did not involve looking for murderous strangers. It involved finding Robin. Given his way, he would just have gone down on to every deck and bellowed her name at the top of his lungs. One way or another, he'd be out of here in five minutes flat.

Tactics also dictated, further, that they should stick together. Which of course only slowed things down even more. But their briefing and preparation had been as detailed as Felix and Yagula with almost military insistence had dictated. And it had been a good, thorough briefing – Richard had been to some in his time and he knew. Even Voroshilov seemed secretly impressed. And they had all agreed to unit procedures and mission tactics as though they were a unit in the SAS. Or, more accurately, Spetsnaz. And Richard had agreed along with the rest. So there was no use trying to change things now.

So they proceeded, in Richard's imagination rather like

Ghostbusters, checking in every work room, day room, office and cabin all across the deck as though there were evil spirits here somewhere. But the only thing on the icy air that Richard could sense other than the stench of the place was the faintest whiff of burning. And all he could hear was a whispering, hissing, scratchy kind of silence. And the occasional, whispered 'Clear' in answer to his own. And the creaking of the body armour as they swung in and out of doorways.

Until the rattle of sub-machine-gun fire from all too close at hand followed by the muffled mortar-round *THUD!* of the first explosion far below.

The death of the generator saved Robin's life. It had taken some time for the water to penetrate the vitals of the solid, reliable German machine, but when it did so, it did so in style. The live circuits fused, of course, but the water penetration was sufficient to set off even those that Robin had switched off earlier, for while she had broken the circuits, she had left them all connected to the machine.

The waterlogged generator fused at last, therefore, exploding with a muffled bang like a grenade. But more to the point it sent out a final surge of power as it gave up the ghost. And the power-surge sped along all the visible and invisible tentacles of cable attached to it. And one after the other, all the light bulbs, bright or dark, flickered, blazed and exploded in rapid series. The flashing and exploding light bulbs looked and sounded uncannily like the firing of a semi-automatic weapon.

And the Englishman guarding Robin, surrounded by semi-automatic weapons as he was, and half-expecting to be attacked with them as he also was, swung round in automatic reaction. Even as shards and splinters of glass came showering down upon him, he was searching for the enemy he needed to kill.

The red dot and the torch-beam left Robin, and although she was almost as stunned as he, she had a far clearer idea of what was going on. So she got on top of things faster than he did. She grabbed the big bolt-cutters lying hidden under her coat and swung them at arm's length with all the force at her disposal. Which, given the firmness of her stance upon her knees, was quite a lot, in spite of the fact that her makeshift club weighed a good five kilos and more.

The solid weight of the sharp-edged, carbon-steel, square-forged bolt-cutters hit the Englishman full force on the shins perhaps a hand's breadth below his kneecaps. The effect was devastating and immediate. He was felled like a tree, landing flat on his face, driving nose, chin, and forehead into glass-covered steel with almost all of his ninety-kilo weight. His torch was by no means the only thing to shatter and several teeth accompanied the Glock 17 as it skittered across the deck. The red-dot sight flickered once and also died.

Robin paid no attention to the gun at all. She had much to do and she was out of time. She hurled herself back on to her belly and reached out with the bolt-cutters unerringly. For, apart from coming to her knees, she had not moved her position at all. She felt the jaws grip the trembling cable and she closed them with all the strength in her upper body. It was easier than she had thought it would be. The cutters were sharp. The cable was elderly, unloved and poorly maintained. It was also bearing a load far beyond its design specifications. Half a dozen brutal pumps with the cutter handles should easily be sufficient to send the lift car hurtling down the shaft.

Robin was pumping the third one in when the door nearby opened and footsteps came crunching across the nearly atomized glass on the deck. There was no light, nor any possibility of light now unless the newcomer risked the torch or the red-dot sight that would turn him instantly into a target. She pumped again, feeling the cable beginning to give.

'Are you here?' came a quiet voice. The voice she feared most. The American's voice. He wouldn't hesitate like the Englishman. If his red dot reached her heart, so would a bullet an instant later.

'Are you there?'

There was a tiny *click!* in the silence that answered the whispered question. The red dot came on. She pumped again, turning her head to see the red dot wandering apparently aimlessly across the deck towards her.

'Are you there?' so quiet she could hardly hear it. Another whispering crunch of a footstep.

She pumped again, bursting to groan or shout or at least pant with the effort. But she didn't even dare breathe.

The red dot defined a shoulder dressed in a black coat like her own. There was a thud of sound, surprisingly loud, although the gun was clearly suppressed. A torch-beam came on and lit up the pool of blood that had suddenly appeared in the middle of the Englishman's back. It also lit up the back of a beautifully barbered masculine head.

'Fuck!' snarled the American.

Robin closed the cutters.

The cable whipped free, howling away up the lift shaft as the car itself plunged thunderously down. Robin dropped the cutters and rolled into the shaft all in one fluid motion. Even in the darkness she knew every centimetre of it. She grabbed the rungs and pulled herself upwards, reaching into her pocket for the Allen key. Then it was in the lock and the doors slid closed and she was scrambling on up again.

The American was beating on the doors level with her feet immediately. Then there was a tiny silence and a spit of sound as the first bullet tore through the thin metal door. But then the lift car hit bottom, and murderous madmen armed with suppressed SIG Saur P226s, red-dot sights and armour-piercing rounds were suddenly the least of Robin's worries.

The lift car only fell three decks. But as Robin had noticed, the breaking system had long since failed. It was also loaded with some of the heaviest and most explosive canisters of fire-fighting liquid, powder and gas that she had been able to find. As it came to the bottom of the shaft, therefore, the car had travelled a vertical distance of nearly forty metres. It was moving at roughly the same speed that Felix's Mercedes had achieved on the run back from the airport, and although it didn't weigh quite as much as the motorcar, it ran full tilt into the equivalent of a big brick wall. The lift car simply crumpled, still contained within the shaft. But then, a nanosecond later, the canisters arrived. When they began to crumple in their turn they let off all their pressurized contents. And, luckily for Robin, the force went forwards rather than up.

There was a simple kind of inevitability about it, though. The lift car was solidly built in its sides and back, but it was of course open at its front. As it landed, the unsupported forward section of the roof gave way first and most. So that the canisters were already sliding forward towards the doors when they exploded. And the force of the explosion penetrated the doors with as much ease as the American's bullets. In fact, it blew them halfway to the cofferdam that sealed the tanks off from the work areas, and sent out a wave of pure force that rolled right through the lowest decks and corridors aboard.

The rats, already unsettled by the fire below the funnel, had gathered near the cofferdam, trapped and frightened. The explosion of the lift shaft killed some, and wounded others. But it sent the rest of them simply insane with terror. And the only way for them to escape was up the companionways towards the main deck.

Robin was right. They had become cannibalistic, lean and mean in the last few years, in numbers as well as in character. But there were still over a thousand of them able to make their escape. And willing to tear to shreds anything at all that got in their way.

The force that came up the tunnel was as nothing compared to what went through the lower decks, but it was still enough to shake Robin as she clung to her precarious position. It was also enough to rattle the door at her feet and send some deeply disturbing jets of air though the bullet holes and into the face of the man with the suppressed SIG. He took off at a flat run, no longer at all hesitant about using his torch and she, shaking her head to clear her pressure-blocked ears, sped up the ladder like an old-fashioned matelot swarming up the rigging.

Robin was reckoning on darkness and confusion on 'A' deck, and planned to add to it if she could. She tore the door open with the Allen key then, faced with only darkness, slipped it into her pocket. One-handed, she pulled out two of the distress flares. She closed her eyes – not that it made any difference – and grabbed the lanyards with her teeth. She tore the flares forward and pitched them through the half-open door, keeping her eyes closed and feeling for the Allen key again as soon as her hand was empty. But she simply couldn't find it and as the sudden blossoming brightness warned her of yet another job well done, she left the door as it was and climbed on up the ladder, teeth aching, lips burning and ears ringing with the approaching scream of a thousand terrified rats. But then she froze. For the noise of the terrified animals was completely lost beneath the disorientatingly violent sounds of automatic gunfire that seemed to burst out immediately above her head.

And that hesitation was simply fatal. Two arms and a torso swung in through the door to the lift shaft. The arms closed round her hips. A bullet head was pressed to her backside and a force far stronger than anything she could resist, simply tore her off the ladder and dragged her back through the gaping door. She hit one shoulder against the rubber door-closer as she came. But she hit the other shoulder and her head against the solid metal of the frame. Even against the brightness of the distress flares, everything went very bright indeed. The last thing she heard was the screaming and she wondered vaguely if it was her own.

Robin had simply misjudged the American. She had thought of him – almost characterized him – as machine-like, cold and calculating. Like a villain from a movie; not like a person at all. He was not a soulless, mechanical fictional psycho-villain. He had a purpose, a passion and an ambition. An over-whelming ambition, albeit a newly acquired one. In the light of the flares that blazed in the 'A' deck corridor he came tearing up the stairway from engineering and into the ruins of his carefully laid trap. Even as he arrived he found his head was ringing with the sounds of an unexpected firefight upstairs that just added to the general mayhem. And there she was in the shadows of the lift shaft. He could easily have just shot her and let her fall on to the wreckage of her makeshift bomb below.

But the simple facts were these. His plans were going to hell in a handcart here and he hadn't even met the men who were coming here to rescue her and due to arrive at any moment now, by the sounds of things. His professional standing, his job and his ability to maintain his lifestyle were all at severe risk. He might well need a bargaining counter if he was still going to come out on top. Or at least some kind of cover while he and his remaining associates took all the approaching rescuers out, which he was still very confident of doing. And after the completion of that increasingly pleasurable-seeming piece of business he would deal with his second, over-whelming, motive.

Which was that he truly, passionately and overwhelmingly, wanted to watch this fucking woman die.

At the *THUD!* of the crashing lift car, Repin shot Paznak point blank between the shoulder blades. He was using Militsia-issue 9mm Parabellum load which was powerful but not, like the military issue, armour-piercing. He reckoned that with them all bunched together like they were, however, he stood a good chance of the bullet going straight through and killing Voroshilov as well. Which was why he avoided the more obvious head-shot. But the armour was stronger than it looked. The bullet tore through the policeman's back, missing the spine and entered Paznak's chest, but it was stopped by the front panel as it came out through his lower right ribs.

Paznak collapsed instantly, but his body convulsed instead of merely dropping to the deck, and it simply got in Repin's way, slowing his second shot. Or shots – for he had already decided to switch to automatic mode. Voroshilov threw himself sideways, using a wall to keep him erect, skidding across the flaky paintwork as he tore his body round. His gun was already up, but he was looking for some other enemy. It simply did not occur to him that the shot had come from Repin's gun. Until, in the moment that Paznak fell away, he saw the smoke oozing out into the customs officer's torch-beam. He fired before Repin, the standard three-tap of a well-trained marksman, but his bullets hit Repin's body armour, a far more substantial proposition than Paznak's. Hit three times at the centre of the torch-beam focused on his heart, Repin staggered back, fighting to contain the shock of impact which came close to breaking his own ribs. An impact that was just enough to knock the earmuffs off his jerking head. His gun came up, torch alongside it, shining into Voroshilov's eyes. Only for his left knee to explode as Richard shot his leg out from under him.

Repin twisted as he fell, his fist closed tight and a spray of eighteen bullets erupting from his weapon as he fell. They screamed and whistled off the metal walls in an overwhelming torrent of sound. Taken together with the detonations of the soaring cartridges themselves, it would have deafened everyone in the corridor. More than deafened them, in fact. Stunned them senseless like eighteen reverberating hammer-blows delivered in a second. Exploded their eardrums and pummelled their brains. Except that they were wearing earmuffs. All except Repin.

The gun fell from his senseless hand and he lay there, twisting and bug-eyed. Richard crossed to him, and knelt by his side, wishing that they had been supplied with some field-dressing kits. Both men needed something in the way of plasma and pressure bandages or they would be lucky to survive. Voroshilov looked up from tending Paznak. Richard saw his lips moving but no sound was coming through. It took Richard a moment to realize that the earmuffs were cutting out the Cossack's words because of the volume of the customs man's screams. Brutally practical, he hit Repin in the head with the carbon-steel club of the Grach in his right hand. The eyes rolled up. The mouth closed.

'. . . must go on,' said Voroshilov. 'They must take their chances. Especially that two-faced bastard! This is war!' As he spoke, he gently removed the fully-loaded Grach from Paznak's hand and slid it into his holster.

Richard nodded grimly. But before he pulled himself back up on to his feet he did two things. He stripped off Repin's armour and swapped it for his own. Then he leaned forward and patted the man's uniform pockets until he found his cell-phone. As he had noticed earlier, it was the same sort he had bought for the twins to take to university with them. He knew how it worked. Good, he thought, slipping it into his pocket.

Now he knew there had been a double agent in their midst, the little device might well be able to help him find out who the traitor had been in contact with in the enemy camp.

Because, like Voroshilov had observed, this was indeed war.

Richard and Voroshilov moved quickly now, side by side, like a battle-hardened team. They didn't need to speak. They had all the important routines down pat. They went down the stairs on to 'B' deck side by side, with torches probing the leaping shadows sent up the stairwell by a guttering bright-ness from below. They swung on to the 'B' deck corridor and paused. They were well aware that their enemies might well have laid an ambush for them here. It would make tactical sense. The main focus of light, noise and action was below and seemingly immediately below. A clever opponent might well try to set a trap just that little bit earlier than expected. And the proposition was given added weight in Richard's mind at least, by the fact that the lift door here was wide open. And a wall of fire extinguishers was blocking the next flight of stairs at their feet.

But their hesitation was overcome almost at once. A kind of rising shriek washed up the still, shadowy air in front of them. The shrieking was certainly animal, but all at once it was joined by more human, masculine screaming. Because of the distance, the screaming did not kick in the sound regulators in their earmuffs. So they both knew in those brief and terrible moments that something truly horrible was going on down there. The human sounds of disgust were joined almost at once by the sounds of gunfire, apparent only to Richard by sudden interruptions to the continuity of what he could hear.

Voroshilov was simply spooked. Battle-ready, wound up tight, witness to the betrayal of his command by a spy and the attempted murder of his friend and right-hand man, he found that this final set of surprises simply pissed him off. In spite of tactics and briefings and everything else that Makarov and Yagula had put into the mission, therefore, he simply shone his torch down the stairwell and got ready to charge. Shone his torch down the stairwell and froze. The stairway was moving, weirdly like a black metal escalator. The illusion was so powerful that it took the disorientated Cossack a moment to realize what he was seeing. But then the light of his torch came glittering back at him. And instead of metal elevator ridges, it came glittering back off eyes and teeth. There were several hundred rats running madly up the steps towards him.

Voroshilov had no words. Like the men below, he simply started screaming and shooting.

Richard hated rats as much as Voroshilov but he had a greater respect for the load in his Grach, and he didn't have an extra gun in his empty holster. He had eighteen bullets left. And he could well be needing them all. So he grabbed the nearest fire extinguisher and he threw it down the stairs. As soon as it landed it exploded, spraying foam out of its stubby little hose. Voroshilov saw what he was doing and threw another. That too exploded into foaming life all over the confused, terrified and suddenly hesitant rodents. A moment later Richard threw the third and that was enough to turn the tide. So the two men could run down the stairway, shoulder to shoulder, on the heels of the retreating rats.

Richard reached the last metre of the companionway wall leading down into the 'A' deck corridor and he slammed his shoulders against it, feeling the unsettling combination of foam and fur washing away from around his ruined Oxfords. His gun and torch were pointing at the ceiling above his head but the torch at least was switched off. The faintest of whispers told him Voroshilov was precisely opposite. 'Back!' he breathed. Voroshilov stepped back up one step. Then another. Richard swung out, Repin's body armour silent in spite of the movement.

The corridor was in darkness and silence. No torch-beams, no pale glimmers of movement, no red dots. Nothing. Even the last of the rats seemed to have deserted the place. All they left behind them was the stench of powder and sloshing wash of foam from the extinguishers. Richard had no idea at all of how many enemies were still down here, whether they were still armed and dangerous, and, if they were, then where they were hiding. But he was impatient to find out those vital facts, to the point of recklessness.

Richard silently pulled his hands apart so that the torch was in his left hand while his gun was in his right. Then, holding the left hand high, he crouched down in the darkness, swinging invisibly round the edge of the wall at knee height. He steadied himself, raised his gun and pressed the torch switch. The beam shone out across the corridor from waist height, where an impatient man might be carrying it. Two pistols spat at once together. Richard shot at the bright muzzle flash presented by the first, and Voroshilov blazed away happily at the other. The guns stopped shooting. Richard switched off his torch and slid flat on to the floor. The foam stank but it was soapy and slippery. He pushed himself silently forward across the length of the corridor separating him from the flashes he had shot at.

And there, huddled in the doorway through into the dining area, there sat a still and silent man. Richard felt down the arms that fell slackly from his slumped shoulders and soaking, shockingly hot chest, until he reached his right hand, where he relieved him of his gun. He flattened himself against the floor, cheek in the stinking wash of the foam. 'Voroshilov?' he called.

Bullets spat over his head and impacted with a range of materials including metal, wood and flesh. The slumped man stirred. Richard heard the spitting of the sounds and reckoned that this opponent was using a suppressed gun. He slid off his earmuffs to make sure.

'Here,' called Voroshilov. The suppressed gun spat again. Richard couldn't quite make out where the shots were coming from. Whatever was on the weapon was cutting flash as well as sound.

'Still here,' repeated Voroshilov, mockingly.

Richard's fingers were working feverishly on Repin's phone. As Richard knew from helping the twins set theirs up, it had a secret mode that switched off not only the sound but the internal light as well. Useful for students at late-night parties who wanted to keep things private; and for spies, come to that. He flicked the secrecy switch full over and opened the phone, confident that even though nothing showed, the little instrument was now on. Then he hit the simple combination of keys that clicked in the callback function. The last number contacted by Repin would ring at any moment.

And so it did. A persistent stanza of Mozart's music from right across the corridor.

'Oh, very clever! Then I guess we're here too,' came a third, equally mocking voice. An American voice. Maybe Boston, thought Richard. 'Though I guess my friend Mr Repin is not,' it concluded, mocking. Confident.

Robin wasn't certain exactly where she was. She simply knew that she was clutched against the front of an iron-hard body with a steely hand around her throat. And the hot end of a pistol barrel kept touching insistently against her right temple. And a piece of *Eine Kleine Nachtmusik* kept repeating and repeating. She was solidly on her feet, having been dragged there by brute force sometime between the arrival of the rats and the exploding of the fire extinguishers that had come rolling down the stairs and told her Richard had arrived even before she heard his voice. Her tool box and her flares were gone, and her coat was bunched uncomfortably behind her.

The fingers at her throat, however, would hardly let Robin breathe, so speaking was, for her, out of the question for the moment at least, while the Russian, Richard and her captor exchanged grim macho banter over the disturbingly out-of-place bars of Mozart. She focused on breathing, which would have been hard enough, given how scared she was, without the pressure on her windpipe. On staying upright. On holding on tight to his rock-solid forearm with both of her hands in case she should slip and cause a terrible accident. On trying to work out where she, her captor and everyone else was in this echoing, deafening, powder-stinking little cavern they all seemed to be trapped in. His breath tickled the back of her neck when he breathed. She could feel his nose on the back of her skull, but the hot barrel of the suppressed pistol kept her mind off any foolish thoughts about lashing back with her head and diving forward into the darkness. She moved her feet in answer to an insistent step forward. And she felt something on the floor.

That one second orientated Robin absolutely. She knew where she was. She knew where the man behind her was. She could even guess where Richard and his Russian friend must be. Because she could feel beneath her foot the little credit-card torch she had last seen in the doorway of the lading office where it opened into the 'A' deck corridor.

Without a second thought, she trod on it with all her might. Out through the utter darkness, a beam of pure white light shone across the foam-covered floor. It came out from under her boot sole and it shone right the way across to the stairwell as though the foam on the deck was suddenly luminous. At once a torch-beam answered from the mouth of the companionway. But it shone back blindingly at head height. The gun barrel left her head for an instant. The gun spat deafeningly in her ear, spraying her with heat and stench. The torch-beam sank to floor level like her own, but it did not waver. And it stayed on. 'He's all yours now, *Angliski*,' croaked a hoarse Russian voice in English.

'She goes first, though,' warned the quiet voice in her ringing ear. 'Unless you go first yourself, of course.'

And she knew that it was true.

*   *   *

Emboldened by Repin's armour and unaware that his enemies' guns were loaded with armour-piercing rounds, Richard slowly pulled himself to his feet. He was aware that his movements would be easily visible in the backwash of brightness from Voroshilov's torch. Therefore, he let the guns lead him up. He had the Grach in his right hand still and the new gun, which he did not recognize as a Heckler and Koch, in his left. Which didn't make a lot of difference really. Richard was fully ambidextrous. Part of the reason he did not recognize the Heckler was that it had a red-dot-sight attachment on its stubby little barrel. He had the Grach's ambidextrous safety in the ready to fire position under his right thumb and believed he had the safety of the unfamiliar weapon under his left.

Richard needed to be sure, because all he could see clearly in the light of Voroshilov's torch was Robin. There was a hand around her throat, and her own hands were clenched around his forearm, elbows high, like wings.

Robin's coat was flapping open, the right side of it folded right back, to reveal the stark line of her tight-buttoned jacket, the flare of her hip and her thigh. Richard remembered wistfully the way she had put on the black lacy all-in-one that afternoon before they had left for the restaurant. It had been so tight that he had to help her settle it as it pulled her slight frame even more firmly in. He looked at her, with her eyes so wide and so calm and so grey, even with the smoking barrel of the SIG pressed hard against her temple. He smiled. It was a farewell.

'You first it is, then,' said the quiet voice. And the gun swung away from Robin's head.

Richard's thumb moved on the side of the Heckler and Koch. The red-dot sight came on. It was shining on Robin's right breast. Right on the outermost slope beneath the tight-buttoned jacket. He moved it a centimetre further left until the red dot plunged past her corseted rib and he squeezed the trigger. Then he dropped the sight ten centimetres and he squeezed the trigger again. Then he dropped the sight ten centimetres and squeezed. Three shots in little more than a second. The doorframe beside his shoulder exploded, but the hand that fired the shot was dead already.

The first bullet missed Robin's body by little more than a

finger's breadth, but it punched a neat armour-piercing hole exactly between the American's right nipple and his armpit and it deflated half of his lung, while the rest began flooding with blood. Then it removed a section of his right shoulder blade as it tore out into the room behind him. The next one was further from Robin's constricted waist but it perforated her captor's liver and right kidney, pulling yet more blood out of his rapidly depressurizing cardiovascular system, and tore the whole of his right dorsal muscle. The last one smashed through the Mozart-trilling phone and the right hip behind it, shattering the ball-and-socket joint before it tumbled out of his back, tearing away a large section of upper buttock. The bullets had destroyed his blood system, several major muscles and his skeletal system in turn.

The shock was simply enormous. The trauma was more than the American's heart could stand. And, fastidiously well nourished, well exercised, well trained and fit though it was, it stopped dead just as surely as Mu'hmud Kamyshev's had done before he was shoved in the freezers with the others. He fell back into the lading office. And just the dead sound that his body made as it impacted with the deck said everything that needed saying.

'Ow,' said Robin, slumping against the doorframe. 'OW!'

'Did I hit you?' Richard was slumped against the shattered doorframe himself. His voice was shaking with horror at the thought. At the thought of the risk he had run.

'No. It's my *ears*. You hurt my ears with all that . . .' She stepped forward, staggered, straightened. 'Well, at least you came for me,' she observed.

'You knew I would,' he answered.

She nodded in acknowledgement of the truth of his words and took another step forward into the full brightness of Voroshilov's torch-beam. 'Hey!' she called, suddenly outraged. 'Look what you've done to my poor coat!' Three neat bullet holes marked where the red dot had rested on the fabric moments earlier.

And Richard pulled himself erect. Stepped forward two steps until they were standing chest to chest, almost leaning against each other. He looked around, with the gold curls of her singed and powder-reeking hair tickling his dark stubbled chin. 'Hey,' he said in reply. 'Look what you've done to my poor *boat*!'

And they started to laugh in a mad, almost Cossack, manner that Sergeant Voroshilov most thoroughly approved of. He reached for his phone while he still had the strength and punched in the first pre-programmed number.

Twenty-Seven

The Moscow flight roared into the air, seemingly just above Regional Prosecutor Bakatin's Zil. The big black limousine was proceeding back towards Archangel at a steady pace, and Bakatin looked up as the plane soared over it with a thoroughly self-satisfied smile. He was still almost girlishly aglow from the effects of his final interview with Federal Prosecutor Yagula. He had already decided that he would purchase a new bowler hat for himself, a pretty Armenian shawl for his wife, and, for his mistress, the kind of delicious confection that the girls at Snezhok wore for the first few moments of their acts on a Wednesday night.

'So,' he said to his companion. 'Moscow.'

Regional Investigator – soon to be Federal Investigator – Elena Onega stretched like a satisfied cat. 'After I have tied up one or two loose ends,' she said.

'Loose ends like Voroshilov and Paznak in hospital? I've seen the chocolates and the *Playboy* magazines. You spoil those two.'

'And the last of the paperwork on ex-Officer Repin,' she said more soberly. For she was not the only local officer destined to go to Moscow. 'You'd never believe the forms that need filling to get someone in to Butyrka.'

'Perhaps,' suggested the Regional Prosecutor drily, 'that's why it takes such a long time for the people already in there to come out again. Even to go to trial.'

The Moscow jet whispered over the Talagi–Archangel road then swung away from the outskirts of the city itself to cross the Dvina River and pass low over the dockyards at Severodvinsk. Richard looked out of the window and smiled gently to himself at the unmistakable sight of *Prometheus* snugged safely in her dock. The early shift had been working on her for hours already. Everything was back on track and proceeding full-steam ahead.

On the table by Richard's hand there lay a newspaper dark with Russian print. He could not understand the language but he knew what the stories said. The main one told of the brutal murder of a watchman and his dogs by a vagrant who had fled aboard the vessel *Prometheus* moored at the end of the Komsomolskaya Pier. Of the heroic efforts of two local Militsia officers in apprehending the individual, even though he was killed and they were wounded in the gunfight aboard the boat. There were pictures of the wounded heroes and of the owners of the vessel, international business leaders Richard Mariner and Felix Makarov, publicly thanking Regional Prosecutor Bakatin for the good work of his department.

Another story told of the completely independent enquiry by local and federal prosecutors into a ring of suspected smugglers in the Customs Division itself. It told of the arrest of one officer who had tried to commit suicide when faced with the full force of the allegations against him. He would be moved to Moscow for further investigation and eventual trial as soon as he got out of hospital. Local Investigator Elena Onega would be promoted and transferred as a result of her excellent work on the case. There was a picture of Elena with Federal Prosecutor Yagula, to whose Moscow office she would be assigned.

Somewhere deep inside was a story so commonplace it didn't merit any kind of comment or more than the most perfunctory of coverage. A body had been discovered in the harbour. It was badly decomposed and eaten by fish. So much so that there was no chance at all of any kind of identification ever being made, though DNA samples had been sent to Moscow for analysis as the corpse was of the Arabic sub-type of the Caucasoid male, in the opinion of local pathologist Alicia Kashin. And there weren't many Arabs in Archangel. The thinking in Regional Prosecutor Bakatin's department was that this was the body of some sailor or stowaway fallen off one of the ships in the busy sea port.

The one story remarkable by its absence was the story about two freezers full of dead bodies.

'It was *extraordinary rendition*, wasn't it?' said Richard.

Yagula looked up from his perusal of the first set of documents preparing for Repin's transfer to the Butyrka SIZO, or

pre-detention prison, where he would be held until his trial.
'The term extraordinary rendition's not really used any more,'
he growled. He glanced across at Felix Makarov who was
looking at Richard's list of the next tankers he could most
easily deliver. None of them were anchored anywhere near
Germany.

'Why do you say that?' asked Felix easily.

'Mu'hmud Kamyshev gave me enough clues to be going
on with. And our discussions after his autopsy supplied
anything that was missing when I got to thinking about our
tour around the ship. If the Russian anti-terrorist authorities
were really worried about poor old Kamyshev they would
have been able to get to him unless he holed up in one of
those Chechen regions you haven't been able to get into yet.
But he didn't. He vanished from Baku, where Bragin's boys
from Constitutional Protection could have had him any day
of the week. So someone else took him. And who takes terrorist
suspects off the street and makes them disappear? Especially
if they have suspected al-Qa'eda links?'

'You think it was the CIA?' asked Felix, his tone showing
how ridiculous he thought the idea to be.

'It could be any of you. There was an American, a Russian,
a German and an Englishman in the team that came out to
clean up after the Germans sold me back the boat.' Richard
glanced across to Robin who was sitting across the aisle of
the exclusive little club-class section that had been put aside
for the federal prosecutor and his influential guests. Her eyes
were closed and she was apparently asleep. But he knew better.
She was listening to every word, intonation and inflection, as
acutely as any lie detector.

It was Robin who had described the men's words, actions
and accents in such detail to him. To them all, in fact. She
was still drained from her experiences and finding it far harder
to bounce back than he was. But that didn't mean she wasn't
still at the sharp edge of things. He really needed to take her
away on a nice long holiday. A cruise, maybe. She raised one
eyelid quizzically, alerted by the silence, caught his concerned
look and gave the ghost of a smile.

Richard leaned forward and continued, 'As far as I know,
though, the only cases brought to court by people who say
they have been taken like that are against the CIA. And it was

the CIA who got into all that trouble for putting extraordinary-rendition flights through British airports a couple of years back. And they hardly made a secret of things like the Quassem affair in Zagreb, the disappearance of Shawki Attiya and the others. But that could all be the result of America's open society and their rights under the Constitution and the Bill of Rights. I'd certainly be surprised if they're the only authorities who do it in the current climate.

'I'd see *Prometheus* being used as a stopping-off point, a holding facility. Maybe even a multi-agency facility. Somewhere that suspected terrorists from all over the world could be held and processed between being secretly snatched off the street and being delivered to the relevant authorities in countries where there is less restraint about interrogation techniques than there is in the West. Right from the start it was obvious that people had been living aboard her. Everything was just that bit too clean. She was still too well equipped – the galley alone gave that impression. I mean, the extractor fans ripped out – so the cooker could still be used. Medical facilities. Clean linen, for Heaven's sake! Not to mention the generator my towing watch found left behind. But whoever was running this little floating Guantanamo, this Abu Graib On Sea, got too heavy handed. People's hearts began to give out. Bodies were stored. The rest of the suspects were moved on pretty quickly. Things were reined back. The whole thing was hushed up. To such an extent that when someone in Berlin said *Hey, there's an Englishman wanting to buy back this boat*, no one else said anything at all.'

'It's an interesting theory,' purred Felix. 'Utterly without foundation, of course.' His fingers went to the knot of the gold tie that reminded Robin of Fabergé.

'And you'd know, *of course*,' said Richard, as lightly as he could frame the words. 'Because you know as well as I do that the double-headed Romanoff eagle crest on your tie is the symbol for the FSB as well as for Fabergé.'

'So much more stylish than the red star with hammer and sickle,' said Felix, seemingly genuinely amused. He glanced across at Yagula's red tie with the gold stars. Then he caught Robin's eye and winked. Robin winked back. It wasn't only Richard who got briefed before coming into a deal. KGB, FSB: it was all a matter of club ties these days.

'But you know all this,' continued Felix gently, speaking

to both of them now. 'You have your own intelligence section. You know where I learned my English. Where we all learned our English. Is it a problem?'

Yagula leaned forward, suddenly, unable to keep out of the conversation any longer. 'Before you answer that, Richard, think carefully. You have said that our agencies were probably not involved – in the death of Mu'hmud Kamyshev at least. We cannot speak yet for the other dead men and their voices, so to speak, will be heard post mortem in secret; secure even against your intelligence. For I assure you that they also are bound for Moscow and the best that my laboratories and pathologists can supply. So even if we are FSB or KGB, what have we done? We have made a bad situation good. We have made decisions that fit with good business. That is what our mission was here. It is still our mission now, for ex-Colonel Felix Makarov, ex-aide to Aleksander Bragin himself *but current chairman of the Sevmash Business Consortium*, will take personal oversight of the rest of *Prometheus*'s breaking. Just in case, eh?'

Yagula turned to Robin and included her in his carefully calculated, overpoweringly enthusiastic speech. 'But it will go well. It will go smoothly. For all of us. Because we also have a mission for the future. There are many more ships to be broken. Our yards will break them. Our economies will be supplied with materials. Our workers with work. Our businesses with profit. And this is the future. *Da?*'

'*Da*,' answered Richard. 'Yes.'

He smiled at Robin. And Robin smiled back. '*Da*.'

Elena Onega stood at the end of the two beds in a private section of a small ward in the Medical Academy. 'Who gets the chocolates and who gets the *Playboy*s?' she asked.

Voroshilov heaved himself up. 'Give Paznak the magazines,' he said. 'I prefer my women real.'

'And on stage at Snezhok on Wednesday nights, yes I know,' answered the Regional Investigator.

'Besides,' continued Voroshilov, 'I can have the magazines after he's finished them. Though,' the Cossack grew expansive, waving his plastered arm as far as the bandaging across his chest would allow, 'he's welcome to the chocolates after I've finished with them too.'

'You've seen the papers?' asked Elena Onega.

'Daily and weekly. We've been on radio and local television. They say our Medal of Bravery ceremony may go nationwide.'

'I'll be sure to look out for it. I'll be settled in Moscow long before you're well enough for public ceremonies.' Elena Onega frowned. 'I made Bakatin promise you both full pensions. Even if you set up in some other business after you're invalided out.'

Neither of them would ever serve again. They'd be lucky to walk properly. Paznak only had one lung, a hunch and a limp. Voroshilov would have one arm shorter than the other for the rest of his life.

'I hear they're short of night-watchmen,' said Paznak.

'Security consultants you mean,' said Voroshilov. 'Everybody's some kind of consultant these days. Even if all they've got is a brother, six dogs and a clapped-out van.'

'And I think Colonel Makarov's Sevmash Consortium people will be looking for, ah, *security consultants*, at about the same time as you become available for work. No matter when you become available for work. There's a man called Fedor Gulin. He's in the phone book.'

'We'll find him,' said Paznak. 'Which is more than we'll ever do for that back-stabbing bastard Repin.'

'He's going to Moscow too, I understand,' said Voroshilov.

'Everyone from *Prometheus* is on their way to Moscow except you two. Whether they're alive or not. Recently deceased or long dead. All of us Moscow-bound. Which reminds me. It's time I was off, I'm afraid. I must pack.'

Elena Onega dropped the *Playboy* magazines beside Paznak and the chocolates beside Voroshilov, turned on her heel and went.

As her footsteps faded, Paznak turned to Voroshilov as far as the traction harness would allow him. Like the Cossack's, the Slav's hands were suspended up above his head. And would remain there until the wounds to hands, arms, shoulders and chests were healed. 'It's just as well we have some incredibly understanding nurses here,' he said. 'No matter how you look at it, we'll need some help to get full enjoyment out of the Investigator's kindness.'

'I hope the nurses come by soon,' agreed Voroshilov. 'Those

look like Belgian chocolates to me and I may not be able to contain myself for long.'

'You think you've got troubles,' mourned Paznak. 'Miss October with her huge pair of "O"s there looks unsettlingly like the amazing Olga.'

'Ah,' said Voroshilov. 'Talking about the amazing Olga, I hope the newly promoted Federal Investigator shares at least one of her amazing abilities.'

'What do you mean?' Paznak was concentrating on other things. Like Miss October.

'Well, from the way the federal prosecutor was eyeing her, their relationship will transcend the purely professional pretty soon after she lands in Moscow.'

'I can see that. He's been eyeing her up like a great white watching a beach full of bathers.'

'But she doesn't strike me as a woman of unusual *capacity*, so to speak.'

'Tight-assed I'd say. And I mean that quite literally. So what?'

'Well, look at the federal prosecutor, my slow, Slavic friend and use your imagination! It may not be vegetable and it's probably not green, but he has to have the biggest goddam *agurets* on the block!'